Beck's Grouse

by

Maeve Kim

*Love Stories of the Burlington Bird
Club, Book Two*

Beck's Grouse

Cover Art by *The Wild Rose Press, Inc.*

The Wild Rose Press, Inc.
PO Box 708
Adams Basin, NY 14410-0708
Visit us at www.thewildrosepress.com

Publishing History
First Edition, 2025
Trade Paperback ISBN 978-1-5092-5957-1
Digital ISBN 978-1-5092-5958-8

Love Stories of the Burlington Bird Club, Book Two
Published in the United States of America

Dedication

To all the bird-lovers who share their knowledge and their passion, and to the potential for romance in unexpected places.

Prologue

It didn't make sense to spend every night on the living room floor.

It didn't make sense that she felt so close to Alain in the double sleeping bag they used only four times, but she couldn't make herself go upstairs to the bed they shared for fifteen of her forty-three years.

It didn't make sense that she could not make herself walk into their bedroom, that she brought all her clothes downstairs and piled them on the living room couch just to avoid seeing their closet, their bureaus.

It didn't make sense that Alain was dead.

****

Grief isn't over all at once. For Beck the first glimmer of the beginning of the start of the easing of grief was on the Winter Solstice, five months to the day after Alain died.

She woke up cold. She was still in the sleeping bag, but the thin backpacking pad was beside her instead of under her and she could feel the cold slate floor.

She stood up and walked upstairs and straight through the bedroom door and she walked up to the big bed and threw the sleeping bag on top and wriggled in, and she fell asleep almost immediately. The next morning, she turned the bag inside out and hung it over the stair railing to air, and when night came, she walked into the bedroom and pulled back the covers and got into the bed.

Beck woke up with Alain's arm around her. She felt the weight of his arm, she felt his fingers splayed on her breast. She heard his steady breathing and felt his warmth from her shoulders to her toes.

She didn't open her eyes, and after a while she moved back toward him, just a little.

The warmth at her back dissolved.

She opened her eyes and watched his hand fade away. *Don't go*, she whispered.

Don't go, she called.

Oh, don't go, she sobbed.

Don't go, she screamed and screamed. *Don't go Don't go Don't go.*

Beck curled into a tight ball and rocked back and forth, her throat raw and her breasts bruised from her fists, her whole self buffeted by waves of anguish and fury. Fury at Alain for dying. Fury at the dentist for rescheduling her appointment so she wasn't there when he died. Fury at herself for not being there to save him.

And then... blessed quiet.

No sounds but her gasping breaths.

She moved her head just enough to see the clock.

The realtor. The realtor would be coming in just over an hour. He would walk through the house and look with dispassionate eyes into all the rooms where she had lived with Alain. Lived, not resided. Laughed and talked and made love and wept and hugged and sat on the couch reading.

The realtor would look into the bathroom where they spent Sunday afternoons in the winter, together in that big tub, touching lazily, half dozing, talking, his deep quiet chuckles mixing with hers to make one sound.

The realtor would look at the kitchen table and their two chairs, and their plates and wine glasses, their soup bowls and coffee mugs, and he would probably say their table was too small or too old or too beat-up and should be hidden away before the house could be shown.

The realtor would see the king-sized bed, still with four pillows, two for Beck and two for Alain. He would see the rag rug that Alain's grandmother made. He would see their boots lined up in the front hall, their coats and jackets, his with hers even though he would never again shrug into his favorite jacket or stuff his feet into his muck boots.

She got out of bed and put on Alain's big wool robe. She brushed her teeth and wound her dark heavy hair into a bun, and then she went downstairs and called the realtor and told him she had changed her mind.

****

Beck read somewhere that every person sheds millions of dead skin cells into sheets and pillowcases. That night she got into their bed naked. She lay on her back and stretched her full length. She turned over and rubbed her belly and legs against the sheets on Alain's side of the bed, trying to feel his dead skin cells all over her living skin, mixing into her pubic hair, gathering in her navel. She breathed him in, his scent, his cells that had already been dead for five months and a day. She slept on those sheets for two more weeks before finally stripping the bed and starting fresh.

The day after the Solstice, Beck cleared out Alain's half of the closet and his tall maple dresser. She could wear his flannel shirts, so she kept them. She kept his woolen socks to wear to bed because her feet were always cold and he wasn't there anymore to warm them.

3

She kept his robe and the tops of his long underwear and his three Irish fisherman's sweaters. She packed up the suit jackets and ties and trousers and dress shoes, the uniform of his life as a college professor. And she folded his heavy black winter coat, the one that made him look so distinguished, and added it to the boxes for the homeless shelter downtown.

She stared for a long time into the drawer with Alain's white briefs. They were all softened with washing and stretched a little in the front, gently cupped to fit a man who would never wear them again. Maybe she would wear them. Why not? They weren't all that different from her own undies. But accidents weren't unheard of in her kind of work. What if she ended up in the emergency ward and nurses cut off her slacks and saw that she was wearing men's briefs?

Did she care?

She made room in her underwear drawer for Alain's white briefs.

****

Grief isn't over all at once. For many people, maybe for most people, grief slowly gets more distant, a little at a time, week by week, month by month. Beck went on living with grief, living in grief, for almost four more years. It wasn't as sharp. It wasn't as painful. But it dulled the bright greens of spring, blurred the colors of summer wildflowers, washed fall's brilliant foliage into tones of sepia and gray. Grief was with her every day, all day. She might have stayed longer in her aching numbness if she hadn't seen the grouse.

Chapter One

I was wearing pantyhose when I first saw the grouse. That would not be memorable for many women, perhaps most women, but that was my first pair of pantyhose ever. In high school I didn't sing in the choir or take part in plays or go to dances or get asked out on dates, so I got by with sandals, or low socks and sneakers, for warm weather and high socks with clogs in the winter. In college no one wore pantyhose, not even the female professors. And most of my adult life required standing on mucky streambeds or wading into water or slogging across muddy fields.

I didn't even wear pantyhose on the most important day in my life, the day Alain and I got married. My legs were bare and my feet were in the sandals I bought to go with the long gauzy dress he picked out for me. I can still see him, the way he looked, so different from his usual professor persona, so youthful in white cotton pants and a loose flowered shirt that made him look like a hippie pirate. He wore sandals that day, too, I think for the only time in his life.

But I wore pantyhose on that frosty spring day when I first saw the grouse. I spent the morning testifying before the Vermont State Water Resources Board in Waterbury, and the lieutenant governor herself asked me to dress up. So I wore my first pair of pantyhose with a long black skirt and a lavender silk blouse that had been a gift from Alain's sister, and I dug out a pair of lady-like black pumps I bought years and years ago, back when I still thought I might someday develop a sense of fashion.

****

My job the morning of the grouse was to describe the possible effects of development along the river feeding the capital city's primary water reservoir. I am comfortable testifying. I know more about my subject than politicians or developers or the vast majority of the public, and I felt almost as passionate as the lieutenant governor about this particular project. By the end of the morning, we were both pleased. The proposal was scaled down from thirty single-family homes, fifteen duplexes, and two office/retail buildings, to a much less intrusive "village" of twenty relatively small homes and eight two-family dwellings—much more fitting for the rural outskirts of the nation's smallest capital city. In addition, the developer agreed to mitigations that would gather run-off before it reached the river.

As I was putting files and photos back in my briefcase, I noticed the developer muscling through the crowd, heading for the Board's lawyer. The man was six inches taller than the lawyer, and one and a half times as wide. That big man must have known coming in that the hearing could cost him thousands and thousands of dollars, but the scope of the required scaling-back might have caught him by surprise. I watched as he approached the lawyer's desk and bent over it, leaning forward on fisted hands, and I decided to use the far exit to avoid walking by two angry men.

But the developer looked interested, not angry, and the lawyer looked up from his papers with a smile. I realized that the developer was asking about the "living machine" mentioned during the hearing. That method of stormwater control wasn't required in this case, but the big man wanted to know what it might cost, and whether including a living machine in the plans for another project, this one in South Burlington, might increase its chances of being approved.

I watched the developer and the lawyer bend their heads together over a sketch or a map, talking earnestly. And for the first time in years, I felt something like a thaw. I felt love, I think, love for the inherent civility of my chosen state. The thaw must have shown in my face because two colleagues asked me to join them for lunch at Guido's. Ever since Alain's death, my immediate answer to any invitation, my automatic response, was no. But that morning, they asked, and I hesitated, meeting their eyes and smiling.

"I, uh, somehow I forgot to put my outdoor clothes in the car. I've got to go all the way home and change out of this finery before heading to East Barre to inspect a private dam." As they turned to leave, I called after them, "Eat some garlic bread for me."

It wasn't true. My muck clothes were in the back seat of the car, and I had plenty of time to eat and change. I thought fleetingly of Guido's eggplant Parmesan, but I wanted to be home, to eat lunch in my own kitchen—our own kitchen—and look out the bay window and see the fruit trees Alain planted in the years before our marriage and all the shrubs and perennials we had chosen together and planted together, kneeling in the dirt together, getting filthy and leaning over to kiss each other.

****

Something was moving in one of the highbush

cranberries along the driveway. Viburnums, Alain always called them, *Viburnum opulus americanum*. The leaves and branches were shaking, heaving, and one of the wild grape vines that had grown up over the shrub was swinging back and forth like a circus trapeze. There was a dark shape that wasn't leaves or branches or last fall's grapes, almost as big as the hens we had for a few years. I rolled down the window and leaned out. It looked like a partridge, hanging upside down and clinging to a branch and stretching its neck to get the very last of last fall's grapes.

"You're a determined one, aren't you?" I whispered.

The bird went right on plucking at the dried-up grapes.

"I'm not a threat, bird. I just want to look at you."

The bird twisted its head around and fixed me with one beady little eye, still hanging upside down. I could see bits of fruit on its bill and the sides of its face.

"You are very handsome, you know."

For the second time in an hour, I felt a pulling of the muscles at the sides of my mouth, a tightening in my cheeks, a narrowing of my eyes. I felt a smile.

****

I had passed the shop several times on my way to the bookstore at the end of the mall, but I'd never gone in. Ivy's Optics and Accessories for the Dedicated Birder. Someone in there would know.

A woman was kneeling on the floor, her back to me, taking books out of a box and arranging them on a low shelf. She scrambled to her feet when she realized I was behind her.

"Didn't hear you come in!" She made a vague gesture toward the doorway. "There's a bell that's supposed to ring but it's iffy. Loose connection or something. So. What can I do for you?"

"I'm hoping you can answer a question about partridges."

Her smile blossomed into a wide grin. "Pah-tritch, to old-time Vermonters. Grouse more scientifically. Cool birds! What's your question?"

She laughed as I described the bird hanging upside down in the viburnum, eating last year's grapes.

"Smart bird. There isn't a lot of food around at this time of year, and there's a lot of sugar in dried grapes. Specialty raisins, perfect for a hungry grouse." She picked out a field guide from the shelf at eye level. "Were you around here? Or up in the Northeast Kingdom?"

"Right here. Well, just outside Montpelier."

"Then it was a Ruffed Grouse." She found the page and turned the book toward me. "Spruce Grouse are birds of boreal bogs and spruce woods, so they're not found around here. This look right?"

"Yes. Exactly. Are you Ivy?"

"I am indeed."

Everything the woman had on was bright, from the quilted patchwork vest in pinks and purples and greens, to the brilliant blue turtleneck and bronze corduroys. I had never worn anything that colorful in my entire life. Maybe if there was a man in my life again…

I had no idea where that thought came from. I had never even wondered if I might meet someone someday. But out of nowhere, in that little shop full of birding books and optics and paraphernalia, I suddenly wondered if someday, maybe, I might want to dress in brilliant colors and try to catch a man's eye.

9

"I spend a great deal of my time outdoors, but there are many birds I don't recognize. And even more facts about birds that I don't know at all. Would you recommend this book?"

"It's the best, I think."

"You're the expert." I took the book. "I have also been thinking about a guided bird walk sometime. If you know of anything like that."

Ivy started nodding after the word *guided*. "Here." She darted behind the counter and drew out a printed sheet with the letters FATSO on the top. "First and Third Sunday Outings. F. A. T. S. and O. The venerable Burlington Bird Club, this country's own BBC, leads two free guided outings every month, one walking and one mostly driving."

"Are they open to anyone?"

"Of course!"

And that was it, the start of my return to life. And all because of a curious developer, a friendly lawyer, a shopkeeper named Ivy, and a hungry Ruffed Grouse.

****

Carpooling makes sense, of course. Both economically and environmentally. But I drove alone, in my own car, to my first outing with the FATSO group. I was not ready to be stuck in an enclosed space with people I didn't know, not even for the short ride to Berlin Pond.

When I saw the water shimmering in the distance, I realized that I was excited. I was going somewhere that wasn't for work or grocery shopping. I was doing something different with my day, something special. I couldn't remember noticing a single morning since Alain's death, but now I was overwhelmed by the many shades of new spring green, by the low clouds over the water, by the brisk breeze whipping the flag on a tall pole near the parking lot. There had been frost during the night and I could see my breath when I got out of the car. But the sun was up, already warming the mist off the water, already beginning to be felt through my turtleneck and fleece vest.

I purposely arrived twenty minutes early, but a little blue car pulled in right behind me and Ivy started talking as soon as she opened her door.

"You came! Excellent! We're hoping to meet up with a giant feeding flock of warblers, so you'll get hooked on birding." She looked around and grinned. "And here come the other stalwarts. Every single regular FATSO birder is one of those human beings who, if they're not early, worry that they might be late."

A tiny woman was getting out of the other side of Ivy's car, her bouncy white curls dazzling in the early morning sun. The old pick-up truck beside my car held a boy, maybe twelve or thirteen years old, and a man with a yellow and silver mustache that drooped a few inches past his jaw on both sides of his mouth. The last vehicle, a miniscule two-seater, disgorged a sturdy man with a round face and a broad grin.

"Beck—Charlie, Sean, Molly, Jack. Everyone—Beck."

I decided I could sort out later which male name belonged to which male.

Ivy wrestled a tripod out of the back seat of her car, talking over her shoulder. "The BBC—Burlington Bird Club—has a few hundred members, and big groups turn out for a few specific outings each year. Usually, though, it's just five to ten of us for Montpelier outings." She turned and grinned at the chunky man. "With a few more for Jack's trips, the first Sunday of every month."

"What can I say?" He beamed at me. "I'm a popular dude."

"Or maybe some people just prefer driving around instead of slogging through swamps." The small woman, Molly, kissed her fingers, reached up to pat Jack's cheek, and turned to me. "Ivy leads us up hills and through rutted fields. She makes us bushwhack through dense forests and leech-infested wetlands. Grueling, positively grueling. Jack is much kinder. Car birding all the way."

"This morning will be totally non-grueling." I recognized the role that Ivy dropped into as she looked around. She was the leader, the educator, like I am when I'm ushering groups of legislators or community members around a building site or beside a dam or along a stream. "Just a leisurely stroll along the pond, keeping an eye on the water and checking the foliage on both sides of the road for any bird activity. If the place is hopping, we'll spend the whole morning right here on the road. If not, we'll head up onto the Irish Hill Trail. Everybody ready?"

Ivy and Molly led the group onto the dirt road. When the boy started to dash ahead, the man with the amazing mustache reached out and hauled him back. A lesson learned, for the youngster and for me: One doesn't get ahead of the leader on a birding walk.

The other man trotted beside me, his broad face cheerful, almost dancing as he walked. "Ivy said your name is Becka?"

"Beck. B. E. C. K."

"Welcome to the group, Beck. Jack here. You're in for a treat. This group has been together for a few years now, and we see something astonishing just about every single outing." He raised his binoculars and called out, "Loon on the pond!"

"Good eye, Jack. I completely missed that!" The rest of the group stopped and everyone had binoculars up. "I won't set up the scope unless…" Ivy looked back at me. "My spotting scope will give you a feather-close look at any bird you want, Beck. Would you like to spend a few minutes with the loon?"

"Oh. Thanks. I often get close looks at loons when I'm working. I'm fine for now."

"Working?"

We were walking again, slowly.

"I'm a hydrologist for the state, Jack." I suddenly felt expansive. "Just last week, I watched two loons on Waterbury Reservoir. I thought they might be a breeding pair."

"It's getting near that time of year, that's for sure. Loons—"

Everyone came to an abrupt stop. The four in front had their binoculars aimed at a good-sized white pine tree. Ivy's voice was quiet as she told us to watch an odd-shaped lump on the right side of the main trunk, about twenty feet up.

"I don't see anything, Ivy." The boy was frowning, almost frantically twisting the focus knob on his binoculars. Then he gasped as a small bird separated from the bulge on the tree and flew toward us.

A swallow, I thought. Long, pointed wings, forked tail.

Then another swallow… and another… and then the "lump" dissolved as birds began pouring out of the relative dark near the tree trunk, twittering as they passed overhead.

"Holy shit." The awed whisper was from the boy, and the man with the mustache immediately touched his arm and frowned. "Sorry. But wow!"

"Wow indeed!" Ivy turned to us all with sparkling eyes and a wide smile. "It got really cold last night so all those swallows clustered together for warmth. Now, with the sun starting to heat things up, they've got to find bugs to eat and rebuild their energy, their strength." She looked around. "Did anyone see anything other than Barn, Tree and Northern Rough-winged?"

Head shakes all around, except for me. The only one I recognized was the first one, with the forked tail. "Barn Swallows are the only ones I know. Like the first one."

"Forked tails, right. Tree Swallows at this time of year have iridescent blue-green backs and white bellies."

"And no fork."

"Right, Sean. No forked tail. Northern Rough-winged Swallows are quiet colored birds…"

I stopped listening. Later I would look up swallows in my new field guide. Now, I just lifted my head and watched as a hundred swallows circled overhead and moved out over the water, and I was happy.

****

It was past my usual lunch time when I drove up our driveway, my stomach growling and my mind spinning with new knowledge and with the unfamiliar experience of having been with other people for hours and doing something other than work.

The dried grapes were completely gone when I passed the viburnums but I looked for the grouse anyway. I didn't look for it nearer the garage—but there it was, beside the driveway, its head cocked as it watched the car getting closer and closer.

"It is possible that you're not the brightest creature on this earth," I muttered. "Although you're not right in the driveway." I stopped, turned off the engine, and lowered the window. "Were you waiting for me?"

No answer from the bird, but I thought it leaned its head a little more to one side.

"Wait. I might have something for you." My lunch bag from the day before was still on the seat beside me. "Not much, but..." I crumbled two crackers in my fingers and tossed the crumbs toward the bird.

"Sesame seed crackers. Tasty and nutritious."

The grouse seemed to consider the cracker crumbs. After many seconds, it hopped closer and pecked at the ground.

"Good grouse! Eat them up. Oh!" I reached into the bag again and opened a small plastic box. "Gorp. Not much left, and the chocolate chips might not be good for you, but here are, um, two pieces of peanut and three raisins."

The grouse hopped back in alarm when I reached out the window and scattered the gorp, but this time it approached the food more quickly.

"Ah. So the nuts take precedence over stale crackers. Wise bird."

Both of us were silent, the grouse and I, as it finished the food I'd tossed out. Then it twitched its tail, turned, and disappeared into the foliage beside the driveway.

"Thank you, bird," I whispered. "You were a wonderful ending to a wonderful morning. Stay safe."

Chapter Two

It started, my time with Josef, with sparkles on fast-moving water and sun making my dark hair almost too hot to touch.

The stream was only a few inches deep by the near bank, running fast and clear and smooth over pebbles. A thin root reached out and made a tiny eddy where a bright green leaf spun round and round and round. The far side of the stream was very different. Last month's windstorm had loosened the soil around a huge willow and the tree had fallen into the stream. Most of the roots were exposed but the tree still held onto its new spring foliage. Leaves that were meant to unfurl and photosynthesize in the sunny air now bobbed sometimes on top of the water and sometimes beneath. The swirls around the thick trunk had scooped out a deep hole. That part of the stream was dark brown, the bottom hidden. I needed to collect samples from both sides, including that deep pool, and hip boots wouldn't cut it, so I went back to the car for my old chest-high bib waders.

I am an expert at changing clothes outdoors. I use what Alain called Beck's Patented All-purpose Field Cabana. With the front and back doors open on the same side of the car, I sat on the edge of the back seat to take off my shoes and socks. Then I stood up between the two doors, unbuttoned my khaki work shirt and draped it over the driver's side headrest.

Alain used to tease me about my wild under-secrets, the glowing t-shirts under the somber work clothes. Khaki or blue or olive green or gray on top; fire-engine red, school bus yellow, or neon green where no one could see. That day the poppy on my blue t-shirt was a bit faded but it still glowed in the filtered light under the trees.

The old waders didn't have any leaks, so I hadn't replaced them, but they were too tight to pull on over baggy field pants. I peeled off my chinos, spread them on the front passenger seat, and started the task of getting the bib waders up past my waist and the straps over my shoulders. After several minutes of shimmying, yanking and tugging, I straightened up, took a deep breath, picked up a bag full of little collection bottles, slammed the car doors, locked up, and hung the keys around my neck and under my t-shirt.

Now the hard part, and my favorite part. I waded into the stream, maneuvering over rounded stones, hidden branches, and unexpected sections of mud, feeling with one foot, inching forward, feeling with the other and inching forward again, the current trying to push me sideways with every step. The water was all around me, and I felt like I was part of it.

It was the job of half an hour to gather water from six locations, lift rocks and collect samples of invertebrate life, and spend a few unproductive but deeply satisfying moments watching a school of small fish under the fallen tree.

When I ducked under the willow to start my cautious slog back across the stream, a branch caught my hair, my head jerked back, my hair clip fell off, and I foolishly grabbed for it. My feet went out from under me and I sat down hard, icy water pouring into my waders. Gasping, sputtering, muttering, chuckling, I made it across the stream, clambered up the slippery bank and waddled toward the car like a toddler with a load in her pants. After struggling out of the chest-high waders and dumping a few gallons of water out of each leg, I stood for a minute, wringing out my heavy hair and making a rough braid. My t-shirt, bra and panties were drenched, and the cool breeze made me shiver. After a quick look around, I pulled the t-shirt over my head, took off my bra, and gratefully thrust my arms into the sun-warmed work shirt. Now for chinos, shoes and socks.

"'Scuse me."

I straightened up so quickly that I smacked my head on the door frame.

A man was standing only a few yards away, holding a camera with a long lens.

"Sorry to startle you. I just wanted to ask your permission to use some of the photos."

I purely hate being surprised, and I had just hit my head hard. My voice was icy. "This is not my land. You will have to ask the farmer."

"Photos of you."

I stood up, holding the dry chinos in front of my legs. "What? Where were you? I didn't see you taking pictures."

"On the other side." He gestured. "It's easy to get across the stream up there a ways." He grinned and I was suddenly aware that he was astonishingly handsome, like an actor or a model, with olive skin and white teeth and black hair. "You looked great. The stream. The trees. All that dark hair."

"And you want my permission to use the photos? The pictures you took without asking? For what?"

"I'm here now, asking. I'm working on a book. A photo essay about working women." He raised the camera. "I've got an auto mechanic and an indoor carpenter so far, and a couple of farmers." He grinned, a wide white grin that looked like he could be on a toothpaste commercial. "One is twenty or something, the other is eighty-seven. Great contrast."

I scowled and sat back down to pull on my chinos, socks, and shoes.

"You are doing your job, right? You're not just mucking around in a stream for fun?"

I stood up, flipping my braid over my shoulder. "I am a hydrologist. Please put the camera down."

"Would you like to see some of the photos of you?" He took a step closer. "The sun is going to make it hard to see them on the screen but maybe you can get an idea."

"Hand it to me."

He turned the camera around and carefully placed it in my hands.

"Tap here to move to another photo."

I saw myself wading into the stream, bending to fill collection bottles, standing near the far side, grinning as I watched the school of fish.

"You probably want to skip over the total immersion." He took his camera back, fiddled with something, and handed it back to me. "I'll delete those later."

Now the screen showed me with my head tilted, braiding my wet hair, t-shirt plastered to my front and droplets of water on my face and neck.

"A few great shots there. If you have any more stops today, I'd like to tag along."

"I don't particularly enjoy having my picture taken.

I never have."

"I'll stand at a distance. Once you get busy, you'll forget I'm there."

I stared at him, frowning, until most people would have given up, but this man just kept looking at me with a slight smile on his handsome face.

"If I stop noticing you after the first few minutes, you can stay. If that's not the case, you'll have to go on your way."

"Fair enough. I'm Josef, by the way. Josef Andrews." He exaggerated the YUH sound at the beginning of his first name. "Used to be Andreyev, way back. Probably changed on Ellis Island." He smiled again. "Your name?"

"Beck."

"Beck? Just Beck?"

I nodded and turned abruptly to get into my car.

"Beck it is."

****

At my next stop, Josef stayed far back from where I was working, partly hidden behind a big oak. I didn't see him again until after I waded ashore.

"Thanks, Beck. Beck—interesting name."

I took off my waders.

"There's a form for you to sign, giving me permission to use some of the photos in the book. But I don't have a copy with me. If you tell me where you live, I'll stop by your house with one."

I hesitated.

"Or you could write down your mailing address. Or I'll write down where you can find me. I live and work right in Montpelier."

I took a deep breath. "27 Gorham Hill. East

Montpelier."

****

I am not sure, even now, how it happened, what was first and next and third, what I said, what he said, what either of us did. Josef came by that evening, and then he was in my house. In my bed. He showed up at supper time the next night too, and he made love to me again.

No. That's not right.

It was never making love. I don't think there's a good term for what we did so often in those first months. He did sex to me? Again, and again, and again, almost every day. And I reveled in it. I reveled with my whole body. Every single cell felt as if it had been parched and was now swollen and alive. I felt as if my eyes were brighter, my hair shinier. I wasn't in love. I don't think I even liked him. But I loved those months of sex.

It was never the same as it had been with Alain. Sex with Josef was never slow and quiet. It was never so intensely intimate that sometimes we both would cry. I would never have chosen sex with Josef over sex with Alain.

And, to this day, I don't understand me. It. I don't understand the whole thirteen months. I had spent four years grieving, four years yearning and aching to see Alain again, to look up and see him across the kitchen table from me, reading in his favorite chair, reaching up to get a book or a mug or to straighten a picture on the wall. Alain smiling, his eyes crinkling. Alain somber, thinking hard about something I'd said or something he was writing. I ached to feel him again, to smell him, to kiss him and be kissed by him and make love with him and fall asleep against his body, sated and happy and so incredibly lucky.

I never thought, for a moment, that I also missed sex, just sex, the act itself.

****

"Been thinking, Beck. I'm paying rent downtown and I'm almost never there. That's dumb, when I could be living here."

I put down the grater and the last huge cabbage from my garden. "I think... That's a bit abrupt, Josef. We've known each other less than a month."

"Not talking commitment here, Beck. Just common sense. When my book comes out, I'll probably do some sort of speaking tour or something. Or I'll want to move to a bigger city. But for now, I'm driving out of my way every single day to get clothes or stuff. If I bring everything here, I can just go to work and come straight here. I'll split the money I save on rent and gas, half to you and the other half saved for my future. Help you out, help me out. It's a win-win, Beck."

"I... I've lived alone for quite a while now, Josef. I've come to cherish my privacy. These last few weeks have been... exciting..."

"Putting it mildly."

"... but that's probably temporary, until it stops being so new."

"Maybe. Probably. But my crashing here would be temporary too." He stood up suddenly. "I know! I'll put my stuff in that little upstairs room, the one at the end of the hall. There's a bed in there, right?"

"Yes, but—"

"The place I'm renting is furnished, so I don't have any furniture to clutter things up. We can share a bed whenever we want or sleep separately whenever we want. It'll be pretty much the same as it is now, but..."

His voice was soft, cajoling. "It'll be better for both of us, Beck. Better for both."

At first, having Josef living in my house didn't change much of anything. I worked days, he worked at the Photo Emporium in downtown Montpelier evenings and Saturdays. He was often gone taking pictures all day Sunday. The only change at first was the nights, when he would get back from work at 10:00 or 11:00 or even later and come into my bedroom. And afterward, he would go back to his own bed.

****

When I came downstairs on the morning of my birthday, there was a spotting scope set up in the living room, on one of Josef's tripods, with a garish pink bow. We weren't the kind of lovers, or even the kind of friends, who gave each other extravagant gifts.

"Big discount if I bought three items, Beck. So I got the scope for you, plus that scope cover even though it's sort of the wrong size, plus that pricey lens I've been wanting. Win-win, Beck. Win-win." He grinned. "I'm gonna want the tripod back when I move out, but you can use it with your new scope for now."

****

"You going out with the bird people today?"

I looked up from making the morning coffee. "Yes. Of course."

"I'm coming with you. See all the excitement for myself."

"Oh." I turned away from him and got out two mugs. "How do I introduce you?"

"What?"

"I'm not entirely comfortable announcing to this group of people that I'm living with you." I felt foolish and I am sure I looked it. "Many people do, of course. Live together without being married. But it makes me uncomfortable."

"What about 'this here's Josef'? Why does it have to be any more detailed?"

"Oh. No. I suppose that is all that's needed."

He grinned his lopsided, glistening white smile. "Or you could tell them we met a few weeks ago and we been fucking like rabbits ever since."

"Do you want eggs this morning?"

****

My fretting about how to introduce him was totally unnecessary. At least thirty birders were waiting in the big pull-off when we arrived, many more than the usual group, all setting up tripods and scopes or staring through binoculars at the field in front of us. Ivy said hi to me, looked at Josef, he said his name, she grinned, and that was that.

"The annual Snow Goose expedition always attracts lots more club members than most of the FATSO walks," she told me as she finished setting up her scope. "We're in luck today. Sometimes the whole flock is way over there in a ditch or a gully and we don't see them at all unless something scares them up."

Josef had his camera out, muttering as he adjusted it and took a few practice shots.

"Hey, babe. If we ever come down here again, remind me to bring a sheet."

"What?"

"Great shots if I was lying on my belly. Real money shots. Look right into their faces."

I had never seen so many birds at one time. I had never seen that many of any kind of animal at once. And the last time I'd seen an equivalent number of humans in one place was the weekend Alain and I spent in Montréal, and we were outdoors on the streets at midnight on New Year's Eve. Now the goose noise was constant: subdued honks, whistles, grunts, high-pitched quacks. The big birds were having conversations, exchanging information. I thought about trying to count them but someone near me said there were about 6800 in all, and it was more enjoyable to watch than to try and get my own count.

"Hey." Josef was sitting cross-legged on the gravel now, snapping photos at almost the same level as the birds' heads. "What's up with the gray ones?"

Ivy answered. "They're youngsters. They just fledged, a few weeks ago. They stick with their parents during migration."

"Young and adults in the same frame. Money shots, babe."

"Is this a young goose also? Or something different?" I moved aside so Ivy could take a look through my new scope.

"Ah! Good eye! That is a Snow Goose even though it doesn't look like one. It's a different morph. People used to think they were a different species, called Blue Goose, but th—Whoa!"

Without warning, all 6800 geese took to the air with an enormous whoosh of air and wings, an enormous racket of honking and croaking. The flock went over our heads, heading toward the road, circled over the next field, and then wheeled and started back.

I was breathless, unexpectedly choked with emotion. Next to me, Ivy had her head tipped back and was laughing, a belly laugh of delight and excitement.

"Oh, yes! Oh, yes! The best sight and sound in the whole world!"

A few geese, and then a few small groups, and then the whole flock came down again just a few hundred yards west of where they were before.

"Huh." Ivy was scanning above the birds' heads with her binoculars. "Usually something sets them off, like a Bald Eagle. But I don't see one." She turned to me, still grinning. "Maybe they just needed to stretch their wings or… Hey!"

She was looking beyond me and she was no longer laughing or smiling. She brushed past and started walking, almost running, along the fence line.

"Hey! You! Come out of there now!"

Josef was several yards inside the restricted area, crouching beside a sizeable patch of burdock. He was my responsibility. I brought him.

"Josef!" I bellowed. "Get OUT of there!"

He straightened up, walked back toward the fence and ducked under it.

"They would have come right next to me. Golden opportunity. What's all the yelling?"

Ivy turned on her heel and headed back to her scope.

"I snuck in there fast while they were flying. Gotta be alert for chances like that, babe, if you're gonna be a real photographer."

"It's posted every few yards, Josef." My hand shook a little as I pointed to one of the white signs. "Restricted Access. No trespassing. You are tagging along on a BBC trip. You should follow BBC rules."

"What the hell is BBC? I thought you guys were fat-something."

"If someone from Fish and Wildlife had seen you,

you could have been hit with a hundred seventy-five dollar fine."

"But they didn't see me. And I got some great pic's. What's the big deal?"

I turned and started packing up my scope and Josef's tripod.

****

There was a grouse in the driveway. I slowed way down and coasted to a stop.

"Honk your horn, Beck. It'll move."

"It's a Ruffed Grouse."

"I could give a rat's ass. I gotta pee." He leaned over and pressed the horn, and the grouse took off. "Floor it, Beck. I really gotta go."

Chapter Three

"Time to get serious about the book, Beck. Treat it like a job, a real job."

I was only partly listening, intent on the grocery list, amazed anew at how much more food two people ate.

"I've got most of the photos, babe. Now I've got to spend mucho hours organizing, putting it in order, adding some text. Not much logic in yakking about doing a book and then not really doing it."

"That makes sense," I said absently.

"It does to me too. So last night I told the boss I'm going to cut down to two evenings a week."

Now he was around almost all the time, shuffling down to the kitchen while I ate breakfast, around almost every night for supper. For a week or so he was interested in sex whenever he got bored or ran into a problem with the book, and for the first time since I met him, sometimes I wasn't.

****

Josef's second outing with the Burlington Bird Club was no more successful than the first. Jack wasn't available to drive the rented van for a boreal bird outing and asked Josef if he would take over. We got lost, the van got stuck, and every single person in the van ended the day grouchy and irritated.

His third outing was even worse. Josef wasn't interested in the birds, only in getting some pictures that he could sell to the calendar company he'd worked with before, or maybe frame and sell in the Photo Emporium. And he was impatient with anything that got in the way of that goal.

Things started out well when we all got great looks at a Bald Eagle out on the ice in Lake Champlain, feeding on a duck.

"This is gonna be one great photo. A money shot." Josef pulled a digital camera from a pocket along with a small black device. "My new toy. Adaptor. Don't have to bring my big camera. Gettin' in on that thare digiscoping thang." He elbowed me out of the way and screwed his camera and adaptor to the end of my new spotting scope.

The group watched the adult eagle and an immature eagle, and a huge raft of diving ducks, while Josef took picture after picture. Then the newest member of the group spotted two Barred Owls in a tree not far from the bluff where we were all standing.

"Yes!" Josef's voice was almost in my ear. "That's what I came for, babe. Whole lot better than distant dots of ducks!" He fiddled with the scope and camera, muttering about "the money shot" as he headed across the frozen field.

The owls swiveled their heads, watching his approach, and Ivy called out, "Not too close, Josef. With the nest right there, they can be easily agitated."

"Nah. They don't care." He kept walking, closer and closer to the two owls.

There was a grunt from the man with the mustache that looked like a bushy Fu Manchu, and he abruptly left the group and headed toward Josef. Those of us on the bluff couldn't hear what he said, but Josef whirled around, his face tight and angry. He shouldered the heavy tripod, hitting the other man with the metal legs, and stalked across the field to my car. We all watched as he tossed the scope and tripod in the trunk, got in, started the car, and left.

"Next time I won't leave the keys under the seat." I tried to sound calmer than I felt. "There goes my car and my new scope."

Charlie's face was grim as he rejoined the group.

"What did you tell him?"

"Same as you would've, Ivy. BBC-sponsored trip. No harassing birds."

"He's not going home, you know." I watched my car disappear into the distance.

"Beg pardon?"

"Josef. I am willing to bet that he will stop a little way south of here and give us time to leave. Then he'll come back and he will just about climb up into that tree to get a good picture." I tried a little laugh, but it came out more like a gasp. "Gotta get that money shot."

"Well…" Ivy stared out at the road, frowning. "Well, then, we'll just outlast him. He'll come back and we'll still be here. Then he'll drive by again, and we'll be here then too. And then maybe he'll give up."

No one else was in a hurry to get home, but I was done. "I will need a ride home later, Ivy. May I go sit in your car until you're ready?

"You don't think he'll come back for you?"

"He's… Josef is focused on Josef's interests. So no."

"Here are the keys. Turn it on if you want heat."

****

As I pulled into the driveway a few days later, I

30

could see Josef out by the chicken coop. I didn't want him mucking around with anything Alain built, but I was too cold, wet, and muddy to investigate. I wanted to go inside, strip, and stand under a hot shower until I stopped shivering and my toes thawed out. I had spent two full hours walking the fields with a farmer who used to spread manure on fields right next to the river. Three years earlier, under pressure from the state, he agreed to a wide buffer zone of willows and scrub as well as a catchment ditch, and the water samples I took downstream from his fields proved that his improvements were working. The man was as proud as if the whole project had been his idea from the start. He wanted me to walk the length of the ditch. He wanted me to see how well the willows were doing. He wanted me to walk with him through cold ankle-deep mud while he talked and talked and talked.

It wasn't till I was halfway home that two possibilities came to me. The man was lonely, or he was enjoying a little bit of wet and muddy revenge against one of the people who cost him part of his hay fields.

By the time I was washed, warm, dry, and dressed, Josef was in the kitchen.

"I did something today you're gonna love, babe! You know that farm with the big silvery silo?"

I nodded, wary.

"I took a run this morning, and I got to talking with the woman there. She's moving out of state so she sold her chickens to me."

"Chickens?"

"Laying hens. Well, four of 'em anyway. Fresh eggs. You've got the coop and now we've got the chickens. It's perfect!"

"Just four?"

"Ten, actually. The others are for roasting, she said. Orlinghams or something."

"Orpingtons? Buff Orpingtons?"

"That's it. Jeez, babe, you really know your birds. The Buff ones lay eggs too. Just not so many as the other ones. It was all or nothing, so I took 'em all."

I walked stiffly to the refrigerator and got out a dish of leftovers. "Chickens are a lot of work, Josef. That's why Alain and I gave up on them."

"So? I'm home all day. I've got time to burn. All you've gotta do is eat eggs whenever you want." He put his arms around me and nuzzled my neck. "Four Barred Rock hens, babe. Good layers, the woman said. And besides…" He reached past me and grabbed a bottle of beer. "You like birds."

He plopped himself down at the table and grinned that wide, beautiful smile. "Oh. My car needs some brake work before it'll pass inspection. I need you to pick me up at Moody's Garage when you're done work tomorrow. And maybe you can drop me off at work for a few days." He lifted the beer bottle to his mouth. "Maybe a few days, maybe a week."

"Moody's is going to take that long with an inspection? They're usually pretty fast."

"Yeah, well. I can't pay him until Friday. Payday."

****

I have thought and thought and thought about why I let Josef live with me in the first place. About why I went right on allowing him to stay in my house, for months and months, in the house I'd shared with Alain. I tried to tell myself that I'd been lonely, even though I hadn't realized it, that I was swept away by the excitement of sex again after so many years, that I was impressed by Josef's talk about a book deal, that I thought of him as a famous photographer, a professional author. I reminded myself how pleased I was that day at work when I noticed all the calendars hanging in offices and cubicles had six of Josef's pictures.

I didn't actively dislike him until Jack's accident.

It had not even dawned on me that Jack had become an important part of my life. I wondered at the beginning if his endless cheer would become irritating, but that hadn't happened in eleven birding expeditions. I liked and respected the bouncy man with the ready smile. And now that sunny, always enthusiastic man was in Intensive Care.

Ivy called early in the morning, her voice shaking, to tell me that Jack had a freak accident just after I'd pulled out of the parking lot after the last FATSO outing. I didn't understand her whole story, but apparently a dumpster slipped off a forklift, demolishing Jack's little car and hitting him.

"Oh, my god. How is, how is he doing? What did it do to him?"

"Just a knock on the forehead and a scrape on his leg. He was sitting up and talking and lively when the EMTs got there. Molly and Hugh were amazing, Beck, like a team who'd been first responders together a hundred times. But then Jack contracted some sort of superbug in the hospital—" Ivy stopped to inhale. "He's—" Her voice broke. "Jack is fighting for his life, Beck."

I felt my eyes fill with tears, and I could not say anything.

"So we're…" Ivy's voice strengthened. "Rose is

spending most of her time at the hospital. We can't visit him because he's in quarantine. So we're organizing a food drop-off. At their house, so Rose won't have to worry about cooking."

I found my voice. "When?"

"This afternoon. We've got a key so we'll let ourselves in. About four?"

"Yes. That sounds good. Yes. Thanks for calling."

There wasn't much in the freezer or refrigerator, and Josef had my car. He said he'd be back around 3:00, which wouldn't leave much time for me to run to the store. Maybe I could pick up something at Guido's or Jorge's on the way to Jack's house.

No. I wanted to make something. I wanted to bring Jack's wife something that I had spent time on.

I dithered for at least a half hour, trying to come up with something to make, something to bring that Rose could reheat for a quick meal. I was staring out the window when I realized the chickens were in the front yard. Josef let them out every morning and lured them back into the coop every afternoon. He would shake a can full of cracked corn and they'd come running from all over, desperate to get at the corn even though they'd been eating bugs and seeds all day. Josef called the corn chicken cocaine.

The Buff Orpingtons were meat hens. I didn't like the idea of killing and plucking one, at all, but I knew how to do it from when Alain and I had our flock.

****

Josef got back at 3:40. For the first time since I met him, he was in a foul mood. He snarled when I met him in the driveway. He hated his job, he hated his boss, he was angry at Moody for something about his car, the book wasn't going as fast as he had hoped. His face dared me to say something about his being late. And as he handed over the car keys, he reminded me that I had to drop him off at the Photo Emporium at 5:00.

"You'll have to come with me, then. To Jack's."

"Why're we going there? It's out of the way."

"Jack is in the hospital. A superbug, Ivy said." I put my bag in the back seat. "We're bringing food for his wife."

"Grocery stores deliver, you know. You order online. It's the twenty-first century, even up here in the boonies."

I started the car before Josef was all the way in the door. Neither of us said anything on the drive to Jack's. Three members of the FATSO group were already there, Molly in front of the open refrigerator and Charlie and Hugh unloading grocery bags on the counter. I lifted my canvas tote onto the butcherblock island.

"Is there room in the freezer for two casserole dishes?"

Josef peered into the bag. "Two dishes, Beck. Nice! What's in 'em?"

"Chicken cacciatore." I took one of the foil-wrapped dishes out of the bag. "For later."

"Visiting hours? The wake?"

Molly's gasp was loud in the sudden silence.

"What? I'm being realistic. Lot of people don't beat those superbugs. That's why they call 'em super."

I took the second dish out of the bag. "This is for when Jack is home again. It's his favorite casserole."

"Where'd you get the chicken?" Josef's voice was cold, harsh.

"What?"

"You heard me."

I could see the others stiffen at his tone.

"It's one of the Buff Orpingtons."

"Uh uh. Not acceptable, Beck. Not acceptable at all. Those hens were still laying. I got them for eggs."

"A few of them are laying hens. The others were bred for meat." My lips were stiff. My whole body was stiff. "Jack is a friend. You were gone. You had my car. I couldn't go to the store. I killed one of the chickens. Watch your head, Molly."

There was dead quiet while I opened the freezer and put the two dishes inside. I couldn't turn around. I couldn't see the others' faces. "Chicken cacciatore is Jack's favorite."

"And you know that. Touching. Jack foolin' around on the side, huh? With you, Beck? Cheatin' on his preggers wife?"

I wheeled around then. I didn't even see the others. I picked up the empty bag off the counter and I made it out of the kitchen, made it to the car, got in, and I left.

****

My one year and one month with Josef started because of photography, and sex. It ended because of photography and sex.

He never mentioned the cacciatore again. He never told me how he got to work that evening, or how he made it back to my house in the early hours of the morning. I barely saw him at all in the week after that day in Jack's kitchen. He got his car back, he went to work, I went to work, and he spent a lot of time in his room presumably sorting and cropping photographs. But one day when I got home, he was at the kitchen table. His laptop was set up in front of him and he was smiling at me almost as beautifully as he had in the early days, his dark eyes glowing with excitement.

"Break out the champagne, honey babe! I got myself a book deal!"

"The book about working women?"

"Yes indeedeo."

"Congratulations." I might have said more, might have asked him when his book would be published, if I hadn't caught sight of his computer screen. It was a photo of me, one I hadn't seen before. I was standing, framed by the two blue car doors, my wet braid over one shoulder. Sparkling drops of water poured out of the waders that I held out to the side, water glistening on bare legs and feet. My torso was bare, nipples hard and raised.

"What... What is that?"

"Great pic, huh? Panties and those big rubber waders. Sexy as hell."

"You... I thought you showed me the pictures you took that day."

"Not all of them. Duh. You would've freaked out."

"Where were... You must have been straight out from the car."

"Yeah." He looked up at me and grinned. "I took a lot of shots from the other side of the river and then I found a place upstream to get across, and lo and behold. There you were. Right smack in front of me, taking off your clothes. Lucky photographer break." He turned back to the computer. "The publisher loved these shots. A hard-working woman, outdoors, looking like a woman. Big nipples and all. Great stuff."

I took a step backward, away from the table and the computer and the pictures. "What about ethics, Josef? Aren't you supposed to get permission before sending photos to, to editors? Aren't the models supposed to be told?"

"You're not a model, Beck. You were an accident. Those photos were an accident. A lucky opportunity."

"You took those photos without my knowledge or permission, and other people have seen them, again without my knowledge or permission."

"Artistic license, babe. The photos are part of my artistic portfolio. And you're one of my muses. This book, with your image, is gonna make me famous." He scrolled through his photos again, absorbed, murmuring to himself. "Your image and all these other images. The editor thinks I need a few more nude or almost nude shots. Different kinda body than yours. For contrast. Maybe that prof in the college photog program could send someone…" He looked up and raised his eyebrows. "No need for you to be jealous, babe. Naked models aren't sex objects. Not for artists. They're just collections of curves and shadows."

****

The next day I got home earlier than usual, muddy again, wet and cold and smelling like stagnant water and probably a bit like cow manure. I dropped my backpack beside the front door and then stopped dead when I heard two voices coming from upstairs.

"One more session, Samantha." Josef's voice. "Not tomorrow because it's supposed to rain and the light will be wrong. What about Thursday, first thing in the morning? Seven-thirty?"

"Got it, Josef." It sounded like a girl, not a woman. "I'll be here with bells on. Or off, as the case may be."

I ducked into the kitchen.

"Oh! Wait." Josef's voice came from the front hall.

"I said I'd pay you at the end of each session."

I could see his hand reach out and pick up my backpack, and I heard him unzip it. "Here you go."

"Thanks. Thursday."

Josef closed the door and turned toward the kitchen. "Beck! You're home!"

"You knew I was home. You just took money out of my backpack to pay that girl."

He opened the fridge and got out a bottle of ale, holding it up toward me with one eyebrow cocked.

"No, thanks."

"Good. Only one left anyway." He twisted the cap and took a swig. "Samantha's perfect. She's a welder, would you believe it? I called the human figures instructor at the college, and he sent her over. I could not have chosen better myself."

He set the half-empty bottle on the kitchen counter. "And now, let's spend a little couple time. You. Me. Right now, right here."

"I don't—"

"Yes you do." He rubbed against me. "I'm hard as hell."

"You said models aren't sex objects."

"They're not. Ask any artist."

"You were turned on by that young model. Photographing her made you horny."

"She looked damned fine naked, and that's a true fact. She's got a lot stuffed into that small body." He took me by the shoulders and looked me up and down. "Guys have a phrase for bodies like yours, babe. All that meat and no potatoes. Sometimes a guy likes lookin' at taters." He took a step forward, pushing me back against the counter. "But taters or no, you and I have had some fine times. Fine."

"Not now, Josef. I stink."

"C'mon, babe. I know we haven't been exactly burning the sheets recently, and that's probably on me. Busy with the book and all. But that means we're both needing it. Bad."

I looked at the man who had lived in my home for over a year, at his dark hair and dark eyes and beautiful, beautiful smile. And I wanted him out of my life.

"Win-win, Beck. I get a major load off, and you get a good hard fucking from a good hard man. Win-win."

"I want you to leave, Josef."

"What?"

"You were going to leave in a few weeks anyway, when your book comes out. I want you to leave now." I straightened my shoulders. "I want you to gather up your belongings, put them in your car, and drive away."

Josef's face hardened. For the first time, I saw something frightening in his eyes. But I could feel the kitchen counter behind me, and my right hand was near the block holding all the knives. I refused to be afraid.

"I am going upstairs. I am going to take a shower and get into dry clothes. Then I'm coming downstairs to get something to eat, and I want you gone by then."

****

I wasn't completely stupid. I locked my bedroom door and also put a chair under the handle. I debated locking the door to the master bathroom too but I wanted to leave it open so I could see into the bedroom, so I could keep my eyes on that locked door.

Nothing happened while I undressed, while I tossed my filthy clothes into the hamper, while I showered, while I dried off and got out warm clothes and put them on. But I could hear movement from downstairs: doors and maybe drawers opening and closing, something heavy being pulled across a floor, Josef muttering.

I waited, upstairs in my bedroom, until the house fell silent and I heard a car door slam. Then I cautiously opened my door and tiptoed, feeling foolish and angry because of it, to the window at the end of the hall.

Josef's car was making the turn-around in front of the house. And then he was heading down the driveway and away.

I find this hard to believe, but it's true: I went downstairs, I got some leftovers out of the refrigerator, I put them on a plate and reheated them in the microwave, I took the plate and the rest of Josef's bottle of ale into the living room, and I never even noticed the chickens.

Chapter Four

The next morning, I left the dead chickens where they were.

I tried not to look at them. I tried not to see the hen in the downstairs bathroom, on the toilet seat. The one at the kitchen table, in my chair, head flopping sideways on its broken neck. I tried not to see the dead hen on the counter with its bill in the butter dish.

I made myself take a quick look at the living room, but there were no hens there. I made myself look into the porch, and there were two hens in the rocking chairs, their limp bodies like feathered seat cushions.

The scope and tripod—my spotting scope, Josef's tripod—were on top of the cabinets where I put them the last time I washed the floors. He must not have seen them. He would never have intentionally left his tripod for me.

"Bird Walk" was written in the calendar square for the day. I would go. I would leave the chickens. I would deal with them later. I was going birding.

****

Several cars were in the parking lot when I got to the meeting place but there was no one around. They must have headed down the trail to the place where a drawdown by Fish and Wildlife exposed a wide area of mudflats, a place Ivy promised would have oodles of shorebirds.

I would enjoy this morning. I would think about nothing but birding. I would listen to Ivy talk about shorebirds, and I'd listen to Sean asking excited questions, and I'd hear Charlie's deep quiet voice, and if silent Hugh said something I would listen to that too, and I would not think about anything else. I would be birding.

But I couldn't get the scope fastened onto the tripod. Josef always put them together. Josef always acted as if they were both his, his toys, even though he said the scope was a present for me. Now I couldn't get them together so I could use them. It was ridiculous. I was ridiculous. I was panting, almost in tears. After many infuriating minutes, I gave up and telescoped the tripod legs and hauled the heavy thing across my arms with the spotting scope on top. I hurried along the path, my body slightly bent at the waist and both arms cradling the awkward weight.

Ivy said it was only a half mile to where we would be birding but I felt as if I walked, stumbled, three times that far before I caught up with the others.

"I am sorry. I'm late. I had… I had difficulty leaving the house. And then I could not get the scope onto the tripod."

Ivy took a step toward me. "I'm glad you could make it, Beck. You haven't missed anything yet."

"Are there any shorebirds?"

"Some of us tried the regular spot without success so we're heading down to the end of the trail. Maybe there's more exposed mud there."

Charlie took the scope out of my arms, handed it to Hugh, and lifted the tripod. He extended the legs, set it on the ground, and examined the top. "Yeah. Thought so." He took back the scope, brought it to the top of the tripod, pushed two levers, and handed it back to me. "Now you can carry the whole shebang easier."

"Thank you."

"Is Josef coming?"

"Josef is not coming. Josef is gone."

I hoisted the scope and tripod over my shoulder, the way Charlie and Ivy always carried theirs, the way Josef had always carried my scope, and I marched off down the trail.

****

There were scores of little birds, their cryptic coloring making them almost invisible at first glance. Some were walking around on the mud, stopping frequently to probe with their bills. Others huddled motionless, each behind its own little root or bit of tree trunk.

I opened the too-large case on my scope and froze. My voice sounded loud to my ears.

"Josef always acts like this is his. He bought it, but he said it was a present for me."

I felt a touch on my arm and looked down at Molly.

"Then you should use it, Beck. And what better use for it than to ogle shorebirds?"

"I can't."

Josef's digiscoping adaptor was attached to the scope. Josef's. I grabbed it, holding it with my fingertips as if it might burn me, and wrenched the thing off and threw it far out into the water.

About two dozen small tan birds took flight in alarm, and all the birders were silent.

"I apologize. I frightened the shorebirds away." I turned to the others. "And I threw litter into, into a wildlife management area."

I had a sudden urge to laugh, but then I saw Jack. Jack! I had forgotten all about Jack. This was his first outing after his accident, and I hadn't even noticed him, hadn't welcomed him back. He looked a good deal thinner and his face was pale, but his eyes sparkled and he looked kind, like a dear old friend.

"Jack. I didn't see you. How are you feeling?"

"I am better than good, Beck. I'm alive and I'm happy and I'm birding. What could be better?" His expression changed, and he looked closely into my eyes. "Do you want to tell us what happened?"

"Josef is gone. It's not a big deal." I looked around at the group. "You all know he wasn't very… He wasn't a pleasant human being. Having him in my life was a stupid mistake. I am not upset about Josef. I am upset about the chickens. But I will be fine in a moment." I turned back to the birds, back to the scope that was supposed to be mine.

"Chickens?"

"It is not important. We are here for birding."

In silence, the others turned again toward the mud and the water and the birds. Sun broke through the clouds and bathed the flat sheets of shallow water beyond the mud with silver light that was almost blinding. I didn't realize I was shaking until Charlie stepped closer and took off his flannel shirt, and I stood motionless while he draped it over my shoulders.

"Thank you." The shirt was warm, body warm, and I wanted to wrap myself in it, hug myself with it, bury my cold face in it. "He killed the hens."

"Eh?"

"Those hens he bought. Josef wrung their necks. Some of them, anyway. Maybe all. I didn't finish looking."

"Oh, Beck. I'm so sorry." Molly and Ivy moved closer as if they could protect me with their nearness.

"He didn't just kill them and leave them out in the coop. He put them... Before he left, he put them around the house. For me to find." A few minutes earlier, I was afraid I might cry but now my eyes were dry and I even gave a short laugh. "They were displayed for me. One in the kitchen, propped up on my chair. One on the counter with its head in the butter dish."

I was shivering again, even with Charlie's warm shirt.

"In the porch. On chairs..." I shook my head hard. "It doesn't matter. We are here to watch shorebirds." I bent and looked through my scope.

"Lots of little birds! Confetti! It looks like confetti!"

Sean's excited voice helped focus me. There was a flock of shorebirds coming fast, and we all tried to get them in our sights.

"At about twelve o'clock, heading right. Six feet or so above the water. Flying fast. Now two o'clock. Now three." Ivy glanced around at the others. "Don't try to find them in your binocs. Just watch in the air for glittering bits of confetti, like Sean said. They've circled around. They're in front of us again, about halfway to the opposite shore. Maybe they'll come down closer to us."

"Why don't they just come in and land?"

"Probably checking for dangers. Come on down," Ivy murmured. "Your fans are waiting."

In unison, a half dozen pairs of binoculars were lowered and focused on a nearby mudflat.

"Sandpipers." Ivy watched for a few seconds and then turned to adjust her scope. "You can divide shorebirds into two broad categories, those with long legs and those with short legs. Many of the long-legged ones can be distinguished from each other by color along with the length and shape of their bills. The short-legged ones, which are often called peeps, are more challenging to identify. They split into two other groups, plovers and sandpipers."

I heard Sean mutter "peeps" and giggle.

****

"It's getting near lunch time. Ready to head back?"

I was. I grabbed my scope and the tripod and hefted them over my shoulder and marched down the trail, with Charlie only a few steps behind. I didn't want any questions. I wanted to relive the last few hours, relive birds and quiet and sun sparkling on muddy water. I didn't want to think about what was waiting at home. But before I realized I had come to a decision, I was talking, raising my voice so all of them behind Charlie and me could hear.

"I could hear him downstairs, moving around. Going outdoors. Coming back in. I thought he was taking his camera equipment out to the car. His other stuff. I never thought of the poor hens. That's what he was doing. He was putting the hens around."

I stumbled, off balance with the heavy scope over my shoulder. I felt Charlie's hand grab my elbow and I shook it off.

"I heard his car going down the driveway and I felt relief. Alone again, in my house. MY house. I locked my bedroom door and I slept like a baby all night long."

"What did you do with the chickens, Beck? Where are they now?"

"Nothing. I didn't do anything with them. If I'd

known last night, known that he had killed them, I could have used them. Cleaned them. Put them in the freezer." I was suddenly overwhelmed by the waste. "By the time I found them, they had been dead for hours. Now they are nothing but compost."

The parking lot was visible ahead of us, and we were all walking a bit faster.

Charlie turned to me. "Following you home."

"What? No! Why? Of course not! I am fine."

"Not up for discussion."

Ivy nodded. "We have to know you're safe, Beck."

I felt fierce and defensive and hassled. I wished I had never mentioned Josef and the chickens. Now they were talking about coming home with me, and changing the locks, and helping me with the dead fowl. And Charlie said he was going to stay overnight.

Ivy reached out and touched my arm.

"Charlie's being sensible, Beck. That's an isolated house. You shouldn't be alone."

"Josef is long gone. He is not a threat." I wanted them to understand, wanted them to know how it was between Josef and me. "He's not broken up about us. I'm not either. I was… It was a convenience for him to stay with me. That is all. And he didn't want me to end up with the chickens he paid for." I felt another surge of fury. "Even though I paid for almost everything else."

Molly usually looked ready to smile, ready to be amazed and amused by humans and delighted by nature. But now her huge eyes were worried.

"Hurting animals is a symptom, Beck. It's recognized as a frequent precursor, a sign that there's potential there for sadism. For hurting humans and enjoying it."

"Josef didn't *hurt* the chickens. He didn't torture them. He wrung their necks, the same as I did with the one I cooked. It's just—"

Ivy interrupted. "It's just leaving them around like he did. That's not normal, Beck. It's creepy."

She was right. It wasn't normal. I felt suddenly weak, almost limp.

"All right. Stay tonight, Charlie. Thank you."

As Ivy and Hugh started toward the cars, he put his arm around her shoulders and bent close and said something, and she looked up at him with such a glowing smile that it startled me.

"I thought those two were barely speaking to each other."

Molly looked like her old self again, with twinkling eyes and a mischievous grin, not at all like the somber ER nurse from a moment ago. "Believe me, Beck. It was THE surprise of the morning. Even better than the White-rumped Sandpiper."

I should have seen it. It had been obvious all morning, but I missed it, just as I hadn't noticed Jack was back, that he was on his first birding outing since he almost died.

"I should… I should be happy for them. But I'm not. I'm anxious for her."

Charlie growled. "Hugh is a good man."

"And Josef isn't."

"No."

"You all knew that."

"Yes."

****

I love the house, the house that Alain built, the house where we were so happy. I hated, hated, hated that when

I turned in the driveway, I did not want to go inside. I was almost tearfully grateful that Charlie, Hugh, and Ivy were with me.

Under normal circumstances, I might have been amused when the group split up along traditional male-female lines. Ivy asked if she could "forage" in the refrigerator and put together some lunch, and Hugh asked for plastic garbage bags so he and Charlie could gather up the dead chickens. And I headed upstairs, leaving all the mess and bother to the others, to see how Josef had left his room, the guest room, where Charlie would sleep that night.

The small bedroom looked as if no one had stayed there for a long time. Josef had even pulled the sheets off the beds and the towels out of the bathroom. I wondered if he'd thrown them in the hamper or taken them with him, but I didn't care. He was gone.

I remade the bed, got out fresh towels, and went back downstairs. Ivy's "foraging" had resulted in two piles of sandwiches, each one neatly cut in half. Extra bread and peanut butter and jam were on the counter. She'd even found a very old box of Girl Scout cookies.

"Oh, good." She looked up from making a pot of coffee. "I didn't want to go poking around your home but I really need a toilet."

"Take your pick. There's a half-bath off the laundry room, down that hall. And there are two full baths upstairs, one for each bedroom." I took a somewhat shaky breath. "Alain loved the comfort and privacy of lots of toilets."

"Alain?"

"He was my husband." My eyes abruptly filled with tears. "The love of my life."

The door opened and Hugh and Charlie came in, Hugh already talking. "We've got a plan for the—" He got a look at my face. "Oh. Sorry. We can come back later—"

"No. Of course not." I shook my head. "What were you saying about a plan?"

He glanced at Ivy and then back to me. "We considered burying the chickens but we decided against it. The hole would have to be quite deep to avoid attracting wild animals."

"Oh. Yes. That makes sense. Are all nine of them… Are they all dead?"

He nodded.

"Oh." I looked around the kitchen as if searching for the ideal place to stash nine dead chickens. "The dump is open tomorrow. I can take them."

"No need. We put 'em in Hugh's car. He'll hit the dump tomorrow."

"I… Thank you, both of you." My eyes filled with tears again, and Ivy immediately stepped in, her voice brisk and competent.

"I've got the bathroom first. You guys can wash up when I'm done or use this sink here. Let's eat lunch before we tackle the locks."

****

The last time a group of people, a group of friends, sat around our kitchen table was a few months before Alain died. We hosted the members of the anthropology department, including the interns, and the conversation was fast and lively and professional and I felt giddy with pride every time Alain talked.

Now, Ivy and I got down plates and mugs and I put a few knives on the table while the two men washed up.

I handed her a bag of chips—salt and vinegar, Josef's favorite—got out half-and-half and sugar, and opened a jar of pickles.

"Yours?"

"What?"

"The pickles. Did you make them?"

For a brief instant, I looked at the jar as if I had never seen it before in my life. "Oh. Yes. Of course. Every year I make sweet pickles and dills. There's a good-sized vegetable garden out back."

"They look delicious. I used to make pickles when I lived in the commune." Ivy carried the coffee pot to the table and looked up at the two men. "All right, everyone. Have a seat, have a sandwich, have some coffee." She put the pot on a trivet. "It's perfectly legit to peek into each sandwich and pick what you like. And if you hate them all, there's good old P. B. and J."

She had sliced up the remains of a ham and had found Swiss cheese, a container of hummus, lettuce, a red onion, mustard, and mayo.

"This is wonderful, Ivy." I sat down. "Thank you so much."

"Your food, your hospitality, your dishes, just a bit of my time." She blessed us all with her sparkling grin. "And your pickles."

****

It took less than an hour to replace the old locks with shiny new hardware, on the front door and the kitchen door and the door to the porch. Then Hugh and Ivy left, and Charlie made a quick trip home to take care of his dog. I washed the lunch dishes and then wandered through the house, touching the back of Alain's favorite chair, putting a book back in its place. I gave a few minutes of thought to some sort of supper, but I was still full from lunch and I didn't like the idea of an intimate supper, just Charlie and me at the table.

The others thought I should stay inside the locked house, safe in case Josef came back, but I couldn't. When Charlie returned, I was out on the porch, a magazine open on my lap while I stared out at the yard. I always felt warm on the porch, as if Alain would come out of the house in just a moment and he would join me and we would sit in the two rockers, our quiet conversation merging with the sounds of robins finding insects in the garden and crows away in the fields.

"Mind if I sit?"

"Yes. I mean no. I don't mind. Of course not."

I'd never been alone with Charlie, just the two of us.

"How... How's your dog doing?"

"He's fine. Likes it better if I'm there but he's okay alone."

"Good." Silence again. "What kind of dog do you have?"

"Mutt. Part mastiff. Huge."

"I can imagine. What's his...? Oh! Look out there, near the corner of the chicken coop. Something's... Yes!"

Charlie leaned forward, his eyes intent under the bushy brows. "Grouse?"

"I think so. I've seen one here a few times before."

The two of us watched, leaning forward in our chairs, as the tall weeds wiggled and parted and moved and then stopped.

"I think at least one grouse lives in the woods next door."

"Makes sense. Good habitat."

"Yes. I—" I stood up so suddenly I almost knocked over the little table between the two rockers. "Let me show you the guest room, Charlie. Upstairs. Where Josef slept. There's a full bathroom right next door."

I was sure they all thought Josef and I slept together, in the same room, but what I had done with Josef all those months was my business, not theirs.

"You got a couch?"

"Of course. But—"

"I'm here because you might be in danger. Not going to be much help if I'm sleeping upstairs."

"Oh. All right then. I'll bring down sheets and blankets and a pillow. Then I think I'll head upstairs. It's early, but I'd like to lie in a bath for a while and then maybe read a little and, uh, check my work e-mail. And then I'll go to sleep early." I turned back toward him. "You can have anything you find in the refrigerator or cupboards, for supper."

****

Charlie stopped dead in the back doorway, his arms full of kindling wood. I hadn't even realized he was awake.

"It's too warm for a fire, Charlie." I twisted around to find the other sleeve of my robe, uncomfortable in my long nightgown and nothing under it. "You're a guest. Sit down. I'll have coffee ready in a few minutes."

I opened the refrigerator. "I was going to make scram..." The eggs were from the chickens that Josef killed. "Scrambled eggs. Or maybe oatmeal."

"Whichever." He sat. "Sleep all right?"

"Yes. Thank you." I got out the bacon and the bowl of eggs. "How about you?"

"Fine."

A whole breakfast to get through, and then maybe he'd leave. I didn't know this man at all, except for a few words during birding trips.

"Three for you? Eggs?"

"Fine. Yes."

"Josef is not coming back, you know. I'm safe here, on my own."

"Good."

"So you'll be heading home in a little while?"

"Yup."

"Good."

Chapter Five

The answering machine was blinking when I got home from work.

Left some stuff behind. Stopping by to get it.

Josef's voice. The tripod. Of course.

And there were clothes in the hamper. A winter coat in the downstairs closet. The ridiculous fur hat with the ear flaps. Two photography magazines. Dental floss, mouthwash, a box of condoms. Cans of sauerkraut, canned soup, Vienna sausages. A package of venison jerky. A half-empty bottle of schnapps.

I put the clothes through the washer and drier and then filled three grocery bags with his belongings and put them outside in the recycling bin. Then I spent far too many minutes dithering. I had to tell him where he could find his things, but I didn't want to hear his smooth voice asking me about the chickens. I didn't want to talk to him. Ever.

He worked evenings, so I decided to stop by the Photo Emporium in the morning and leave a note.

—Josef. The digiscoping adaptor fell out of the scope case and was damaged. I will buy you a replacement. Let me know brand and make. Everything else is in the recycling bin between the house and the garage.—

****

The bin was empty except for a price tag from the

Photo Emporium for an adaptor. I dropped off a check a few days later.

I wondered if he would start working full-time again, now that he no longer had rent-free housing. But I didn't care.

And then I forgot him, totally forgot him for hours and hours out of every day. My house was mine again, mine and Alain's. I think I stood up straighter when I was home. I breathed deeper. I slept a glorious nine hours a night.

****

The grouse was in the driveway again. Or a grouse. This one walked with a hitch in its gait, almost a limp. I wondered if the bird's odd gait was normal for grouse, if maybe they all walked that way when they were feeling anxious.

"What's going on, grouse?" The bird didn't move as I cautiously opened the car door. "Are you nervous about having a great big car nearby? And a human being? If so, you might be smarter than that tiny head would suggest."

The bird moved a few steps to the side, and I could see that its right leg was crooked, deformed.

"What's wrong with your leg, bird?" I pulled my cell phone out of my pocket. "If you'd stay right there for another minute or two, I can take a picture. I know some experts. Maybe they can help us."

The bird cocked its head to one side. Its beady eyes were bright, its plumage looked luxuriant. Maybe it wasn't sick. Maybe it had adjusted well to its crooked leg.

"Was it you who ate the remaining paste tomatoes yesterday? My favorites. I hoped they'd be good until this weekend's frost. Gilberties, bird. Bred for making tomato paste, not for feeding grouse." I held out my phone and snapped a few photos. "Gilbertie Grouse. How does that sound? May I call you Gilbertie Grouse?"

I took a step closer and the bird took to the air, wings whirring.

****

I skipped the September and October birding outings. The first was hawk-watching and Jack said that meant hours of sitting around while other people identify distant dots that the average human being wouldn't even think were birds. Besides, I hadn't bought a new tripod for my scope yet.

I called Ivy the day before, though, to ask if Jack's baby had been born yet.

"Jack is a more-than-proud papa, and everyone is fine."

"What did they have?"

"They had a baby!" Ivy erupted in laughter. "One time in the commune, one of the little kids kept staring and staring at a humongously pregnant lady. Finally the kid asked, very seriously and very worried, how the woman knew she wouldn't have a bunny." Gurgling laughter again. "Or a baby chicken! How did the lady know?"

"The concept of species hadn't quite sunk in yet."

"Exactly! But Jack and Rose had a little girl. A human little girl."

"Well, that's good. I have bought very few baby presents in my life, but I will enjoy buying one for them."

"You should check out the new bird-themed booties and little tiny hats in the shop."

"I will indeed."

****

Most of October was cold and wet and windy. On the day of the FATSO walk, I stayed in my warm house with the wood stove going, soup on the stove and bread in the oven, and I read an entire book. Ivy called in the afternoon and told me I hadn't missed anything, but I thought she was checking in, to find out if I was okay.

I could have ordered a new tripod online but I wanted to talk with someone knowledgeable. I took a chance and dropped in at the Photo Emporium at a time that didn't match Josef's old hours, and one look around showed me that I'd lucked out. There were just the owner and a young woman who rushed up to me as if I were the only customer she'd seen in hours. Forty-five minutes later, I walked out with a used lightweight tripod and the information that Josef quit when he found out he couldn't have his old full-time job back. I put my new purchase in the car and headed for Ivy's.

****

The shop looked as if a mini-cyclone had hit. The sale shelf near the door was almost empty. The counter was buried in bits of paper. Molly was sitting on the floor with open boxes on both sides of her, and she and Ivy looked mussed up and a bit sweaty. And, to my surprise, Charlie was in the doorway to the backroom, holding a few yards of what looked like old-fashioned adding machine tape.

"I've… I have come at a very busy time."

Ivy looked up, her hands full of receipts, and beamed at me. "One of our best days ever! Ever! It's going to take a while to put things back together, but we are definitely not complaining."

Molly picked up a paperback field guide and waved it at me. "See this book? We sold twenty of them today, all at once. It's lucky a new shipment just came in."

"Twenty! What's behind this sudden interest in bird identification?"

"One nature-loving middle school teacher. She ordered twenty pairs of binoculars a few months back and today she came back for birding guides!"

"And she brought with her three members of the PTA, and they bought several books for the school library." Ivy gave an exaggerated sigh of pleasure. "Ahhhh… A day any retailer would love!" She turned to smile at Charlie. "And our wonderful and long-suffering accountant was here to see it!"

I had never even wondered what Charlie did for a living. He didn't look like an accountant. He looked like an aging pirate, a gracefully aging one, with those broad shoulders and sturdy build, the huge mustache pale against his tanned skin. and the frequent twinkle in his bright blue eyes. But his usually terse conversation was a good fit for someone whose life was numbers rather than words.

Ivy was looking at me again, and I had the sudden conviction that she was going to ask about Josef.

"I've been busy, too," I said quickly, and then rattled off a string of completely unnecessary details. "October fifteenth. It's the deadline for farmers to get reimbursements for HOFHOW projects, and it's almost here. It seems like half the farmers in the state waited till the last minute and they all want water samples now. Right now! It's always like this in the fall but since HOFHOW it got even crazier."

"Wait. Hoff—What?"

"HOFHOW. Help Our Farmers Help Our Waters. Farmers add fencing to keep cattle away from streams, or they plant trees for bank stabilization, or…" I was temporarily distracted by a plastic doodad next to Ivy's elbow, with a price tag that seemed absurdly high for nothing but a coiled-up bit of spring. "… or they upgrade their manure pits. And if water samples after two years show that the mitigation had a statistically significant effect on the quality of a nearby stream or pond, they can get back up to sixty-five percent of the initial cost that year with an additional twenty-five percent possible in the future—What IS that thing?"

Ivy picked it up. "It's a twist mount. So you can attach a camera or a cell phone to a branch, or a tree, or a rock. Then you can set the timer and take a photo from a distance."

"And it works?"

"Very well, apparently. We sell a lot of them."

"Amazing." I shook myself. "But that's not why I'm here. I need advice about a grouse. My grouse."

"Your grouse, huh?"

I knew humans shouldn't behave as if wild animals were pets, but I just dug my cell phone out of my pocket and started fiddling with it.

"Take a look. I have seen a grouse on my property a few times now. Does this one look like his right leg is injured? Or deformed?"

"Whoa. You might be right." She held out the phone to show the others. "Does the bird walk all right?"

"He lurches, like a person with a wooden leg. I think he flies normally, though."

"What do you think, Charlie?"

"Leg got caught in something?"

"Maybe." Ivy was holding the phone again. "Or maybe it's some kind of birth defect. I suppose birds can

61

have birth defects."

"There are a few more photos."

She scanned all of them. "Well, some birds live fairly well with bum legs. Sometimes even with only one leg." She looked up. "Unless of course it's a raptor. Those birds need all their talons to catch enough prey for survival. So. Have you named it yet?"

I could feel myself flushing. "Well… yes. Gilbertie. Gilbertie Grouse."

Charlie's eyebrows shot up his forehead. "Pretty high-brow for a wild thing that can't even walk straight."

"Something pulled down one of my tomato plants and picked open the last tomatoes. Gilbertie Paste tomatoes."

Molly groaned from her position on the floor. "You've done it, Beck. You've done what Ivy calls Jumping the Line. You are no longer a disinterested bird watcher."

"Is that bad?"

"Not at all!" Ivy shook her head, her short dark curls flying around her face. "Some folks say so, but I think it's almost always a good thing. Caring about one specific bird can break your heart but it also deepens a person's enjoyment of birds in general."

"You sure Gilbertie is male?"

"I'm not, Charlie. If the bird shows up with a dozen little ones, I'll start calling her Bertie instead of Gilbertie." I turned again to Ivy. "What about the winter? I thought of trying to lure him into the chicken coop, where he'd be safe from predation and where I could feed him, but it's not heated. The chickens had each other for body warmth but he'd be alone."

"Cold's not a problem for grouse. They just burrow

under the snow at night."

"That works?"

Charlie answered. "Stayed in a snow cave once, overnight. Snow's a big warm blanket. Holds body heat close to animals, birds. Humans."

Ivy and Molly were looking at their friend with wide eyes.

"You stayed in a snow cave? Why?"

"For the experience, Moll. For the experience."

"For the insanity, Charlie. For the insanity."

I interrupted, needing to regain Ivy's attention until I had all the information I wanted.

"Should I spread some food around for him every morning? Just during the winter?"

"Fish and Wildlife aren't crazy about feeding game birds because feeding stations can gather a lot of grouse or turkeys in one place, and the soiled feed can spread disease. But it's not illegal." Ivy looked thoughtful. "Is there a lot of woods around your property?"

"There's a patch between my house and the nearest neighbor. Maybe three acres. Then there's a bigger forested area two miles away, past the neighbor's house and barn."

"You might not have a good-sized population of Ruffed Grouse right close by." She looked again at Charlie. "What do you think? If the grouse is injured, it might give it an edge to make it through the winter."

Charlie took the phone out of my hand and looked again at the photos. "Could be. And if it looks like the bird's going downhill fast, Beck'd know about it."

"And then what? Could I get him into a trap and take him to a rehabilitator?"

"Mebbe."

"All right." I took a deep breath. "That is what I'm going to do. There's more than a half bag of cracked corn left in the chicken coop. Will grouse eat that?"

"With glee."

"I have a plan then. Thank you, all of you." I smiled. "Thanks from Gilbertie Grouse and me both."

"Wait a sec, will you? Got a question." Charlie disappeared into the back room and came back without all the paper. "You've done some camping, right?"

"I... Oh. Yes. I went on digs several times with Alain. My husband."

"Got any advice about equipment?"

"Alain had all the camping gear before he met me, Charlie. So I had nothing to do with choosing it. But you are welcome to come out and look at it. Maybe it will give you some ideas about what might work for you. Better yet, you can borrow any of it if you want."

"Good. Thanks. Some Saturday morning?"

"That will work. Just call first to make sure I'm home."

****

"I am utterly baffled, Charlie. It was all right here. All our camping equipment was always here. Alain made these shelves especially to hold it all." I turned toward Charlie. "There was a tent. A two-burner stove. Lanterns. Pots and pans. Dishes. I..."

He was walking away, something tinkling and crunching under his feet.

"Stuff didn't take off on its own."

"What?"

The shed's back window had no glass in it.

"This... This doesn't make any sense. Why would someone break into a shed and steal nothing but old camping equipment?" Alain's woodworking tools still hung on the right wall, over the workbench and the table saw. Our electric lawnmower was by the door, and all the garden tools, and the tractor we used for hauling mulch and topsoil. "Surely many of these items are worth more than an old used tent and—"

"Not if it's camping equipment you need."

"Damn." I looked back at the shelves. "I am really angry, Charlie. Maybe I never would have used those things again. But they were Alain's. We used them, together." I reached out and ran my hand along one of the smooth metal shelves. "He put up these shelves specifically for all of it. He…"

My fingers touched a wrinkled piece of paper, and I moved a step back to look at it in better light.

—I need this stuff more than you do, babe. If you hadn't changed the locks, I could have gone in and taken the key and I wouldn't have broken the window. But now you know. Locks don't do any good.—

Charlie took the note out of my hand.

"Josef?"

"It's his handwriting. Yes."

"Direct threat, Beck. That bit about locks."

"He's… Josef's showing off. Macho."

"No. The man is telling you he can get into the house anytime he wants." His face was grim. "Go inside and call the cops."

****

Charlie knew the Montpelier police officer who showed up an hour later, and for several minutes I was irrelevant as the two men discussed the Montpelier high school football team, a new alderman, and a break-in at the downtown bakery. When it was finally my turn, I told the officer everything I could think of. I gave him Josef's name and described what he looked like. I gave him the note we found in the shed, along with a list of the missing camping equipment. I told him where Josef used to work, and what kind of car he drove. I even told him the name of the company that was going to publish Josef's book.

"He took everything that might have his DNA on it, officer, but you are welcome to come inside and dust for fingerprints."

The man looked at me solemnly and then closed his notebook with a decisive snap. I guess forensic teams aren't called out for petty theft.

****

"You want my dog?"

"What?"

"My dog. I can leave him with you for a few days. Barks at anything bigger than a field mouse." Charlie was sitting at my kitchen table, looking sturdy and safe and earnest.

"I think… I am not happy about it, Charlie, but I am beginning to think you're right. About Josef trying to threaten me. I don't believe he'll follow up on the threat, but he might enjoy frightening me. Showing me who's boss."

"He ever hit you?"

"No. But I think he might have, someday. I—"

The phone rang and I froze, not breathing until after the beep sounded and I heard a woman's voice urging me to renew my car's extended warranty.

"Scam call." I gave Charlie a weak smile. "I get them a lot."

"You were scared."

"Nonsense. I just…"

66

"You been getting prank calls?"

I took a deep breath. "Not pranks, no. But Josef has called a few times. The last time he must have been right outside. He said he just watched me go in."

"Threats?"

"Not directly. No. Every time he calls, he says he needs a place to live and, and I'm alone in this big house and it would only be a few weeks…" I stood up and walked quickly into the living room. "The calls are still on the machine."

I pressed the flashing button.

I made a big mistake, Beck, with the hens. I was angry. Upset. We had some good times. And we might have good times ahead. What about it, babe? You put me up for another two, three months, until the book comes out. You get some good loving, but only when you want it. On demand, Beck. Just think about that. Give me a call.

I'd forgotten about the good loving part, and I wished Charlie hadn't heard it.

"This was mid-September."

Another chance, babe. For both of us. I need a place to stay and it just makes sense to stay with you. Maybe I can get us some more hens, Beck. How about that?

"You didn't call him back."

"Of course not. The next one was early October."

C'mon, Beck. You're just playing hard to get. You know you're gonna give in. I'm here living in a tiny room above a gas station, and you got that big house. Winter's coming. Wouldn't it be good to have someone to shovel the driveway? Get the icicles off the eaves? [The voice on the answering machine got deeper, softer.] *Keep you warm at night?*

"This is the last one. The day before Halloween."

I know you're there. I just saw you go inside. So pick up.... All right, don't. I know you're listening. All I need is a week. Maybe two weeks. Then I'm moving to Philly. C'mon, Beck. You're in that big house alone. It's a hell of a lot warmer in there than in my car. I'm not going to grovel, Beck. Don't expect me to walk up there and knock and say pretty please. Just open the door.

"Don't delete 'em. The cops should hear 'em." Charlie looked like a fierce Viking in the dim light. "You should be staying someplace else."

"No! I won't be chased out of my own house!" I made myself speak more calmly. "I am not going to leave Alain's house, Charlie. Our house. If you..." I squared my shoulders. "All right. If you go get your dog, and if you and the dog would both stay here tonight, just until I hear what the police say about the calls, then..."

He stared at me, his jaw set. "A few nights. Not just one. Until the cops locate Josef."

"A few. All right."

"Lock up. Stay away from windows. Hold onto your phone and dial 911 if you hear or see anything." He started for the door. "I'll blow the horn when I turn in the driveway. If you're okay, flash the front door light a few times. If I don't see that, I'm calling my buddy at the Montpelier police. And the state police. And the sheriff."

"Front door light. Got it. Charlie?"

"Eh?"

"Thank you."

****

"You don't have to make breakfast. You're a, a temporary bodyguard, not a cook."

"Hungry bodyguard. Scrambled or fried?"

"I… Scrambled. Thank you."

Charlie was standing at the stove, my favorite mug raised to his mouth. His gigantic dog completely covered the front door mat and then some. It raised its head, eyed me, and flopped back down on the door mat as if the slightest action was exhausting.

"Does he always have that much energy?"

Charlie picked up a second mug and filled it. "Devon can be a regular whirlwind."

"Right."

"Part mastiff." He handed me the mug. "Breed's famous for calm. Dignified."

"How much does he weigh?"

"One twenty."

"Yikes."

Charlie deftly broke six eggs over a bowl. "Company garb?"

"What?"

"That. Is that what you wear for company?"

I think it was the same nightgown and robe I had on last time, and he hadn't said anything about it then.

"This is what I always wear."

"Fetching." He turned the bacon.

"It's…" It was time, past time, to make something clear. "I didn't wear this to 'fetch' anything, Charlie."

"Huh."

I took a sip from the mug. "What did you do with the coffee?"

"Dash of salt, dash of cinnamon."

"Oh." I took another sip. "It's delicious."

"Wife's trick."

"I didn't realize you were married."

He lifted six strips of bacon onto a paper towel. "She

died. Long time ago."

"Oh. I'm sorry."

"Ditto. Still."

"Sit, Charlie. Eat your eggs while they're hot. I'll finish the toast."

The silence as we ate, as we got up to refill coffee cups, was surprisingly comfortable. The huge dog lifted his head and watched every forkful that went from Charlie's plate to his mouth, but he didn't move off the mat.

"Devon badly wants some of your food."

"Trained him. Won't come close to the table."

"That's fortunate. He could knock it over."

Charlie gathered the empty plates and carried them to the sink.

"He'll come over now that we're done eating. 'Cept he thinks you don't like him."

I watched the twinkle in Charlie's eyes. "Sure. Right."

"It's true. You haven't made him feel welcome."

I looked at the gigantic beast. "Devon. Come here, boy."

Devon heaved himself off the mat and padded across the kitchen.

"That's a good boy." I reached out to pet him, and the dog plopped his huge head in my lap with a mastiff-sized sigh.

"Okay, Charlie." I laughed. "You were right. Your dog was feeling unwelcome." I bent closer to the animal's face and rubbed his ears. "I am sorry, huge beast. You are a welcome guest. You are welcome here any time."

"Told yah."

"Alain would have loved this dog. He always wanted a mastiff. Or maybe an Irish wolfhound. But we were gone too much."

All of a sudden, I wanted Charlie to think of me not just as the woman who was dumb enough to have been with Josef. Words came tumbling out without thought.

"Alain was smart. He was wise. He was an amazing teacher. He understood his colleagues and his students, all of them." I blinked to clear my eyes. "He understood himself. He understood me. Alain knew I loved him when I would have sworn I still thought of him only as my favorite professor. Professor Charbonneau. Not Alain, not the core and center of my life." I sat up straighter and dug a tissue out of the pocket of my robe. "He was married when we met. He didn't say anything to me until he was holding his divorce papers in his hand."

"Might've cost him his job, talking about love to one of his students."

"It wasn't caution. Alain wouldn't say anything to me until he could do it honestly. He was honest. Honest to a fault." I blew my nose and laughed. "Why honest to a fault? That doesn't make any sense."

Devon looked up at my face.

"He doesn't like it when people cry."

"I am not crying, Devon. I am just blowing my nose."

"Heat up your coffee?"

"Yes, please. Alain cared about other people, their feelings, their… their happiness. Their mental health. Josef doesn't care about anyone but himself."

Charlie filled my cup and then leaned back against the counter and watched me.

"Everyone respected Professor Charbonneau, Charlie. No one respects Josef. Not once they get to know him. Handsome but useless. Always trying to sell those pretty little pictures that looked just like millions and millions of other pictures taken by thousands and thousands of other people all pretending to be artists. Great artistic Josef. Pretending his pictures were great art when most of them, the vast majority of them, were identical to thousands of others."

"You said he got a book deal."

"Sixty photos out of a hundred thousand." I shrugged. "Although I guess it does say something about his artistic eye that he picked out those sixty. That he sent those few around to publishers." I took a deep breath and stared straight ahead, my hands clenched on the table, my shoulders pressed back against the chair. "Alain was one hundred percent different from Josef. How could I have had Alain in my life and then let Josef live here?"

"Lonely?"

I looked at him then, considering, frowning.

"I wasn't… No. I wasn't actually lonely. Not for the whole four years after Alain's death. I was… The only thing I felt was loss. Huge, all-encompassing loss. There was no room for any other emotions."

Charlie dipped his chin in what I'd come to know was his version of nodding. "Yes."

"You know. You lost your wife."

"Hate to tell you, but that sense of loss still comes, sometimes. And it's been almost twenty years now."

"She was young when she died, then."

"Too damn young."

"I'm sorry."

"Thanks."

I took a sip of coffee and went back to petting the dog with my other hand. "For me, it started breaking up suddenly. The deadness of losing Alain. One day I found something amusing, just a little. In a hearing before the Water Resources Board, of all places."

Charlie raised his eyebrows.

"And that same day I saw the grouse, hanging upside down next to the driveway."

"Eh?"

"He was eating grapes, trying to get the very last ones."

Charlie's huge mustache twitched.

"I was curious about the bird, and that led me into Ivy's shop, and that led to going on FATSO walks." I shook my head again, knowing I wasn't explaining myself well.

Charlie nodded again.

"And there it was, Charlie."

"There was what?"

"Life. Again. I had been breathing, eating, working. Grieving. And then, I was alive. Again."

"And you met Josef soon after?"

I frowned. "Yes. But how did you... Why did you assume it was soon after?"

"Makes sense. Coming alive again."

"Oh." I lifted my chin. "I thought it would be for only a few weeks. Stupid." Suddenly I wanted it all out. "And I liked the sex."

"Sex is important."

"It was good for a while, even if it was just sex. But the fact remains, Charlie. I had perfect love and happiness and then I took up with a man who, who... A man I didn't love, at all. A man I didn't even like. A man who certainly didn't love me and who was just using me." I gulped back a sob. "It makes me wonder what's wrong with me."

I blew my nose again, and wiped my cheeks, and Devon made a little groaning noise.

"Human-ness, Beck. You've got a case of human-ness. Serious malady."

I surprised myself with a spurt of laughter.

Chapter Six

Charlie's friend from the Montpelier police listened to the phone messages and took the tape with him. But Josef had disappeared. He hadn't been back to the Photo Emporium. His car wasn't spotted anywhere. He had been renting a room over the Shell station but when the owner climbed the stairs to ask about late rent, the door was open and the room was empty. And the publishing company representative told the police she hadn't heard from Josef recently and didn't expect to for at least six weeks.

On TV shows and movies, police get detailed information by tracking cell phone signals. Either Josef wasn't using his phone at all, or police don't bother to trace signals for something as minor as stolen camping equipment and a few possible but not very specific threats.

Charlie and Devon stayed at my house for three nights, the man on the couch and the giant dog on the doormat. It no longer felt awkward to make supper for the two of us humans, to sit and eat together, to play Gin Rummy while Devon rested his huge head on my lap. But each of those three nights I went upstairs early, taking a book with me and reading in the bathtub and then in bed until I fell asleep.

After the man and the beast left, it was a delight to be alone again, to sit in the living room after supper, to start a fire in the woodstove on chilly evenings, to sit on the porch when I got home from work and the sun was heating the bricks and it felt almost like a sauna. By late November, I was confident Josef was gone from my life forever. Maybe I would see his book featured in the window of the Downtown Bookstore and I would be embarrassed, thinking that someone who knew me might buy a copy and would recognize me. Or maybe the book deal would fall through.

****

"There's no FATSO walk this weekend and it's supposed to be gorgeous. A rare end-of-November beauty. Want to join Molly and me and check out that new nature preserve by the reservoir?"

Ivy, as usual, sounded energetic and bubbly. I opened my mouth but she was still talking.

"It's hunting season but Jack and Rose walked there a few weeks ago and Jack said there are signs all over the place." Ivy deepened her voice. "No Hunting! No Trapping! No Fiddlehead Picking! Do Not Remove Any Plants! Stay on Trails! No Dogs! No Fires! Do Not Pick Up Fallen Twigs or Branches! Leave No Trace! Carry In, Carry Out!" She went back to her normal voice. "Jack said the woman who donated the land insisted on all that signage. Every few yards around the whole perimeter. Every eco-friendly warning and slogan she could think of."

"So we'll be safe from hunters as well as dastardly fern pickers and litterbugs?"

"Sure thing. And just in case some scofflaw decides to hunt there anyway, I'll bring three of the blaze orange vests we carry in the store. Are you in?"

"Ivy, my to-do list for today is exceedingly boring.

I am delighted to have an alternative. Where and when should I meet you?"

****

The sun was fully up when Ivy parked and we two tall women got out of the front seats and Molly wiggled herself out of the back. We donned orange vests, put on our binocular harnesses, and started up the wide trail. Russet and brown oak leaves clung to their branches as if reluctant to admit that winter was on its way, their colors looking all the richer because of the brilliant blue sky. The wood chip trails were brand-new, making a yellow sweet-smelling path ahead of us.

"The old reservoir's about three-quarters of a mile ahead. Jack said the trail goes around it, with another loop that's all wooded."

"How many miles in all? Of trails?"

"I think it's between four and five, but I'm not sure." Ivy stopped and lifted her binoculars. "Some sort of thrush. Probably Hermit, at this time of year."

A robin-sized bird was scratching around in the leaf litter at the base of a big maple. I could see smudgy blotches on its pale chest and then, a few seconds later, the chestnut-colored tail.

"Yes," I whispered. "Hermit Thrush. What are you still doing here, bird? Don't you know winter is just around the corner?"

"Hermit Thrushes are the only thrushes that winter in the U.S.," Ivy whispered. "Besides robins, that is. Some Hermit Thrushes are seen in Vermont every single Winter Bird Count."

"Hearty souls."

"You bet."

When we got to the reservoir, Molly said she wanted

to investigate a side trail that led to the water. Trees on the far side were reflected in the still water, deep green conifers, still-blazing maples, yellow aspens, and brown oaks. The reflections became wavy as we walked out onto a little wooden pier over the water.

"Well, would you look at that."

In the middle of the reservoir was a miniscule swimming bird, almost hidden in the tree reflections.

"Pied-billed Grebe," Ivy said. "What a cutey."

We watched the grebe diving, bobbing up like a cork, diving again, then paddling farther away into dense shadow.

"That's my first grebe," I said. "Thanks for inviting me today, Ivy."

A half hour more and we were deep in woods. I looked around. "Ah. A conveniently wide tree trunk for me to duck behind. Even better, a nice fallen log in back so I can sit instead of squatting. You two go ahead. I'll catch up."

I heard Ivy say one time that some of her most intimate bird experiences happened while she was peeing. I doubted that, because she also said that sitting for fifteen or twenty minutes is needed for nature to forget you're there, and no one would stay quiet that long just to pee. But I had barely dropped my pants when a tiny dark bird appeared at the other end of the fallen log. It cocked its head, as if surprised to find some other being in its private world, and then it dropped to the ground. A second later and it was back up, still on the log but closer to me.

And then again. Fluttering to the ground so I couldn't see it and reappearing on the log, closer. The bird was plump, with mostly brown plumage and a faint whitish line above its eye. Its short dark tail was held almost straight up.

"I think you might be my first Winter Wren," I barely whispered—and it cocked its head again and took two hops along the log toward me. I held my breath, watching as it came closer, closer, finally stopping only two yards away. The bird turned its head and studied me with one bright little eye. Then, its birdy mind made up, it fluttered sideways off the log and flew away.

I took a deep long breath. "Thank you so much. That was lovely."

My legs were stiff after several minutes in an awkward half-crouch position. I hauled myself up by grabbing onto the tree and stepped out into the clearing, looking down to fasten my pants.

"Beck."

"Good god! Josef! You startled me!"

He was as upright as always, head held high, but his clothes were covered with bits of dead leaves and dirt and he hadn't shaved in several days. Even though the day was warm, he was wearing the big fur cap with the flaps.

"What are you doing here?"

"I live here."

"You can't. It's a nature preserve."

Josef's smile looked even whiter than before, against his dark facial hair. "Maybe I can't live here legally. But it's possible. Of course." He glanced toward his right. "Camping out. Over there."

"Why… Why?"

"C'mon, Beck. You're smart. Why should I use all my money on a room? Cash is going fast enough just for food, and it'll be a while before I start getting royalties from the book." He reached up and took off the ridiculous hat. "Lucky for me you happened by."

I took a step to pass him. "I am walking with Molly and Ivy. They will be wondering where I am."

Josef moved just a little, blocking me without getting too close. "It's still relatively warm, Beck, even at night. And those two sleeping bags, one inside the other, are very comfy." The smile again. "Thank you for the equipment, babe. I knew you wouldn't want me sleeping out in the cold."

"What happened to your car?"

"Oh. You think I should be sleeping in my car, like other homeless people?"

"I just wondered if you sold it."

"No way! That car is my biggest asset. Assets, debits. Spreadsheet. A few things in that first column. But no debits, lucky me. Neither a borrower nor a lender be." He frowned and then jerked a thumb over his right shoulder. "Car's hidden. About a mile from here. Sometimes I sleep in it but mostly I use it as a..." He grinned. "That car is my deluxe four-door pantry, closet, and storage space. My camera stuff and food supplies are locked in the trunk." He looked to both sides, quick darting glances. "Bears," he whispered. "There are bears all around so the food's locked up. And I walk away from camp to bury the cans." He tapped his forehead with one finger. "Smart."

Josef had never mentioned taking drugs, and I don't think he was high or stoned or drunk in the year he lived at my house, but now I wondered if he was on something.

"Gotta gun, though. In case they come." He gave a half-smile. "Homeless people need guns, you know. Protection. No. Of course you don't know. You got a home. A big home. But if you was homeless, Beck, you would need a gun. Bad things happen to homeless people." He chuckled. "I made a super smart transaction. I sold my tripod and the little camera. Don't need the little one anymore. Sold it and the tripod and got myself a nifty little weapon. Plus ammo." He patted his pants pocket.

I took another step, and this time he reached out and grabbed my arm.

"Winter's coming, babe. You don't want me sleeping in the woods all winter. Or in my car. Not after our, uh, romantic history together."

"Let me go."

"In just a minute. I'll let you go, I will. But listen to me. Just give me a chance."

Josef had always been compulsive about brushing his teeth, flossing, using mouthwash. Now his breath smelled like something rotting.

"You let me stay with you for two months. I'll sleep downstairs, on the couch." He smiled again, the big white beautiful smile that made people like him, at first. "The lumpy couch. Then when the royalties start rolling in, I'll pay you rent. Lots of rent. More than anybody else would pay for sleeping on a lumpy couch." His forehead wrinkled in a deep frown, looking past me at the tree trunk. "Royalties. Royyyy-ul-tees. Why're they called royalties? Sounds like money that goes to the king or something."

He looked back at me and his eyes widened, as if he'd forgotten I was there, and he reached out and grabbed my other arm.

"Let me go, Josef."

"Say I can follow you home. Say it."

"Absolutely not. Let me go."

I thought, for a split second, that he would, that he'd let me go. He released my arms, but then he put his fingers around my throat. I wrenched my head sideways and opened my mouth to scream, but his hands tightened. He hooked one leg around me and pulled me in closer, and his hands kept getting tighter, and my binoculars were digging into my chest, and I couldn't breathe.

"Tell me you won't scream and I'll let go. Tell me. Tell me now, Beck. Now!"

I clawed at his hands, gasping, taking in pinched breaths of his awful smell, trying to tighten the muscles in my neck so I could keep my airway open, trying to move my hips forward to make extra room for my chest.

"No use, babe. Calm down. We'll…" He tried his captivating smile again. "We'll go home together, and we'll maintain our distance for a few months and then I'll be outta your hair. Outta your hair forever. C'mon, babe."

I stopped reacting and started thinking. I dropped my arms and wedged them between us, twisting to one side and then the other, knotting my hands into a tight double fist, and then I brought them up hard between his legs. There wasn't enough room for me to hit as hard as I wanted, but Josef fell backward, landing hard on the ground, gasping and crying.

"Bitch! Bitch, bitch, bitch!"

I moved to get past him, but he grabbed my ankle and hauled me closer and then he got his other hand on my leg and yanked, and I fell on top of him.

"Gonna pay," he gasped. "Gonna pay for that little move, bitch. Gonna pay."

I'm strong and I was furious and desperate, and I

lashed out with both arms, both hands, all my fingernails, my knee, my heels pounding against his legs. But he was stronger. He flipped us both over, grabbed my hair, pulled my head up off the ground, and slammed me back down.

My head was ringing. I could no longer see him clearly. He raised his hand, his fist, and drove it into the side of my face.

I watched him raise his fist again. Then I saw something that made absolutely no sense, something black and thick that whistled through the air between me and Josef and smashed into his jaw.

"Get away from her. Now."

I squinted up at the sky. Ivy was standing above the two of us, holding her folded tripod in both hands like a golf club.

Josef rolled partly off me, pushing both hands down on my rib cage to get into a sitting position. His mouth was hanging open and blood was pooling behind his lips and spilling over. I felt it hot on my throat and I put both hands up and they were covered with his blood too.

"Gonna…" His speech was garbled, bubbly. "Kill you. Both of you. Two bitch women." He wiped the back of a hand across his mouth. "Both gonna pay."

Ivy took a step back, swinging the tripod back as if lining up another shot. "You okay, Beck?"

"Yes," I gasped. I scrambled sideways on elbows, butt, and feet, scrambled from under him, scrambled to get away.

"Two against one. No prob. Even things up." He lifted one hip off the ground, clawing, trying to get his hand into his pants pocket.

"Gun! Ivy, he's got a gun in that pocket!"

She stepped close, lifting the tripod, but Josef held up a small dark pistol, clutching it with both hands, and she hesitated.

"Evens things up, huh, bitch? Makes things fair." He grinned, his teeth very white against the black beard and red blood. "Got it for protection. Guess I was right. Woods're dangerous." He turned a little and pointed the gun at me. "You first, babe, 'cause you hurt my nuts."

Ivy lunged toward him with the tripod but he didn't even seem to notice. And then, from nowhere, tiny Molly was behind him, between him and the big tree, her binoculars held high in both hands, her binoculars crashing down on his head. The gun went off, astonishingly loud for such a small thing, and Josef fell forward onto his face.

"Beck? Beck! Did he get you?"

"No. I, I—Oh god, Ivy. He shot you!"

In slow motion, Ivy dropped the tripod on the ground, raised her right hand, and grabbed her left shoulder. Bright red blood poured through her fingers, all over the blaze orange vest.

Molly morphed in that instant from warrior to trauma nurse. She stumbled around Josef, thrusting her binoculars at me and getting to Ivy and gently pulling her fingers away from her shoulder.

I realized, later, that it was the gunshot that quieted all the birds, but right then it seemed that the forest was holding its breath along with the three of us, holding its breath until Molly finished her first probing examination.

"It went past, the bullet. It grazed your shoulder, Ivy. It's not inside. Beck!"

I jumped.

"You always have a bandanna. Give it here." When I didn't respond at once, she snapped her fingers. I think she stamped her foot too. My brain fumbled to make sense of what she was saying, what she wanted me to do, and then I handed over my pink bandanna and watched it turn bright red.

"Put pressure on it, Ivy. Hard." Molly turned to me again, yanking her cell phone out of her pocket at the same time. "Beck, you take Ivy's tripod. If Josef so much as twitches, hit him with everything you've got. Velma Whiting Nature Area," she barked into the phone. "The woods trail. Probably a half mile past where it branches at the reservoir. We need ambulances and police. A woman's been shot. Bleeding from her shoulder. Second woman with facial wounds and probably in shock. Attacker is on the ground with a head wound. He's temporarily out of the picture, but hurry. Please hurry."

Chapter Seven

I couldn't make sense of the sunshine streaking the polished wood floor. It had to be nighttime. We had spent hours in the woods. Hours more in the hospital. But sunlight was streaming almost horizontally through tall windows. The stripes and bars on the floor made my head ache. I thought we might be in Hugh's house, in Hugh's living room, Hugh from the FATSO group, and that didn't make sense either. Hugh and Ivy and me and Molly and her husband. Molly's husband. I thought I probably knew his name but I couldn't remember. Charlie was there too, and that made even less sense, that he was there, that he was standing near the front door, apart from us, his back against the wall, his arms folded, glaring and silent.

I thought Molly was talking but it took too much energy to pay attention. I closed my eyes and I was back in the woods, waiting for the police and EMTs.

****

We waited for a long time, and Josef didn't move. Once, I think, Molly went close to him, touched him. She might have tried to reach the gun but I'm not sure. The three of us clustered together past his head so he would have to twist around before he could shoot us.

Ivy's blaze orange vest was on the ground, wet and heavy with the blood from her shoulder. I struggled to get out of mine, desperate to wad it up and throw it as far as I could. But it was sticky with Josef's blood and maybe my blood too and I couldn't bear to touch it, so I finally shrugged out of it and dropped it at my feet and then I lurched away from the others and threw up onto dry leaves and moss.

The taste of vomit stayed, all the rest of the time in the woods and in the hospital and afterward. I wanted to brush my teeth. I wanted a mirror, so I could look at my face and see if I was getting a black eye, so I could find out what pinched and hurt on my cheekbone. I think I raised my hand several times to touch, but the pain made me queasy.

I never heard any sirens. I never heard anyone coming. The woods went from breath-held quiet to noise, instantly, suddenly full of noise and people and activity. Two police officers were near Josef. One, a woman whose yellow hair stuck out every which way from under her dark blue hat, lifted the gun from under Josef's body. She turned in my direction and I felt panic that she was going to shoot me, but she dropped the gun into a plastic bag held by the other cop and then she looked at her wristwatch and wrote something on the bag.

They were asking us questions, the two officers, maybe more than two. They were touching us, asking more questions, and I don't know if I answered at all. My head was rhythmically expanding and contracting and then expanding again. I had to hold my breath to stop my brain from growing bigger and bigger until it exploded.

A light flashed in my eyes. My arm was squeezed. My cheek was swabbed, dabbed, washed. I was on a stretcher that was bent so I was partially sitting, and I was in a crowded, claustrophobic ambulance, and someone was asking still more questions that didn't make sense so I closed my eyes again.

I don't remember the ambulance ride. I don't remember arriving at the hospital. I remember lying flat, at last, and feeling a wave of comfort, a bliss so powerful that I started weeping. More people probing, touching, asking questions. I remember being wheeled through miles of halls and into an elevator and into some sort of machine. Then the halls again. And Hugh was there, in the examining room. Ivy's Hugh, from the bird walks. I didn't know why he was there, or how he got there. I watched through barely opened eyes as someone in scrubs talked to him about concussion care.

After a while, I asked for a bathroom and a pleasant woman helped me walk a few steps across the hall and then back, and I told her I could smell vomit and maybe blood and she helped me get out of my flannel shirt and my turtleneck and she washed me and gave me two short hospital gowns and helped me put them on, one backward and the other frontward.

Then I was being pushed in a wheelchair to a waiting room, and Hugh was pushing Ivy in a chair too, and Molly was there, sitting on a couch with a man who had all four of their hands in a knot together on his thigh. And more police officers. The yellow-haired woman was replaced by an older one, this one with a neat gray bun. More questions, for all three of us at once. I couldn't see clearly out of my left eye. I couldn't think clearly. I felt apart from the others, in an envelope of apartness.

A few days after, I came up with a description of that feeling, a description to help me make sense of it. I felt, in the hospital waiting room and later in Hugh's house, as if there were thin curtains a few yards in front of me, ten or a dozen of them, walling me off. Sometimes the curtains swayed or rippled, and the movement made me nauseated. I could see, but not well. I could hear, but only some sentences. I knew that if I just closed my eyes, I could stop trying so hard to see, trying to hear, trying to understand. But I was afraid that if I closed my eyes I might never wake up.

****

Now I was wearing an unfamiliar sweatshirt over the two short gowns from the hospital, and someone had wrapped a heavy wool blanket around me. I was much too warm one minute and shivering the next. My left eye was swollen closed and the whole side of my face felt raw. A small bandage on my cheek itched and stung. If I leaned my head back against the chair a knot on my skull hurt, I suppose where he slammed my head against a stone, so I sat upright even though I had to concentrate hard to keep from falling forward.

I still smelled vomit. I still wanted a toothbrush. I still wanted a shower.

Molly was talking and I thought she might have been talking for some time but I wasn't sure.

"… my life helping people." She was huddled on a sofa in Hugh's living room, her eyes huge and tragic. She looked like a sad child in a curly white wig. "It's not right for me to clobber a man over the head. I'm not supposed to send anyone to the hospital. I—" Her voice broke. "I'm one of the people who take care of them once they get there."

I pushed the blanket away from my chin so I could talk, and leaned forward a bit more. "You saved…"

I wasn't talking; I was yelling, unbelievably loud. But when I tried to be quiet, I ended up whispering.

"You saved my life, Moll," I whispered. "You

probably saved Ivy's life too. And your own. You have to know that."

"I do know it, rationally. I just can't do rational very well right now."

"Me, I don't feel one bit guilty!" Ivy was much too loud too. She pushed herself to her feet, as fierce and determined as she'd been in the woods. "I don't feel guilty about hurting him! What I regret, regret, REGRET is that I didn't hit him a few more times! I should have completely knocked him out with my tripod, knocked him out cold." She looked at the tiny woman huddled on the couch. "Then you wouldn't have had to do a single thing, Moll. Josef would've been laid out on the ground and you could have…" Ivy looked as though she was fighting not to laugh, and that was something else that didn't make any sense. "You could have just checked his vials—his vitals, just like you really did." A half-smothered giggle escaped her. "You, you clobbered him like a, like a prizefighter or something. No! Like an avenger. Yes! You were an avenging angel! And then you knelt there and checked his vital signs like, like Florence Nightingale. And she was another kind of angel!"

I tried to understand the joke. No one else was laughing, though.

Oh. Ivy must have been given something for pain. I remembered. I was proud that I remembered. She told us back in the hospital waiting room that she had a furrow. A furrow, she called it, in the top of her shoulder, a half inch deep in front and a few millimeters deep at the back.

Just a half inch, she said. That's all. Only a half inch of her flesh blown away by a speeding bullet.

I was glad she had been given something so she

wasn't feeling the pain. I hadn't, though. Hadn't been given anything. Because I had a mild concussion. Another fact I was proud of remembering.

Ivy was still giggling. "Did I tell you, I told you, didn't I? I told all of you that a very serious doctor—a VERY serious doctor—told me I can't wear a bra with straps for three weeks. He looked about fifteen years old. It's true. A teenage doctor." She snorted. "He was embarrassed to be talking about bras!" Hugh pulled her back against him, his arms around her middle. "So for three weeks I'm gonna be droopy. And right now I'm loopy. Loopy, droopy!" She gasped and was abruptly solemn. "But I shoulda hit him again, Molly. I shoulda knocked him out cold. I shoulda ob, ob, ob-LIT-er-ay-shed him."

"It's not your fault!" I might have been yelling again. I wasn't sure. "Not yours either, Molly. It's my fault!" It hurt so much to lean forward, to talk so loudly, but I couldn't stop. "I should NOT have let Josef into my life. I should not have introduced him to all of you. If I hadn't done that, none of this would have happened. I wouldn't have had to be…" My voice wobbled. "Had to be rescued. None of us would be sitting here."

"Lord God Almighty!"

Charlie's bellow startled everyone in the room. He was still standing against the wall, his back straight, clenched teeth showing through his huge drooping mustaches. He looked from one of us to another, spitting out hard and angry words. "Beck. What happened today is your fault. That's what you think. Because of something you did umpteen months ago." He turned and glared at Ivy. "And the whole thing is your fault. Because you didn't beat the man to a pulp. And Molly, you're…

you're agonizing over what you did out there in the woods today. Which was exactly what you HAD TO DO." He abruptly shoved himself away from the wall. "You three were in the woods with a dangerous man. He had a gun. Ivy was injured by a bullet from that gun. Every one of you could have died. Every one of you acted bravely." His voice went from growling to hoarse. "Immensely brave. You all showed courage. You all are alive. Celebrate it!" He grabbed the door handle. "Lord God Almighty!"

The door slammed. There was complete silence. Then Molly let out a deep breath.

"Charlie never gets angry. Never. Ever."

"Well," Ivy was struggling between shock and giggles. "That's just not true, Moll. We just saw. He does get angry. Charlie got… He got snarly. Snarly Charlie!"

Hugh tightened his arms around her. "Three people who are important to him were threatened. That's enough to make anyone angry."

"How…" I leaned forward and winced when the abrupt movement made my head throb. "Why was Charlie here? How did he even find out?"

"Charlie has a secret vice." Molly's whinnying laugh wasn't as hearty as usual, but it was a laugh, and it sounded like Molly. "He has a police scanner in his office, and he listens whenever he's working."

"But still… How did he know it was us?"

Ivy nodded and went on nodding, her face overly solemn. "He knew we were going to walk at the Whiting Nature Area. That's it. That is igg-zacc-ly it. Charlie heard about three women at Velma Whiting Nature Area and so he knew they were us." She leaned back, still nodding like a bobblehead doll.

Molly looked up at Hugh. "Did the police say how he's doing? Josef? Did they say anything about him to you?"

"We'll probably have to wait for the evening news. I doubt that anyone from the hospital will contact any of us directly."

"Of course not. Not me for sure. I'm the woman who hit him. One of the women. I'm the woman who might have killed him. I'm—"

Hugh's deep voice interrupted her. "Out into the kitchen. All of you." He turned Ivy toward the doorway. "No one has had anything to eat since early this morning. There's a crockpot of minestrone in the kitchen. We are all going to have hot soup and bread. Now. Get going."

Molly's husband joined him in herding us all into the hall and then into the kitchen. I had been nauseated only a few minutes before, but I was ravenous the instant I smelled Hugh's minestrone. Starving. Shaky with hunger.

"Beck!" Ivy was still too loud. She patted the chair beside her and called loudly to me. "Sit here, Beck! Beside me! Because we two are the wounding... the walky... how does that go?" She giggled. "Wounded Walkies!"

****

Molly and her husband left after Hugh's minestrone with bread and cheese and glasses of seltzer. Ivy went to lie down and Hugh stood in front of me, stern and determined, talking about doctor's orders and concussion and waking me up during the night. I sat at their kitchen table and watched his face and didn't even try to understand. After a while I blurted out that I needed a shower but he said it wasn't safe because I might get dizzy and fall. So I filled the bathtub with hot water to my shoulders and drifted in a haze until Hugh pounded on the door and handed in some of Ivy's clothes. I don't remember getting out of the tub, or getting dried off, or putting on the flannel pants and t-shirt. I was warm: inside from hot soup, outside from hot water. I was not cold for the first time since I looked up and saw Josef there, in front of me, in the woods.

I have no recollection of Hugh waking me up in the night. I remember, instead, a long period of uneasy slumber, bits and pieces of dreams, wanting to change positions but it hurt too much to move my head, wanting to wake up because I was in danger. Then, finally, hours of nothing.

And then it was daylight. Hugh and Ivy were in the kitchen, both looking tired and a bit subdued. She sang out "good morning" almost as cheerfully as her usual self, and pushed a bowl of cut fruit toward me. I gobbled down fruit and a plate of pancakes and ham as if I hadn't eaten for days and then I went back to their guest room and fell asleep again.

The house was quiet when I woke up for the second time. I wondered if Ivy and Hugh had both left, but I found her standing at the kitchen sink. She whipped around when she heard me, the expression on her face both guilty and defiant.

"Oh! I thought you were Hugh." She turned back to the suds, and I saw that she was trying to wash dishes with only one hand. "He said I should take another pill and go back to bed. But I hate that muzzy feeling. So we had words."

"Oh dear."

"I took only half a pill and I slept only an hour and

now I'm wide awake and starving but I felt I had to get the breakfast dishes out of the way before I start on lunch."

"How does your shoulder feel?"

She grimaced. "It hurts. Truly. It hurts like hell. My whole arm hurts."

"I'll wash the dishes. You sit at the table and talk to me."

"Deal." Ivy dried her hands, sat down, and heaved a big sigh. "Thank you, Beck. It seemed like a good idea to be tough and independent and all, to show that I don't take orders from anyone, not even Hugh. But mostly it just hurts." She frowned. "How are you feeling? Your head?"

"If I don't nod, it's not bad. And if I don't shake my head. And if I don't look down. If I just keep it balanced and still."

"I have to say it, Beck. Your face looks awful. And very painful."

"I expect it will look bad for days." My little laugh came out more like one of Ivy's snorts. "I will avoid mirrors."

We were quiet as I washed and rinsed dishes and stacked them in the rack.

"Balanced and still. That's a good phrase for you, Beck. You always seem balanced and still. Serene." Even with my back to her, I could tell when she grinned. "Young Sean, Charlie's grandson, said you remind him of Sacajawea. I can see you like that. Standing on a bluff, shielding your eyes against the sun, picking a route to lead all those men safely through untold dangers."

My already hot face got hotter. I had never been alone with Ivy, just the two of us. We had never just chatted, like friends.

"Where's Hugh?"

"He got a call right after breakfast from the contractor who's building one of his houses. Something about a ledge of bedrock being almost six feet east of where they thought it was and maybe requiring some revision in the plans. He had to go out to the site."

I turned toward her, drying my hands. "Hugh is an architect?"

"A very good one! He's won all sorts of award." Ivy beamed and waved her good arm. "He designed this house!"

"I am impressed." I hadn't noticed much the night before, but now I could see the beauty and quality in the heavy sliding door leading out to a patio, the slate floor, the appliances, the wide front hall. "It's beautiful."

Right on cue, the award-winning architect came through the door. He didn't ask Ivy why she wasn't in bed, or if she had taken the pain medicine. He just bent and kissed her.

Then he took my shoulders and looked closely at my eyes. "You look better."

"I am."

He glanced at the sink. "I usually do the dishes whenever I cook. But—"

"I know. Ivy told me. How did things turn out?"

And then all three of us were talking about the problem with the new house, and about a sale coming up at Ivy's store, and about the birds coming to feeders just outside the windows. While we talked, Hugh got out a huge griddle and made tuna melts on rye, one of my most favorite sandwiches. Cut in half, they made an impressive pile, and I didn't feel the least bit shy about eating three halves and a pile of dill pickles and then two lemon bars washed down with freshly made coffee. And when we finished lunch, he said he thought it was safe for me to go home.

I wondered, I had to wonder, if it was the conversation or my appetite that convinced him. Maybe he was thinking ahead to what he and Ivy planned for supper, and how much of that food I was likely to inhale all by myself.

But Ivy ate as much as I did, at breakfast and again at lunch. Maybe recovery needs calories.

****

Alain built the first part of our house when I was still in middle school, living with my parents, with no knowledge at all of central Vermont. Now that first building might be called a Small House, maybe even a Tiny House, but then it was all he needed and all he could afford. After he married his first wife, they more than quadrupled the dwelling, enlarging the kitchen, building on a separate living room, adding another bedroom and two more bathrooms, making an upstairs office.

The porch was ours, added after we found each other. Alain had it built as a surprise the first time I went with him on a dig as his wife, not as a student or an intern. The two of us and a crew of interns spent three weeks digging into an ancient Haudenosaunee village near Syracuse, New York, and while we were gone a construction company built a porch all down the southwest side of the house. The afternoon sun always poured in there, and the bricks of the house acted like a heat sink, and most years the porch stayed warm into December.

Later that afternoon, the sun would light up all the

old brick and paint the narrow floorboards golden, but when I got home from Hugh's house only one corner was warmed. I dragged a rocker into that patch and I exulted. I was home! Home! On our porch, where Alain and I used to spend hours, usually in the afternoon or evening. Once, though, in the very early morning, we made love on the floor with mist swirling in through the screen and making droplets in our hair. The porch floor was cool on my back. Both of our robes were open, his hanging down on both sides of us. I kept his robe after he died, and I still wore it sometimes.

I was not only back home. I was back to *me*. The fogginess, the confusion, the blurred curtains that separated me from reality, were gone. Abrupt movements still made my head pound, and I still wasn't seeing clearly out of my left eye. My face was swollen, reddish-purple, and painful. But I was no longer dizzy, or queasy, or baffled about every single thing around me.

It wasn't even three o'clock in the afternoon, but I was ravenous again. I didn't want to leave the porch, though. I felt warm and drowsy and happy, in the rocker in the warm sun, on the porch that Alain had built for us. A flicker of movement caught my eye, something moving near the chicken coop. I leaned forward, wincing from the sudden stab of pain but intent on whatever was out there. An animal was moving from the coop toward the garage. It was mostly hidden in the high weeds so I could see only an occasional bit of brown, but I was immediately convinced that it was the same grouse from weeks ago.

The bird's head was visible now, floating above the weeds as if unattached to a body. Its crest was sticking straight up, just a few little feathers sailing above the foliage. Then the bird emerged from the grasses, and I could see all of it, warm reddish brown and tawny brown and lighter gray-brown, with the head looking much too small for its rounded body.

"Hello," I whispered. "Are you the same grouse? Or is there a whole army of you out there in the woods?"

The bird kept moving closer to the house, moving with a lurching gait, rocking from side to side like a cartoon pirate with a wooden leg.

"It IS you, Gilbertie Grouse! You are still alive!" The grouse was close to the far end of the porch. "I put corn out for you a while back, Gilbertie, for two or three days in a row. But you didn't come to get it and a gray squirrel gobbled it all up."

I wondered if the grouse roosted under the porch. Alain had put trellis all around to keep out skunks, but maybe part of it was broken and I hadn't noticed.

"I'm hungry, grouse. Are you hungry too?"

The bag of cracked corn was still out in the chicken coop. I didn't feel like walking that far, and it was going to take an energetic heave to get the warped door open and the effort would make my whole head hurt. I tried to remember what I read about a grouse's diet. Fruit, obviously. And nuts. And Gilbertie ate cracker crumbs that day in the driveway. Or maybe that was one of his kinfolk.

"Stick around, bird. I'll be right back."

The phone was ringing as I reached the kitchen, and the blinking light showed several messages. I would check them later. Maybe. Maybe the next day. If I felt up to it. But I could at least find out who was calling now.

"Hello?"

"Beck! What a relief to hear your voice! We all saw

the news and we're all worried about you. How ARE you?"

Sally had the office next to mine. I might not have recognized all my co-workers' voices but her rushed, breathy delivery was unmistakable. I wondered if she had been appointed to get details from me.

"I am doing fine, actually. A bit of a headache—"

"I should think so!"

"—and my face looks dreadful, but I'm feeling…" I looked for the words. "Hale and hearty and healthy."

"You are one strong woman! Well, I won't keep you. I just wanted to say that I'll be by in about twenty minutes."

I wanted to tell her I wasn't ready for visitors, but she was talking again.

"We all put together some supper stuff so you won't have to cook anything. Enough for several meals. All you have to do is sit there and wait. Bye!"

Well. That answered the question of what to do for my supper.

Now to the grouse.

I took a stale baguette out of the bread box and then got out a box of raisins and dumped some on a plate.

"Hmmm, grouse," I muttered. "We might have a problem. These raisins are hard as rock. Maybe soak them in hot water? That might help."

What else?

Nuts! Of course. I had a whole bag of unsalted mixed nuts. I poured out a cup or so and got a knife and had just finished chopping them when I remembered that Ivy said grouse eat whole acorns. Well, maybe an occasional treat of pre-cut nuts would be welcome.

"All right, bird." I drained the raisins and dumped

them in a bowl along with the crumbled baguette and nuts. "Special Grouse Gorp today, cracked corn tomorrow."

I didn't see the bird but I heard movement around the corner of the house, so I scattered some of the food along the side of the porch and the rest of it under a nearby shrub. I was back in my rocker when my co-worker's car came up the driveway and screeched to a halt. People at work called her Speedy Sal and I always thought it was because of how fast she talked, but maybe she did everything at high speed. She threw herself out of the car and almost ran up the walk, a box in both hands and a canvas bag hanging from her shoulder.

My stomach started growling the minute I got a whiff. Tomato, cheese, oregano, basil, garlic. Lots of garlic.

"That smells incredible, Sally. Thank you so much!"

She smiled, and I had the fleeting thought that I might never have seen her smile before. I probably did, ages ago, but for so many years the people I worked with were background, just background. Ever since Alain's death, I never saw them socially. I never went into their offices to chat and laugh and complain, like everyone else did. As I looked at Sally's lined face, her broad smile, her bright little brown eyes, I promised myself that I would be a better colleague in the future.

"Guido's eggplant parmesan," she was saying. "Nick said, Nick from the office next to yours, he said you used to order it, years ago when you and…" She stopped and looked appalled.

"When Alain and I used to join some of you after work on Fridays. Imagine Nick remembering what I ate, after so long." I ushered her up the stairs and into the kitchen. "Come in, come in."

The box held two servings of what was, at one time, my favorite food in the world. There was also a bag of garlic bread, the sides shiny and damp from melted butter.

"Oh my goodness, Sally. This is a feast!"

"There's more." She plopped the bag on the table and took out four closed containers. "These two are salads. And these are frozen stuff, for tomorrow or the next day. I'm not sure what we ended up getting. They probably should go into the fridge right now because they got a tad soft." She poked the foil with her fingers "Or maybe they can go back into the freezer. I'm never sure what's safe to refreeze."

"Me neither. But nothing's going to last very long anyway. I have been hungry this whole day."

She nodded sagely. "My hubby was like that after his hip replacement. The doctor told him he needed some ridiculous number of calories a day while he was healing. Five thousand or something." She smiled that transforming smile again. "He took it as an open invitation to wolf down pints of the most expensive kinds of ice cream, every single day."

"A true Vermonter." I smiled too, even though it hurt. "I've got to peek."

One of the other foil containers held Guido's famous Italian sausage lasagna, and the other had penne with shrimp in lobster sauce. Alain's favorite. I wondered if the amazing Nick had remembered that also.

"What wonderful food you all chose! I can't thank you enough, Sally." For an embarrassing moment, I thought I might cry. "The fish probably shouldn't be refrozen, but I'll put the lasagna and the extra eggplant parmesan in the freezer."

She left after just a few more minutes. I felt immeasurably grateful to her, to all the people in the office, for the incredible food. I was also grateful to be alone again, alone in my home. I got down one of our trays, filled a bowl with salad, piled a plate with eggplant parmesan and garlic bread, picked up a water bottle, and took everything back out to the porch.

The afternoon sun was now shining directly in, and the whole porch was deliciously warm for November. Alain used to take down the plywood at the north end every spring, but I left it up all year since he died because it blocked the prevailing wind. In a few weeks, I would move the sliding glass panels to cover the screens, and lock them in place, and the porch would be ready for winter.

As soon as I settled into the rocker, I saw Gilbertie Grouse again. He was under the shrubs beside the driveway, his head bobbing up and down as he ate.

"Good little guy! You eat, and I'll eat, and we will both be stuffed and happy."

The bird looked toward the porch, briefly, and then it headed for the other patch of food. I wished I had my binoculars outside with me.

"Maybe it's hard for you to find natural food, with your leg bent the way it is. Maybe that's why you're coming so close to the house. Maybe that's why you hear me but you don't get scared off. You are determined to get that food, aren't you?"

The grouse attacked the second pile of grouse gorp as if it couldn't eat fast enough, the silly too-small head bobbing up and down almost as fast as a sewing machine needle.

"Or maybe you're just a hog."
The grouse looked up again, for just an instant.
"Either way, grouse. Either way. Enjoy."

****

Grief isn't over at once. I will always feel sadness about Alain's death, always for the rest of my life. But there on our porch, sharing a meal with a solitary bum-legged grouse, eating wonderful food chosen for me and brought to me by friends, I sloughed off a bit more of the leaden sadness that had been part of my life for so many years. And I sloughed off a bit of the dread and fear that began the day before, in the woods, with my friends and a man and a gun.

Chapter Eight

I almost gave in and reheated the penne with shrimp and lobster for breakfast. I could still taste the garlic from the day before, and my mouth, my stomach, my whole body craved more of that soul-satisfying food. Alain would have told me to go ahead and indulge. He would have come up with a quote from a source as varied as Rousseau or Will Rogers or Siddhartha Gautama, about the importance of yielding to temptation for balancing one's life and being whole.

But Alain wasn't here, and I am not good at ignoring the voices in my head that tell me what I "should" do. So I settled for a breakfast of toast, sliced apple, and some cheese.

By 10:30 my stomach was growling again. I was getting food out for a very early lunch when I got a phone call from the Montpelier police station; an officer was on his way to talk with me and would be here in about twenty minutes.

Damn. I did not want to talk with another police officer. I was doing well. I was almost forgetting the hours in the woods, the hours at the hospital. I wanted to go on forgetting.

I scowled at the phone and then took a deep breath. All right then. If I couldn't sit on the porch and fill my belly with garlicky pasta, then I would listen to all the old messages. I would spend two hours, no more, doing things I didn't want to do, things I should do, and then I would eat more of the extravagantly delicious food and go back to living my real life.

There were four calls from colleagues at work, two from a local TV station, two more from newspaper reporters, and one from a woman who said she was a spiritual healer and wondered if I needed her services to rebuild my chi. I deleted them all. I didn't want to talk with the press, the chi woman made me shudder, and Sally would have shared news of her visit with everyone else in the office.

Then I went outside to wait.

The officer turned out to be Charlie's buddy again, the solemn sergeant who'd come about the theft and later about the phone calls. Josef's car had been found and was being towed to an impound lot. The camping equipment had been "recovered," which sounded like TV cop-speak, and would be returned to me in a day or two. But that wasn't the real reason he was there. He wanted to question me again about what happened in the woods because, he said, "You seemed to be, uh, having difficulty recalling the exact sequence of events."

I led him onto the porch and told him I would bring out some coffee. Safe in our kitchen, I spent a few minutes looking out the window, my back straight and my chin up. Then I filled two mugs and put them on the tray I used for my feast the night before, added the sugar bowl and a container of half-and-half, opened a bag of store-brand fig cookies, and took two deep breaths.

"Here you go, officer…" I had no memory of the man's name.

"McCauley, ma'am."

"Officer McCauley. There's more coffee in the

kitchen." I sat down. "You are quite correct. I was having difficulty recalling anything. I felt… foggy, I guess is a good word. Addled. Baffled." I tried a small smile. "And my head hurt."

"You had a concussion, correct?"

"Yes."

"How are you feeling now?"

"I am much better. Thank you. I woke up the day after…" I tried to remember if Officer McCauley had been at the hospital. "The day after the, the event, and most of the fogginess was gone."

"Your face still looks very painful, if you don't mind me saying."

Now I almost smiled for real, and it hurt. "That is the truth, officer. I look awful."

"May I get a picture, the way your face looks now?"

"Why? What for?"

"I doubt that Mr. Andrews will ever prosecute."

For a split second, I had no idea who Mr. Andrews was. Josef never used his last name. Once he said he was going to change back to the Russian original and call himself Josef Andreyev because it would go better with his professional image.

"But if he ever does, it will be good to have a record of what he did to you. The damage he did. A lawyer could get the x-rays and show that you had a concussion, but we…" He looked uncomfortable, unable to meet my eyes. "We neglected to get a photo at the hospital. It was a serious oversight."

"A picture taken today will be more colorful anyway."

"Thank you for being so understanding." He met my eyes. "The chief wasn't."

"Oh dear."

"Ready?" He held his phone in front of him.

"Don't tell me to smile for the birdy."

That startled a grin out of him.

The questions, I suppose, were the same that I was asked in the emergency room, and again in the waiting room with Ivy and Molly. I told him about being startled by Josef when I was alone and about his asking if he could move back in with me because winter was coming and he was camping in the woods. And then I had to explain how I knew Josef, that he lived with me for over a year until I asked him to leave.

"Was he ever abusive, ma'am?" Officer McCauley had his little notebook out, the one he had when he made the list of stolen camping equipment.

"No. Not really. But he called several times. Oh. You know that. You took the tapes. You and Charlie thought he was making threats." I took a deep breath. "I gave him a place to stay when he needed one. He needed one again so he wanted me to allow him back."

I told him about trying to get past Josef, and how he first blocked me and then grabbed my arm and then put his hands around my throat. The officer's pen made little scratching noises before he looked up.

"Then what happened?"

I tried to remember the exact order, the sequence of events. "I struggled for a minute or two, I think, and then I got my hands between us and I hit him in the, I hit him between his legs. That made him let go so I tried to get away, but he grabbed my leg."

"Then what?"

"He pulled me down onto the ground, I think. Yes. I tried to hit him, to scratch him, but he rolled on top of me. That's when he slammed my head into a rock."

Scratch, scratch. More writing.

"And that's what caused the concussion?"

"I… I don't know. I didn't think to ask, at the hospital. Josef punched me, too, on this side of my face. I thought that might be the cause of the concussion. But I guess I'm not sure."

"Were the other two women there the whole time?" He looked down at his notebook. "Ms. Pritchard and Mrs. Russo?"

Ms. Pritchard. Mrs. Russo. No one in the FATSO group used last names.

"No. I thought you knew that. I thought I told you. Ivy and Molly had gone on ahead."

"Oh. Yes. You did say that. When did they come back?"

"I'm not a hundred percent sure. But I think Ivy hit Josef with her tripod right after he punched me. I think."

"The tripod. It's metal?"

"Yes."

"And heavy?"

"Yes." I suddenly had to say something normal, something that had nothing to do with fear and pain and confusion. "She has been wanting to buy a new tripod, a lighter one, for months and months. I guess I am lucky she didn't find one yet."

"What happened next?"

"I… I got away, out from under him. But then he, he pulled a gun. Oh! The gun! I don't think I told you. He said he bought a gun because he was homeless, because he was camping out in the woods. He said the woods were dangerous."

"Had you seen the gun before? Before he pulled it,

I mean?"

"No." I felt, idiotically, as if my forgetting to mention the gun would make him think I was lying. I felt as if I were on trial, as if I was guilty of something.

"So Mr. Andrews had a gun. What happened next?"

"Well." I needed a lot more air. I needed time to think, to breathe. "He turned toward me. He aimed at me, aimed the gun. The pistol, I guess. It was small. And gray."

"Go on."

"And then all of a sudden Molly was there, behind him, with her binoculars. And she hit him."

"Mrs. Russo hit Mr. Andrews with her binoculars."

"Yes."

"Did she hit his head with the binoculars?"

"Yes. And the gun went off, I think right then, when he fell forward."

"One shot?"

"Yes. At least I think so. I am pretty sure. I suppose another shot could have gone off into the woods. But I didn't hear it. Didn't hear more than one." I started talking very fast, wanting to be done. "And Ivy was bleeding. From her shoulder. Molly ran to her and gave me her binoculars and started looking at Ivy's shoulder and asked me for my bandanna and… and sometime, I don't remember when, she went over and felt Josef's pulse." There. I was done. "Oh! And she called 911. And we waited."

"Did Mr. Andrews move at all? Make any sounds?"

"No."

Once again, there was silence except for the officer's pen moving across paper.

"Just a few more questions. Did Ms. Pritchard hit

Mr. Andrews more than once with her tripod?"

"No."

"Did Mrs. Russo hit him more than once with the binoculars?"

"No. Only once."

"You're sure?"

"Yes."

He closed his notebook with a snap.

"Why? Why did you ask about Molly and Ivy?"

"If this comes to court, and it might not, ever, it will be good to show that the three of you used necessary force to get out of a bad situation. But not unnecessary force."

"Oh." I watched his face. "Do you think Ivy or Molly will be in trouble because of this? Because of saving me?"

He stood up. "I very much doubt it, ma'am." He smiled again, and I thought that he was quite a pleasant-looking man. "I know this hasn't been easy for you. Thank you for taking the time, and for being careful about going through it all again."

"You're... You're welcome." Again, I felt a need to make things normal, to be someone other than a woman who had felt another person's blood all over her, a woman who had heard gunfire and had seen her friend dazed and injured. "It's almost lunchtime, Officer McCauley. I've got food from Guido's in the kitchen. This, this has been hard, as you said. I would rather not be alone. Would you join me for lunch?"

I expected him to say he had to get back to work, and I was inordinately pleased when he said yes. But then, almost immediately, I wondered if I had just done something foolish, if he might think up more questions.

When he followed me into the kitchen, I told him I'd get salad ready if he would uncover the penne and put it in the microwave.

"Oh. Fish."

"Yes. Shrimp and lobster, with a lot of garlic and a lot of white sauce and a little smoked provolone. Absolutely sinful."

"I'll have salad with you, ma'am. Just salad. I don't do well with fish."

I turned away so he wouldn't see how relieved I was. I was going to have all that garlicky pasta for myself. I didn't have to share it.

"Here then." I handed him the leftover bread and a plate. "Take this out of the foil and put it on the plate and give it a few minutes in the microwave."

I got out a big bowl, dumped in what was left of the first salad, added all of the second one, threw in some black olives and garlic croutons, and got out two kinds of dressing and a few bottles of seltzer.

"My wife will be pleased," he said as he sat down and carefully tucked a napkin into the top of his uniform shirt. "She thinks I don't eat enough salad."

"Maybe it would be best if you don't mention the croutons or the shaved parmesan or the buttery garlic bread."

"I think you're right, ma'am."

****

Officer McCauley's car was just turning out of the driveway when Hugh's car pulled in. Before the car stopped moving, Ivy was leaning out the window and calling to me.

"Why was the cop here?"

I am not often mischievous. In fact, I am almost

never mischievous. But I waggled my fingers coquettishly in the direction of the distant police car before turning to Ivy and Hugh.

"We had a lunch date."

"Really?" She turned sideways to get out of the car and I saw that her left arm was in a sling, with the sling belted tight across her chest. "Exchanged phone numbers in the emergency ward?"

Hugh was holding a white cardboard box, like the kind you get in a bakery, and I was illogically, impossibly, ridiculously hungry again.

"He had more questions. The same ones he asked us before. What's with the sling?"

"I saw the doctor this morning. The shoulder's healing well, he said, but it hurts every time I move." She made a wry grimace. "So I'm immobilized for a few days."

"Come in, come in."

"I wanted to make you some cheesecake but I had to settle for bakery pound cake."

"I love pound cake, Ivy. Sit, sit. Hugh, there are a few packages of strawberries in the freezer. From Cunningham's farm. Would you get out one of the big bags and empty it into a bowl and put it in the microwave?"

I dumped the last few ounces of breakfast coffee. As I fixed a fresh pot, I thought that Alain would have liked Hugh. He would have appreciated that the tall Scot never talked just to hear his own voice, that he always had something to say before he opened his mouth.

"I just barely ate," I said.

"With the cop, yes. But Hugh says it won't hurt either of us to put on a few pounds."

I turned and looked at the slender woman sitting at my kitchen table. "I hated going over those questions again, Ivy. I hated remembering, describing what happened, one more time. I asked him to stay for lunch because I wanted to feel normal. I didn't want to feel like the person who was there in the woods that day."

She was nodding before I finished talking. "I know, I know what you mean, exactly. Yesterday afternoon, after we dropped you off, I asked Hugh to take me to the movies for that exact same reason. To feel normal." She laughed. "We were the only adults there without attached children."

Hugh turned from the microwave. "It was the first kiddy show I've ever seen." He did the little lip lift that counted as a grin for him. "And you know? I liked it."

Ivy looked up at him, glowing, and I saw again how much she loved him. "Me too, Hugh. Me too."

"May I get out the pound cake?" I looked at them both a bit sheepishly. "I've been continuously hungry since yesterday morning."

"Our poor abused bodies are telling us what they need."

"Must have calories. Must have sugar." I glanced in the direction of the refrigerator. "Must have garlic and cheese and lots and lots of butter."

"Exactly so, Beck. Exactly so."

Pound cake and hot coffee and warm strawberries and friends. I felt immensely rich. I was even beginning to feel full, at least for the moment.

"So…" Ivy put down her napkin and turned serious. "Molly has a friend at the hospital. A woman who used to work with her in Boston. This morning she got some information about Josef."

"And?"

"He had a stroke early Monday morning."

"Oh, no. Poor Molly."

"No. Not poor Molly. Not at all! Josef was operated on sometime Monday, and it looks like Molly hitting him with her binoculars might not have had anything to do with what's going on." She glanced at Hugh. "Interrupt me if I'm not getting this right, Hugh. Molly hit him near the top of his head. But there was an earlier injury down near his jaw, a fracture that never healed properly, maybe from years and years ago. The nurse didn't share all the details but she thought a bone chip from that earlier injury was causing bleeding inside, in his skull, and that's what caused the stroke. And that's probably what's causing him to be unconscious this long."

"Does Molly know that yet?"

"She's the one who talked with the nurse."

"Oh, of course. I wasn't thinking. Well…" I shook my head and winced. "I don't want him permanently injured, but… but I was hoping to see him in court. I was hoping to see him held accountable, for attacking me, for pulling a gun, for shooting you. Even for stealing Alain's camping equipment!"

"Being unconscious seems like an easy way out?"

"Exactly, Hugh! Like he's getting away with it. Ivy's shoulder hurts like hell and she can't even…" I blinked against unexpected tears. "Can't even make cheesecake when she feels like it. And Molly probably still feels guilty even after hearing about the other injury. And me!" I tried a laugh. "My face looks like a wobbly bloated balloon, all black and gray and rainbow colors."

"And there's Josef." Ivy was getting a bit giggly again. "Lying at ease on nice clean sheets, with nice clean nurses tending to his every need. And giving him warm sponge baths!"

"Time to head for home, my love."

Ivy passed her right hand over her face and sighed. "You're right, oh wise one." She stood up. "Beck, I am glad to see that you're doing some home entertaining, even with your rainbow balloon face. What did you and your policeman eat?"

"My colleagues brought me a ton of Guido's food yesterday. The officer and I had Caesar salad and garlic bread." I grinned, just a little. "He said his wife will be pleased to hear he had salad for lunch instead of a burger and fries. Oh!" We were on the front steps before I remembered. "Gilbertie Grouse was here earlier, right before the policeman!"

"Excellent!" Ivy giggled again. "Did you have something to eat with him too?"

"Of course I did. He… Oh!" My mind kept leaping to new thoughts. I wanted to keep them both near me, to talk and talk and talk. "The bag of cracked corn is still in the chicken coop. It's going to hurt me, a lot, to open that door. Hugh, would you mind getting the bag and putting it up here in the garage?"

I could see that he didn't understand why it should hurt to open a door, but he nodded and immediately started walking down the driveway.

"I'm pooped." Ivy laughed, but she did indeed look tired. "Too pooped to pop. Am I needed for this endeavor?"

She sat in the car as I raced indoors, got the key, ran down the driveway and unlocked the chicken coop. Hugh needed both of his hands to hoist the door up off the warped sill, so I didn't feel quite so silly about asking for his help.

"You were going to do this yourself, with that head?"

"With no other, Hugh. I am very grateful that you did it instead."

****

After Hugh and Ivy left, I cut another slice of pound cake, that third piece that I was too embarrassed to take while they were still with me, and I finished the strawberries, and then I used just a little more cake to mop up the rest of the strawberry juice from the bottom of the bowl.

"Later," I promised myself. "Later I'm going to take that seafood penne out of the refrigerator and I'm going to heat it up in the oven, not the microwave, because I think it tastes better that way. I am going to wait until all the cheese has melted and the sauce is bubbling, and then I'm going to take the whole thing out to the porch with a spoon and I am going to eat until I can't eat any more. And if there's any left…" The second part of the promise was to Alain. "I will eat it tomorrow for breakfast."

Chapter Nine

There was no real reason to take seven full days off from work.

The first two were necessary. I had to eat every two hours and I couldn't make any quick moves without my head threatening to explode. And maybe the next two days were justified as well. I wouldn't have been able to do my office work efficiently, and there was no field work that couldn't wait. I was sleeping ten hours a night and I still needed long afternoon naps on the porch, covered by a quilt and warmed by the sun.

I thought of heading in to work on Friday for a few hours, but Nick from work called to say he was going to drop by with some paperwork that needed my attention. He stayed only long enough to bring me up to date on one project, eat two cookies, and gently suggest that my face might be distracting if I showed up at a hearing scheduled for the beginning of next week. When he got up to leave, he assured me that someone would cover for me and brushed a kiss against my good cheek, leaving me astonished and embarrassed.

Then the temperature dropped forty degrees in twelve hours. I folded up the chaise and put the tarp over it and told myself it was almost time to close in the porch. Then I got a fire going in the woodstove and spent hours in front of it, in Alain's chair that still had the imprint where he used to lean his head.

The Monday morning weatherwoman had dire predictions about unseasonable cold and fierce winds. I called the office and said I needed two more days and was planning to be in part-time on Wednesday. Then I took the last of the Guido treats out of the freezer and put it near the woodstove to start defrosting.

****

I had more visitors during those days spent at home with a swollen face than at any time since before Alain died. Gilbertie Grouse was a regular. Twice a day, I put out cracked corn for him, and twice a day I watched him running from the cover of the woods and weeds with his awkward, lurching gait. I talked to him most days, wondering if he would ever become familiar enough with my voice and my presence to eat out of my hand.

On the fourth afternoon, a noisy flock of Blue Jays got to the corn first. I put out some more and stood guard on the porch until the grouse appeared and had supper. But the jays were back the next morning, just minutes after I spread the food around, and two hungry Mourning Doves were right behind them.

"You are going to have to accept me, grouse, or starve."

There was an old dog dish in the mudroom, left from the brief time when Alain and his first wife had a cocker spaniel. I rinsed it out, dried it, put in some peanuts in the hopes that the smell would be irresistible, and added a few handfuls of corn. Then I sat on the bottom step of the porch with the dog dish on the ground between my feet, and I waited. Two Blue Jays sailed into the tall oak by the driveway and started squawking, but they didn't come down to get the peanuts. I tucked my cold hands under my arms. I thought there was movement by the side of the chicken coop but I wasn't sure.

I waited some more.

Then I saw the ferns and dry weeds part, and Gilbertie Grouse hobbled out into the sunshine. I wondered if I should keep quiet, or if he associated my voice with food. In the end, I decided on talking.

"Hello, Gilbertie. There's food here," I murmured. "I am not going to let those jays get it. This is just for you. Come on. Come on. That's a brave grouse. Don't worry. I'm not going to lunge at you and catch you and make you into fricassee. I promise."

The bird came closer in a series of angled dashes, three lurching steps off to the right, three to the left, getting closer with every nervous dash.

At last, he was at my feet, gobbling the peanuts first, and then the corn.

"This works then, grouse. I will be back this afternoon, right here."

The bird tilted its head and looked up at me and then down at the empty dog dish.

"All right. More next time, I promise. And I am going to have on many more layers of clothing. You stay warm too, Gilbertie. You stay warm."

****

That afternoon, I sat on the steps with the dog dish full of corn, nuts, and soaked raisins at my feet, and the grouse finished it all. I began to think I wasn't offering enough to keep him alive and healthy. He ate even more the next morning. After he emptied the dog dish, the bird startled me by climbing onto my shoe and beginning to preen. I could feel him leaning against my ankle as he twisted to get at his wing feathers. I couldn't believe how light he was. He must have been two-thirds feathers.

"You are becoming very dear to me, bird," I whispered.

****

Hugh and Ivy came again on Saturday, a frigid and blustery day but Ivy had her window all the way down and was calling to me before the car came to a stop.

"Hugh is the best maker of soups in the entire state of Vermont! Wait till you see what we brought!"

Hugh opened the car's back door and lifted out a box that clanked as he carried it.

"Chicken soup for today and chicken soup for the freezer!" Ivy was still wearing the sling, with a heavy jacket draped over her shoulders, but I thought her face had more color.

"Thank you, thank you." I went to meet them. "I do have food, you know."

"I know. I've looked inside your freezer, remember? But Hugh's between major projects and I'm working only part-time at the store, so he wants to cook and I want to visit with you."

"Well, I am delighted to see you, with or without food. Come in."

Hugh's box held three gallon-sized Mason jars of soup, still warm. I opened two and poured the contents into a big pot and then pointed to the breadmaker.

"Caraway rye bread will be done in…" I peered at the timer. "In eight minutes. Will you eat with me? Even though it's a bit early for lunch?"

Ivy laughed. "Are you kidding? We've been smelling that soup for the last two hours. Of course we'd like some!"

"Ivy." Hugh's deep voice sounded a bit apologetic. "We have some at home. This is for Beck."

"And Beck," I said, "would love your company for an early lunch. Early lunches are perfect for me, I have discovered, because then I can have a mid-afternoon snack and still be hungry when it's time for supper."

I never particularly liked chicken soup, but Hugh's looked special, with a great many vegetables, big chunks of chicken, and tiny herb-dappled dumplings instead of floppy fat noodles. I got out bowls and plates and soup spoons and butter while the soup heated and the bread finished cooking, and I opened a gallon of cider.

"So do you think chicken soup can cure just about anything?"

"Well, if it can, I wish it would magically make my shoulder back to normal."

"I wish so too, Ivy. I am so sorry you were injured because of me."

Hugh scowled at me. "We're not going there again."

"You're right. Let's talk about something completely different. The grouse!"

"It's still around?"

"He is, Ivy, still hobbling around with one good leg and one bent leg. I've been feeding him out of an old dog dish, and he walks—well, lurches—right up to it now, even though I'm only a few inches away. And, big announcement…" I drummed my fingers on the table. "Yesterday he stood on my shoe to preen his feathers!"

Ivy reached out and squeezed my hand. "Beck, you have been the beneficiary of some especially pleasing grouse behavior. Young are hatched out in the summer. They're able to walk around with their mother and find food within a day or so, and then the whole family sticks together for several more weeks. But when fall comes, the covey disbands and sometimes one of the chicks gets lonely or something. Your injured grouse might be delighted to make a friend wherever he can find one." She gave a little snort. "At least that's one theory, that they're lonely. But it could be territorial behavior, not friendship."

"It can't be territorial. He stood on my shoe and leaned against my leg."

"Maybe he's claiming you as part of his territory."

I didn't think Hugh ever said anything flippant. "Hugh, if I could grin all over my face without it hurting, I would do just that."

"Well, either way, Gilbertie is one lucky grouse. Now," Ivy leaned back in her chair. "Molly's friend at the hospital fed her more information about Josef's condition."

"Improperly. Unprofessionally."

"Probably so, Hugh. But do you want to hear it anyway, Beck?"

"I guess so. Yes."

"He's still unconscious but he's out of the ICU because he's breathing on his own. There's talk about moving him to an acute nursing facility if he doesn't start responding to stimuli. The hospital has been trying to find next of kin, and someone in the billing office is contacting the Armed Forces to see if he ever served." She grimaced. "Josef didn't have any insurance cards in his wallet, and he's racking up a humongous bill. If he could be sent to the Veterans' Hospital, it might be a good solution."

"I can't imagine Josef taking orders."

"Maybe not."

****

Charlie was my next visitor, showing up just as

Gilbertie and I finished our morning ritual. The grouse hadn't stood on my shoe again, but he usually stayed close after eating, smoothing his feathers and, I was sure, listening to me talk to him.

"Was that the grouse? Your grouse?"

"It was, Charlie." I stood up. "I have officially made him into a pet."

"You sit out here and feed it?"

"I do."

"It's cold, Beck."

"I know that, Charlie. So let's go in where it's warm."

I told him to make himself comfortable while I unloaded all my layers of clothing. By the time I joined him in the kitchen, there were two cups of coffee on the table and he was getting out the half-and-half.

"I been talking to Officer McCauley." He sat down. "You made quite an impression on him. Not every day a cop gets invited for lunch."

"I didn't want to be alone right then. Thanks." I wrapped my hands around the hot cup. "He… I had to go through the whole thing again, what happened last week. I was glad he stayed a while afterward."

"Understood."

"I made pumpkin bread yesterday. Would you like some?"

"I would. Thanks."

There were a few minutes of quiet, and then Charlie got to the point.

"So here's what I learned. Josef's given name is Peter Joseph Andrews. On his job application." Charlie broke off a piece of pumpkin bread and chewed before continuing. "Doesn't have a police record. Just a couple speeding tickets, one in southern New Hampshire and one on Long Island."

"So stealing the camping equipment might have been his first crime. His first time."

"Or the first time he got caught."

"Oh. True."

"He has a sister on Long Island. Bill said—"

"Bill?"

"Officer McCauley. Sorry." His mustache did the slight twist that passed for a grin. "I figured you two were on a first-name basis."

"No."

"Well, Bill said Josef's sister hasn't heard from him in years. Doesn't know where he's been, doesn't know what he's been doing. But she's heading up here. Look through Josef's belongings. Talk to the doctors. That sort of thing."

"Oh."

****

For a dizzying instant, I thought Josef was standing outside my door. Then the world righted itself and I realized it was a woman with his thick dark hair, his narrow face, his high cheekbones, his wide mouth and dark eyes. I couldn't tell if she also had Josef's blinding smile because she was frowning.

"I'm Letitia. Letitia Andrews."

"Yes. You look, you have a strong resemblance to your brother. Come in."

She laid a laptop computer on the hall bench and took off her coat. Then she stood and looked around, at the living room and hall and kitchen.

"May I sit down?"

I chose the kitchen because the chairs weren't as

comfortable as in the living room. I wasn't at all sure I wanted her in my house for more than a few minutes.

"Your face is still bruised." Her hands were knotted together in front of her. "The police officers told me he punched you, that you had a concussion."

"I did. But I will have no lasting effects."

"I just met with Mrs. Russo and her husband. She seems, she was very upset about injuring Joseph."

"I think that's a very normal response."

"I… May I have something to drink?"

"Water? Coffee or tea?"

"Coffee. Thank you."

She sat completely still while I got down one of my least favorite mugs, filled it with left-over breakfast coffee, gave it a minute in the microwave, and set it in front of her.

"Cream? Sugar?"

"Cream. Yes. Thank you."

I sat down opposite her, without a cup for myself.

"The police gave me his laptop. I didn't know he was such a good photographer." She met my eyes. "I don't know anything about him. Dad and Mom divorced when I was six. I lived with her, and he lived with him. I don't even know where they went."

She poured half-and-half into the coffee a drop at a time.

"I saw him only once after he left. It was right after I graduated from high school. He had lunch with our mother and me. He said he ran away from Dad when he was only fifteen." She frowned. "We weren't sure we believed him. Do you have a spoon?"

"What? Oh. Yes." I got her a spoon and watched her slowly stir her coffee, her eyes fixed on it.

"Why do you all call him YO-sef?"

"He said that's his name." I decided I could have a cup of coffee with her and got up to get a mug. "He said your family was Russian and he was thinking about changing his last name back to Andreyev, the way it was before Ellis Island."

"We're Irish! Irish and English! Why would... He used to do things like that. When we were kids. He'd make up stories about how we used to be rich but Dad lost all our money in the stock market. Oh! And once he said Mom was some sort of European royalty!" She shook her head. "Poor Joseph. What we were wasn't good enough, I guess."

I sat back down.

"This is good. Thank you." She took a sip and then carefully placed the mug exactly where it was before. "I adored my older brother when I was little. But when he came back, he seemed, I don't know, closed off. Tough. Like our father." She took another sip. "I am embarrassed to say that I wasn't surprised when I got the call from the Montpelier police. I don't mean I knew he was going to start attacking women. But I've always worried. I've always expected, I guess, some sort of call from some police department. Or hospital."

"I'm sorry." I was still worried that this woman might someday want to sue Molly or Ivy for injuring her brother, and I didn't want to say anything that might prompt that. But I felt sorry for her. "It must be hard having a sibling and not even knowing him."

"It was. Yes. Yesterday when I looked at Joseph in that hospital bed, I... I ached."

It was hard to look into her pained eyes and keep myself from reaching across and touching her hand.

"The surgeon said Joseph has had at least two skull injuries, one of them many years ago, maybe when he was a child." Her mouth twisted. "I wondered if Dad knocked him around. He hit my mom once. At least once. Maybe that's where Joseph's old injury came from. Our father."

Oh god. I wanted to make her feel better. I wanted her to smile, to let me see if her teeth were as white and beautiful as Josef's—*Joseph's*. I wanted to magically erase her memories of an unfamiliar brother and a violent father.

"Would you like your coffee heated up a bit?"

"Oh." She looked down at her mug as if surprised to see it in front of her. "Oh. Yes. That would be good. Do you... This is rude of me, but I missed lunch. I was going to eat in the hospital cafeteria but I forgot. Do you have, I don't know, peanut butter? And toast?" Her smile was tiny, tentative. "Childhood comfort food."

I jumped up. "I'm sorry. I should have offered you something. I have leftover soup if you'd like something hot."

"Soup and peanut butter toast." She smiled again, almost Josef's smile but sweeter. "That will be perfect."

While I fixed her lunch, she told me about her job as librarian and curator for her church diocese, a job she had held for almost fifteen years. And I talked a bit about my job as state hydrologist, and about helping Alain with archaeological digs.

"I went on a dig once. On a whim. I had vacation time coming and I saw an article about someplace in Arizona where people could stay and help out with a dig. It was the best vacation I ever had."

"It sounds wonderful, Letitia." I handed her a bowl

of soup and put a plate of toast on the table in front of her.

"This is wonderful. Thank you."

She was almost finished before she started talking again.

"I probably should have seen Ms. Pritchard first. The officer said she was shot."

"She's doing well. She won't have any long-range effects except a scar."

"She'll be the hardest, for me. My brother shot her. He had a gun and he aimed and shot at another human being. Why did he shoot her?"

"I think the gun went off by accident."

"Is that true? Truly?"

"Yes. Truly."

For the first time, she smiled her brother's glorious white smile. "That makes things easier. Thank you! Thank you. Oh! I haven't finished telling you yet. The surgeon said a fragment of bone was loose in Joseph's head, maybe for a very long time. Joseph was, his brain was bleeding, way before Ms. Pritchard and Mrs. Russo hit him."

"If he... If his brain was bleeding inside, wouldn't he have felt some pain?"

"Oh, yes. The surgeon said Joseph had to have known something was wrong. He probably had headaches, double vision, confusion. Maybe even paranoia." Her eyes filled with tears. "He was living alone in the woods, and all that was going on."

"Oh dear. I... That day in the woods I thought he might have been drinking, or on drugs. But all the time he stayed here, he was so careful about his health, about his body. It didn't seem right that he'd be..."

"Drunk or doped up."

"Exactly."

"So what happened in the woods, with Joseph attacking you and… and you three fighting back, that might have been fortunate. Oddly. Maybe his guardian angel was on duty or something. The surgeon said Joseph could have had a stroke out there, all by himself. It sounds funny but he might have been lucky he got knocked out and ended up in the hospital because then when he had the stroke, he was right there, in the ICU, with doctors and nurses and machinery and surgeons and… With all that around him." Her little laugh was uncomfortable but her hands looked more relaxed. "And another funny thing that isn't really funny. If he comes around, if Joseph wakes up, I'm not going to know him. I might not even like him. I keep feeling like I'm up here under false pretenses. Meeting with his doctors and nurses. Accepting their sympathy." She swallowed and then took a deep breath. "That makes me feel guilty. I'm a Catholic. Joseph was too, at one time. We are good at guilty." The little laugh again. "I'll have to go to confession as soon as I get home. Bless me father for I have sinned. I'm not sure I love my own brother."

I sat, mute.

"One more question." Now her eyes flooded with tears, and she stopped talking until she could get a deep breath again. "I have looked through some of Joseph's photos. I read some of the text. It's going to be a lovely book. How could my brother have that kind of insight, and a real sense of beauty, and still be, still be the same person who would hit women? Hurt women? Do you think the early brain injury did all that?"

"I don't know, Letitia. I can't explain that. People

are complicated beings."

"Yes." She stood up. "I talked on the phone with the publisher. For Joseph's book. She asked me to help with some text and maybe pick out more photos. From his computer."

"Oh." I couldn't think of any way to warn her that she was going to see almost nude pictures of me. "Thank you for coming here. You... You do realize that you don't have to apologize for anyone else's behavior, don't you? Not even your brother's."

"Maybe not." A tiny smile. "But if I do apologize for him, then I won't have to apologize to St. Peter for *not* doing it."

****

I did not expect to like Josef's sister. But later that day, I talked with Molly and Ivy and I liked what I heard about her from them too. I liked hearing that Letitia asked for Charlie's help in wading through Medicaid and Social Security Disability rules, for her brother. I liked that she asked Charlie to recommend a different accountant, just in case she ended up being her brother's guardian and Josef—*Joseph*—woke up and made a fuss about his sister working with a friend of the women who were out there in the woods with him that day.

But I still felt a pang of anxiety when Letitia Andrews came back a few days later. I invited her in but she stood in the driveway and said she was in a hurry.

"I have to get back to my job. But I looked through the book on Joseph's computer and I saw some photos of you and I wanted you to decide if they should... If the book should have them in it."

"Oh. Well. I... Letitia, I was furious with him for taking those pictures without my knowledge, and for sending them to the publisher. But I think they were good. If you do too, then I think… Leave them in. And if you think they're not good, get rid of them."

"They are good. And they fit in that section of the book." She turned to go. "Oh! I talked again with the publisher. The book isn't coming out until September. That's the date the publisher wanted all along because then it will be in stores when people start thinking about holiday shopping."

"He told me it would be out any day."

"Joseph was building his life on dreams, just like he did when he was a boy. If he had listened to his publisher, if he had understood that there wouldn't be any money for several more months, he might have found another job. He might not have been living in the woods, and hurting, and all alone."

I reached out and took her hands, and we both wept for Josef, for Joseph, for her big brother.

Chapter Ten

I will always remember that winter for the unrelenting cold. The whole of January was as cold as the whole of December, one of the longest cold spells in Vermont's long history of frigid winters. The few days with blue skies were the coldest. More often, everything was gray. Medium gray skies, pale gray snow, dark gray tree trunks. Sometimes a front went through and then there was floating mist, and that also was gray.

For the first time in the history of the Burlington Bird Club and its several branches, there were no outings in December. Ivy's shoulder still hurt if she tried to lift her binoculars, and Hugh was gone to a conference so he wasn't available to carry her heavy scope. And Jack canceled his scheduled car-birding in Addison County when thirty-five mile-an-hour wind gusts were predicted.

I wouldn't have gone with them anyway. I thought I was fine, fully recovered, but going back to work left me exhausted at the end of every day and I needed both weekend days to recoup. My job was proving to be both more enjoyable and more tiring than before. It took effort to be a better colleague, effort that didn't come easily to me. I tried leaving my office door open, but the frequent interruptions drove me crazy. So I started going into the staff room once a day and sitting down with my thermos of coffee and listening to the chatter and sometimes joining in.

Feeding Gilbertie Grouse, spending a few minutes with the bird every morning and every evening, soothed and rejuvenated me. I bought another bag of cracked corn and one of whole corn mixed with oats, alfalfa meal, and field peas (for protein, according to the man at the feed store). The bird now came running as soon as I opened the door, racing around the corner of the garage or up the driveway with his rolling, lurching gait. He often leaned against my leg, or bumped my foot with his head in what I took as a greeting.

Letitia Andrews called twice, each time prefacing what she had to say by asking me if I wanted to know how her brother was doing. I wasn't sure I did, in truth, but I liked her so I said yes. The first call was to tell me her brother was still in a coma.

"So now the odds have changed, Beck. There's a higher chance he'll end up brain-dead and also a higher chance he'll die." I heard her gulp. "Sooner rather than later."

Now the gray days were further dimmed by a dull sense of waiting. Molly called it a death watch. I understood, I felt that way too, even though I also thought she was being overly dramatic. We should not feel guilty, not one of us. He attacked me. He pointed a gun at another human being. I didn't feel guilty about fighting Josef—*Joseph*—or scratching or kicking or hitting him between the legs. But Molly and Ivy hit Joseph around the head, and now he was still in a coma. Even knowing about the previous injury, they couldn't stop wondering if what they did that day in the woods might end up killing him.

Letitia called again in late January to tell me she had

become Joseph's guardian and was making plans to have him moved to a nursing home run by her local diocese.

"So I won't be making any more trips up to your area to talk with doctors and such." She hesitated. "I regret not getting to know you better, Beck."

"I am sorry too, Letitia. Maybe when it's nicer weather you would like to come up and stay here for a few days." I tried a small laugh. "I can take you birding."

"Oh. Yes. I would like that."

****

"Beck. Charlie. You got that camping stuff back, right?"

"Hello, Charlie. Yes, I did."

"Tomorrow good for me to head out and look at it?"

"I'll be in all morning."

"Good."

The box was still in the laundry room where I put it the day Officer McCauley returned it. I took the sleeping bags to the dry cleaners the next day, and I put the liners in the washing machine. Now I lined things up on the living room couch: the tent, smelling of wood smoke; the two sleeping bags that could be zipped together to make one; the two sleeping mats; the blackened percolator and nested cooking pots; the two-burner stove and the lanterns, one big and one small. Even the little tin box where Alain always kept his waterproof matches.

It felt like a touch of normal to see Charlie at the door, looking just like Charlie, without the fierce scowl from that day at Hugh's house. His face was still tanned and lined, his eyebrows were still bushy, his mustaches still huge, drooping, and goldy white.

"Camping, huh? In the worst winter in decades."

"Yup. I'm hearty."

"Or crazy."

"Not crazy yet." He got rid of his heavy jacket. "My winter camping's gonna be way south of here."

"Oh!" I felt illogically bereft. I didn't want any of the birding group to go anywhere. I didn't want any changes.

"Come on in. The camping supplies are in here."

"Whoa. That's a lot."

"All we had. Yes."

"You sure you don't mind loaning it to me?"

"Of course not. It's been collecting dust since the spring before Alain died. Well, at least until Josef…"

He picked up one of the sausage-shaped stuff sacks. "Sleeping bag?"

"Yes. This one too. Take them both if you think you might hit some cold weather." I put my hands on two identical cylinders. "These are self-inflating mats. They're not terribly comfortable but they'll do. This, on the other hand—" I touched a big box "—is luxurious. It's a double air mattress that inflates with a foot pump. Josef didn't take this because it was in the hall closet waiting for me to fix it. It's got a slow leak."

"You mind if I try a patch?"

"Of course not. But take the two pads with you, for backup."

He lifted one of the lanterns. "This and the stove would be great." He frowned. "I suppose the tent, too, for when it's nice enough to sleep outside instead of in the camper."

"Camper?"

"Yeah. Can't remember if I mentioned it on the last birding walk."

"Which feels like several years ago."

"True." He straightened up. "Way last spring I bought a camper shell. Fits over a pick-up truck. Owner had a roll-over accident so the shell was pretty bashed up. Took me months to knock out most of the dents, get the door to close, replace a window, paint it, and do the fun stuff."

"Which is?"

He grinned just enough to make his mustache move. "Interior decoration."

"Really. You're into décor?"

"Not Home Beautiful, that's for sure. But I had fun figuring out how to use the space. Putting in cabinets, cupboards. A bed and a table."

"I'm impressed."

"Put a second bed in there too, so my grandson Sean can come with me to the Adirondacks this summer." He pulled apart the nest of pots and pans and lined them up on the couch. "Probably don't need all these."

"But all of them don't take up any more room than the big one alone."

"True."

"Your camper sounds huge, Charlie."

His hands were busy repacking the cooking pans. "When I traded in my truck last August, I got a bigger pick-up. Extended cab. Works great."

"Oh, wait. There are sleeping bag liners." I ducked into the laundry room. "I washed them. And I had the bags dry-cleaned. Where are you going?"

"Florida, eventually. But slowly. Got a friend outside Pittsburgh, haven't seen in years. And my wife's sister lives in Virginia, been asking me to visit."

I couldn't tell from his expression whether he was looking forward to that or not.

"Spend a few days with both of them. Maybe drop in on an old high school buddy in Maryland." He looked up and smiled, a kind of wide, happy smile I had never seen on his face. "And then straight through to Florida, soak up some sun, and then the best part! I'm gonna follow spring north. With the migrating birds."

That smile transformed his face, making him look much younger than the fifty-something Molly had mentioned.

"It is a delight to see you smiling, Charlie."

"Smiling this time, you mean." His face was instantly sober. "I was out of line that day, at Hugh's. Yelling at you all."

"Oh. No. I wasn't thinking of that." I wanted to reach out and pat his worried face. "You certainly didn't look very happy there in Hugh's living room. But you said what you were thinking. I believe that's all right, with friends."

He studied my face and then shrugged. "Not sure myself. But thanks."

Together, we started filling our arms with camping equipment.

"When are you leaving?"

"About three weeks from now." Another un-Charlie-like smile. "Take my time heading south and then start back north tail end of March or start of April. I figure that's when the first migrants'll be leaving Sarasota. Follow 'em to Georgia. Jekyll Island. Always wanted to go there. Then a little west to the Blue Ridge Mountains. Then zigzag east again and spend some time on the Outer Banks. That'll take me to late April."

"And by then there will be lots more migrants. A flood of migrants."

"And it'll be getting warmer. Should, anyhow. If it doesn't, I'll either stay put or go south again for a bit."

"That sounds wonderful, Charlie. I… Wait. I thought you were a CPA. Isn't April your busiest time of the year?"

"I do the books for six businesses. They'll all have their taxes done before I go." He lifted one eyebrow. "Even Ivy." He hoisted the box. "This'll be my first vacation in… Well, ever."

"I am delighted to be able to help."

We walked toward the door. "Will you send postcards?"

"Nary a one. But I'm takin' my laptop and a good camera. Gonna share the birds and the scenery with the whole FATSO group. You included, of course."

"I am looking forward to that, Charlie."

****

Ivy's birding trip the third Sunday of February was another excursion to Addison County, to scan the open agricultural fields for Snow Buntings and Horned Larks and hawks, and then spend time at the Champlain Bridge watching diving ducks and loons. I very much wanted to go, to look at birds, to feel normal again, but I wanted to avoid any opportunities for shared anguish over Josef or questions about his sister's phone calls. I finally decided to take my own car, and on the way home I would stop in Shelburne and stock up on smoked trout pate and three-year-old cheddar.

The drive down, alone, was a balm to my nerves. I stopped to watch a magnificent Rough-legged Hawk perched in a tree, glaring down at the icy ground and then coasting from its perch and hovering in place for a full minute before dropping and coming up with something small and furry in its talons. I stopped again at the Goose Viewing Area in Addison and watched a good-sized flock of buntings, swirling like a wind devil of multi-colored snowflakes.

There was a crowd of people in the big lot under the bridge, all bundled up against the biting wind. I didn't recognize anyone at first but then Ivy turned around and called out, "Beck! Get your scope set up fast! Tufted Duck!"

There were hundreds, maybe thousands, of waterfowl bobbing up and down on the icy water, and every one of them was black and white. As I got out my scope and new tripod, I doubted that I would ever find one duck in that mass, not unless it was bright orange and the size of a German shepherd.

"See the raft of scaup?"

It took me a minute but then I found them, black fore and aft, as Charlie said the previous winter, with gray sides.

"Yes. I've got the scaup."

"Well, scan to the right edge of the raft. There's one bird a little apart from the others... no, wait, now it's with two other ducks. It looks like one of the scaup but it's got... yes... Now you can see it well. A nice long tuft of feathers hanging down over its nape."

"Oh! Yes! I've got it! It looks somewhat like that Ring-necked Duck we saw."

"I think Tufted Ducks and Ring-necks are related." Ivy was intent on moving her scope to the right as the bird moved again. "But I'm not a hundred percent sure."

"I'm assuming Tufted Ducks are rare, from all these people ooh-ing and aah-ing."

The bundled-up shape next to Ivy turned around.

Jack looked like a kid on the playground in a puffy down jacket, snow pants, fleece hat, and wooly scarf. "HELL-OOO, Beck!" His grin was mostly hidden in a scarf but I could see his eyes crinkle and twinkle. "This is not your everyday duck! Tufted Ducks are a Eurasian species. One a year. That's all we Vermonters get. One per winter."

"Almost always on Lake Champlain."

"Right, Ivy." The twinkling eyes again. "And we all go bonkers."

I looked at the distant duck, trying to imagine its flight across the North American continent from Siberia. Or, no, maybe straight up over the North Pole and then down into Vermont. That probably made more sense.

Birders around me were making sure everyone saw every species: the Tufted Duck of course, and Greater and Lesser Scaup, Common Mergansers, one Hooded Merganser, a few Mallards and American Black Ducks, three distant Horned Grebes and three Common Loons in their gray winter plumage. As I panned with my binoculars from one part of the huge raft of waterfowl to another, I saw Charlie and Molly standing close to the water's edge, both of them focused on a mostly empty part of the lake west of the main flock. Molly turned and said quietly, "A late grebe. Pied-billed, not Horned." And every one of the scopes, binocs, and cameras swiveled.

The chunky little brown bird was easy to find, all by itself just beyond the shade of the big bridge, halfway between Vermont and New York. I felt a moment's unease, almost superstition. I looked quickly at Ivy and she nodded and answered my unspoken question.

"It's late for Pied-billed Grebes in Vermont. So this

could be the same bird we saw that day. But maybe not."

Another quarter hour, and the FATSO group was ready to move on. We made a quick stop at the Viewing Area to see if the Snow Buntings were still there, but all we saw were five crows and a dozen starlings. Then our convoy moved to Gage Road, where it took us a full hour to travel a mile and a half. First, we stopped and everyone got out of the cars to watch a female Northern Harrier eying us suspiciously as she crouched over her prey. Then a male harrier drifted by, dancing over the snowy hillocks and corn stubble, looking exactly like its nickname Gray Ghost.

Charlie nudged me. "Your buntings."

This was a huge flock, possibly as many as two hundred, many more than before. They reminded me of Sean's "bits of confetti" shorebirds as they whirled, darted, and twittered over the field on our left and then above our heads and then to the field on our right, finally settling in the dirt road with a fluttery wave just like a line-dried sheet settles when you shake it out over a bed.

"Coupla longspurs."

"What?" I was whispering too. The flock was close enough so we didn't need scopes to get a good look.

"Lapland Longspurs. Darker than the buntings."

"Oh. Yes. I see one. No. Two. I would have thought they were some kind of sparrow."

Behind me, Jack said, "Horned Larks, incoming!"

Five more minutes, and all the little birds—larks, buntings, and longspurs—rose in a twittering cloud and headed toward the distant field beyond the old barn. Ivy turned around with a big grin.

"All RIGHT! The winter threesome. Plus, two harriers!"

"How about some hot chili?"

"Do you have a place in mind, Charlie? That restaurant in Vergennes?"

"My place. All of you." His grin looked uncharacteristically sheepish. "Got something I gotta show off."

Eating together would be another chance for mopey faces and speculation about Joseph. But Charlie looked like an eager kid, so I followed the other cars.

****

The camper was not a work of art, with the hammered-out dents still visible under forest green paint and the main door neon yellow. But the inside was a marvel of creative planning and use of space.

"This has more storage space than my kitchen, Charlie." Molly was opening and closing doors and drawers. "Do you hire yourself out?"

"For you, Molly, any day." He bent, pushing his fingers down into a wide mattress that filled the back of the camper. "Sent away to Canada for this. Coils plus two kindsa foam." He looked past others to meet my eyes. "Got your sleeping pads in the house, Beck. You can take 'em home with you. But I'd like to keep the air mattress for when I use the tent. I patched it and it seems to be working fine."

"Of course, Charlie."

The chili was, as advertised, hot. Temperature and spice both. Molly and I needed piles of buttered crackers to eat it without gasping, but Ivy and the three men savored their first bowlfuls and went back for seconds.

"Thank you, Ivy, for the morning. And Charlie for the chili. This whole day has been a wonderful break in the winter and the—" Molly stopped short. As she got into Hugh's car, I thought she had tears in her eyes.

"I would give two of my Rose's peach pies, maybe even three, to hear Molly give one of those laughs. The ones that sound like a horse whinnying."

"I would too, Jack."

"Maybe spring will snap her out of it."

"Maybe."

"They're waiting for me. Bye, you two."

Charlie's face was somber. "Not like her to be gloomy."

"No." I didn't want to leave. "I've been gloomy too, Charlie. Although it's not as unusual for me as it is for her. I suppose it's the weather, partly. But it's also waiting for another call from Letitia—"

"Who?"

"Josef's, I mean Joseph's, sister."

"Oh. Right."

"And it's also knowing…" I turned my head and watched his face. "It's also knowing that none of it would have happened if I hadn't been involved with someone who turned out to be dangerous."

"You know my feelings about that kind of talk."

"I do. And I know that you are a kind man to feel the way you do. But I also recognize and accept my, my *complicity*, if you don't like the word guilt." I dug in my pocket for the car keys. "It keeps me awake at night."

"Not sleeping?"

"Not well, no. And that *is* unusual for me."

"PTSD."

"Charlie! I have never known you to be the least bit melodramatic. PTSD is what soldiers get, after months and months of seeing unspeakable horrors. Or what someone gets after watching a loved one get murdered."

"PTSD is just what it says. Post-traumatic. You ever had to fight for your life before?"

"Of course not."

"Or had a gun pointed at you? Or been punched in the face? Ever had someone bash your head against a rock?"

"How did... Molly and Ivy have been sharing details, I gather."

"Ever ended up in an emergency room with one of your friends, both of you covered in blood?"

"Of course not, but—"

"That was trauma, Beck. You went through a traumatic event. Not surprising you're having some sort of reaction."

"Maybe." I didn't move for several seconds, watching his craggy face. "You know what I wish?"

"That he'd die?"

"Oh! No. Although, yes, that might be good for everyone. But I was going to say I wish I could go with you. And escape."

He turned and looked at me then, his bushy eyebrows climbing up his forehead.

"That was not a serious suggestion, Charlie. I am not seriously asking to horn in on your wonderful expedition. But I do want to escape." I took a deep breath and looked around at the sky, already clouding up again, and at the snow-covered trees and bushes. "I want to be somewhere else. I want to be someplace where it's not all cold and gray. I want to be looking at different scenery. I don't want to be worried about how bad the roads are. I want to talk with different people. I want to be someplace where not one single person knows me, or has ever heard one single thing about me." I grimaced as

I realized something I hadn't known until that moment. "This is almost worse than after Alain's death. I wanted to escape then, too. But then I did escape, in a way."

"Isolation? Work? Numbness?"

"All of the above."

"That's what I did after Claire died. Wasn't a success."

"It was for me. At least it got me through those first several years." The smile that twisted my mouth felt more like a grimace. "I wasn't living, not really, but I was at least breathing."

"You got any vacation time?"

My short laugh came out more like a snort. "Those several years I just mentioned? I didn't take a single vacation day, starting a week after Alain's memorial service. Even with the days off last November while my face began healing, I have a full month saved up. The maximum we're allowed to accumulate."

"So why don't you hop on a plane and just go? Head for Arizona. See a dozen different kinds of hummingbirds in one day."

"That sounds… I might just do that, Charlie! Thank you."

Chapter Eleven

I saw the feathers in the snow as soon as I pulled in.

I stopped the car and just sat. I did not want to get out. I didn't want to walk closer and study the feathers and try to figure out what happened.

When I finally made myself open the car door, I was hunched over, stumbling. I felt old and bruised. Fragile.

They looked like grouse feathers. A confusion of prints was all around, many from some sort of small dog. Or fox. I'd seen a fox loping across the field only two days earlier. And now there was a line of prints heading straight toward the high weeds near the chicken coop and then out into the field beyond.

The fox prints were mixed with grouse prints. In two places, I could see that the right foot turned out a little.

That evening I filled the dog dish with seed, and I sat on the bottom step until I could no longer feel my fingers or toes or nose.

I tried again the next morning. And the next afternoon. And the morning after that. I sat on the bottom step, with the dog dish at my feet, staring at the unmoving weeds near the chicken coop, trying to convince myself that I could see some movement.

Then I went inside, sat on the bench by the door, and sobbed. I wouldn't cry when Josef died. If Joseph died. But I cried for my grouse.

****

"Charlie? This is Beck. You're…" Now that I had him on the phone, I wasn't sure how to continue. "You are leaving any day now, right?"

"Yup."

"I… I did look at birding tours, as you suggested. And I thought about doing a birding trip by myself. But I haven't found anything, and now I am thinking it might be better to be with someone I know." I took a deep breath and launched into my spiel, my words tumbling out, so different from my usual slow and precise speech. "I have to get away, Charlie. I was being flippant when I asked you the other day, but now I'm not. I would like to go with you. South. In your camper. I'll try to stay out of your way. I'll give you all the privacy I can. I can sleep in Sean's bunk, or… or one of us can always be outside in the tent. Yes. I can. I'll sleep outside. And every morning I'll go off on my own, birding. We hardly have to see each other. And I can do half the driving, if you'd like."

"Whoa. Stop."

I didn't stop. "Oh. That won't… I can't, can I? You are planning to visit friends. And your wife's sister. I forgot. I'm sorry. Ignore me. Have a nice trip."

"Beck!" His voice was almost as loud as it was that day in Hugh's living room. "Stop talking! Take a breath. Listen!"

I had nothing more to say anyway. It was foolish to think Charlie could provide the escape I needed. I should never have bothered him. I sat down hard, angry at myself, illogically angry at Charlie, angry that my eyes were filling with tears, glaring at an unsuspecting chickadee taking a peanut from the window feeder.

"Are you listening?"

"Yes."

"You got a month vacation time. Right?"

"Yes."

"You could meet up with me somewhere, when I'm heading north again."

"Oh."

"What about... Yeah. This'll work. You fly into Jacksonville. I meet you at the airport. Just a short drive to Jekyll Island."

"Charlie." I was having difficulty making sense of the whole conversation. "I just made a ridiculous suggestion, one that would change the whole feeling of your wonderful vacation. You should have just ignored me."

"I'll have lots of time to myself before Georgia. More fun to share some of the great birding places with another birder."

"I... Charlie. I am overwhelmed." I reached for the tissue box on the counter. "Yes. I will do that. I will. I'll go birding with you. When should I be in Jacksonville?"

"Wait. What about your grouse?"

Every muscle in my body went rigid. "What about him?"

"You been feeding him. Who's gonna take over? You can't just stop, now that the bird's used to it."

"Fox. A... Fox got him. Two days ago."

There was a long pause. "I'm sorry, Beck."

"Me too, Charlie."

"Let me look at some dates. I'll call later so you can get flight information and tickets."

****

I worked the next three days from early in the morning until after everyone but the janitor was gone. I needed work to keep my mind busy, to avoid thinking any of the thoughts that had harassed me for three months now. And when Charlie didn't call during those three days, I knew he was having second thoughts.

****

"Beck? Charlie. There's a flight to Jacksonville, gets in around 1:00. Got reservations at the RV camp on Jekyll Island for nine nights starting April 8. I can meet your plane any time while I'm there. Whenever works for you."

"Charlie. Thank you. I'll get a flight today and I'll call you back."

"Good deal."

I was grinning when I hung up. Yes! I was going somewhere! I was going to be in a place where every road wasn't lined with chin-high piles of snow, dirty from road sand and vehicle exhaust. I was going to step outside without boots and wool socks and gloves and mittens and a hat and long underwear.

And I was going to forget the Ruffed Grouse I had named and fed, the grouse that leaned against my leg and listened to my voice.

****

"Charlie? This is Beck. I just made reservations for the eighth, so you can pick me up on the way north and not have to interrupt your time on the island."

"Sounds good."

"Wait! Don't hang up yet." I needed to say what I had planned, and Charlie was not one for lingering goodbyes. "I have to clear something up."

"Shoot."

"When I asked if I could come along on this trip, I was serious about sleeping arrangements. About me sleeping outside in the tent. Or in the bunk you put in for Sean. But probably always in the tent."

"Got it."

"I have been worried that you might think, now that Josef's not in my life, that I might be…. I feel foolish saying this, Charlie. But I don't want either of us to feel uncomfortable. It's good to be clear."

"Understood."

"Good. I'm glad. Your friendship has become important to me."

I hung up and stood unmoving, staring out the window. I had never said that to anyone. I told Alain that I loved him a thousand times, two, three thousand times at the very least. But we were never friends, just friends. We were distant professor and worshipping student, and then, in an instant, we were the centers of each other's lives.

I got myself a cup of some sort of African bush tea that Molly said could cure everything from ulcers to gout to melancholia, and I thought about a childhood with no experience of friendship. I was the only child of much older parents. Father left us when I was eleven, leaving my college prof mother more irritated than unhappy. I don't remember ever seeing any sign of affection between my parents, and I don't remember any real affection toward me. When I watched my classmates, listened to them tell stories about camping with their families, heard them complain that their dads always came to their soccer games and embarrassed them by cheering too loudly, I used to think they lived in a different world than I did.

One time in eighth grade, our teacher told us we were going to put together a list of "personality snapshots" that she would pass on to the ninth grade faculty. The list would have two words for each of us, two words only, and we were all supposed to decide on the two words that best described everyone in the class. Next to other names were words like *always fun*; *amazing friend*; *flirty, gorgeous*; *all-round athlete*; *witty, sarcastic*; and *future mega-success*.

The two words next to my name were *good student*.

****

All through the next cold and gray weeks, I hugged the knowledge that I would be taking a whole month off, soon. It made it easier for me to get up in the pitch dark, to get to work early and stay late, to gradually whittle away at the lengthy To-Do list I wrote right after making my plane reservation. One of the biggest tasks was to finish my part of a report about the success of the HOFHOW project and get it to the governor, who might or might not share it with the press. The other was to meet with the three people who would do some spring water testing in April, depending on the weather. After sitting down with each of them separately and going over the ongoing projects, we all met for the mandatory annual reminder about the dangers of fast-running spring streams. I scheduled that session for noon and ordered pizzas and breadsticks and salads and drinks, and for the first time in years I was part of a laughing and jolly group in the office break room.

I remembered how much I used to love my job, how much I loved bringing stories and little vignettes home to share with Alain. Alain would have smiled at the pizza, at me thinking to order food. And he would have been invigorated by the conviviality, but I was exhausted. I was in bed and asleep by 8:30.

****

After the intense cold that lasted all of December and January, the northeast basked in a few relatively warm days when I think everyone in Vermont got outdoors: skiing, walking, snowshoeing, taking sleds to the nearest hill, or just driving around with the car window cracked and breathing air that didn't hurt. On the way home from work one evening, I even saw three people huddled around a grill, having a mid-winter backyard barbecue.

And then came the snow. Day after day of heavy skies that felt as though they were sitting right on top of us, weighing us down, making us talk more quietly, move more slowly, even breathe with difficulty. Day after day of snow, six inches one day, twelve the next, four or five every day for a week.

Alain always plowed our long driveway himself and his tractor was still in the shed, but I hired a local man so I could leave for work every morning without having to spend an hour clearing out first.

Ivy led a group walk through the snow at Montpelier's Hubbard Park for her March outing, hoping for crossbills or maybe Evening Grosbeaks, but I stayed home. Between twelve and eighteen inches of snow were forecast for the night, and I had to get the car out of the driveway so the plow guy could do his work. I rarely used the small one-car garage, and I had forgotten that it was full of gardening tools I should have taken to the shed back in September, plus a metal garbage can full of bird seed and the two big bags of grouse food.

I got out Alain's old ski pants and stuffed my feet into his work boots, with three pairs of wool socks, and then I grabbed one of the feed bags and dragged it down the slope to the chicken coop. The padlock was easy, but there was too much snow for me to open the door so on my second trip from the garage I dragged a shovel along with the cracked corn. It took me at least a half hour to clear away snow and then lift and yank at the door until I could open it just enough to shove the two bags inside. I knew they were wet by then and I worried that the seed would rot, but there was nothing I could do about it short of hauling them back up to the house and putting them inside for the rest of the winter. And I didn't want them in the house. I didn't want to be reminded of my first-ever pet, my adopted wild bird.

My whole torso was drenched in sweat under my heavy jacket, but my hands and feet were like chunks of ice. I wanted to be back indoors, sitting in Alain's big chair with the fire roaring in the woodstove and a mug of coffee or tea in my hands. I shoved the chicken coop door closed with my shoulder and fumbled in my pocket for the padlock. It wasn't there. I tried the other pocket, then both pockets of my pants. I dropped to my knees in the snow and burst into tears, wailing and gulping and cursing, tears hot on my frozen cheeks, digging around with my hands to find a small chunk of metal in mountains and mountains of snow.

Later, much later than made any sense at all, I realized that what I was doing was idiotic. There was nothing of value in that building, nothing that anyone would want to steal. The door was on the back side of the coop from the road anyway, so no one passing by would even notice that it wasn't locked.

I got to my feet and used a handful of snow to wash the tears and mucus off my face. I shoved at the door one last time and then turned and trudged back to the house, knowing again how much I wanted to escape. Needed to escape. From winter. From waiting for Josef's death. From the absence of a grouse.

****

I could have just checked Ivy's website, but I was already on my way home when I decided that something like her birding vest would be ideal for traveling. Friday was the mall's late night, so Ivy's Optics and Accessories would still be open. She must have fixed the loose connection to the bell over the entrance. It let out a loud and cheerful peal when I walked in, and she looked up from the cash register and grinned.

"Hi, Beck. Come to shop or power-walk?"

"What?"

"Take a gander. As we birders are wont to say."

Eight or nine people were striding purposefully down the middle of the hall, heads up, elbows swinging, a few carrying small barbells in their hands.

"Let me know how you like that book, Mrs. Simpson. I haven't read it yet." Ivy finished up with her customer and looked at me again. "It's a group from senior housing. They are absolutely religious about doing three miles every single morning, as soon as the mall opens, and again almost every afternoon at about 3:00. But on Fridays they come late and they do four miles, and then they go to Jorge's for all-you-can-eat tacos." She grinned. "Thus regaining all the calories they just walked off."

"That's why they do the extra mile, I guess."

Ivy busied herself with the next customer, and Molly was helping a thirty-something couple choose guidebooks for hiking and birding in Arizona. I wandered over to a display of greeting cards and key chains and little puzzles. Maybe I should begin stocking up for next December's office gift exchange. It would be good to be prepared, for a change.

As the Arizona-bound couple headed toward the cash register, Molly caught my eye and let out a heavy sigh. "More people heading south! I'm beginning to think the whole state would empty out if we all had a choice. This winter is just too long, too cold, and too miserable."

"I agree."

"Even Charlie is deserting us. Two months, maybe more, with sun. And heat! And palm trees!"

"I'm—"

"Just a second, Beck. This gentleman has a question."

It hadn't dawned on me that Ivy and Molly might not know I was going to join Charlie for some of his trip. I felt uncomfortable, even embarrassed.

"Beck?"

Both Ivy and Molly were looking at me expectantly.

"Did you come by to say hello, or are you looking for something specific?"

"Oh. Yes. Ivy, I wanted to know where you got your vest. Your birding vest?"

She smiled her dazzling smile. "My mega-pocket vest. The best purchase I ever made." She reached toward a display on the wall beside the cash register and handed me a brochure. "Here. You'll love it!"

"I have been thinking it might be good for air travel. I could stash my passport, driver's license, wallet, cell phone and lots more in all those zippered pockets, and I wouldn't have to carry anything like a purse or pocketbook."

"Air travel, huh. Are you going to join the hordes that are escaping from our beloved state?"

"Escaping. That is exactly the word." I frowned, turning so I could look at both Ivy and Molly. "I want very much to escape, from the cold and the snow and the… From everything."

Molly grimaced. "I hear you."

"So I'm taking some vacation time before spring craziness begins in my job. Charlie is going to take me birding. On Jekyll Island."

"What a truly splendid idea! Good for you!"

It was that easy. They were happy for me. For the umpteenth time since November, I felt the prickle of tears in my nose and behind my eyes.

"I'm going to take just a roll-on suitcase and my backpack." Relief made me talk faster than usual. "The backpack is my one piece of personal luggage so I wouldn't be able to carry a purse anyway."

"Hence the vest."

"Exactly."

"Well, you'll love it, not just for travel but every single time you go birding. I can carry everything I need in mine."

Molly laughed, and her comical whinny filled the little store and filled me with relief and delight. "One time a man asked her if she could camp overnight with what's in her vest. And I think she could!"

****

I felt amused, at myself, for the whole short drive home. I had been worried that Molly and Ivy might see me as some sort of vamp, getting rid of Josef and immediately looking around for another unsuspecting male. The idea of me as a vamp was beyond absurd. I never dated in high school, and I had only one "boyfriend" in college, a fellow student who transferred to a different school soon after our first date and then came back for two weekends. Both of us were virgins. After the first weekend we tried to believe that sex had been the thrilling experience we'd expected. But a repeat the next time he visited was just as awkward and uncomfortable as the first, for both of us, and I never saw him again. By the time I was a grad student, I'd gone out a handful of times with a handful of men, and I slept with one of them once. I was definitely not a wild woman, or any threat to Charlie's solitary integrity.

****

The vest wouldn't arrive until after I left. I had to rethink packing.

My binoculars, camera, cell phone, and charging cables went into my backpack, with toiletries in Alain's old canvas shaving kit. I added some tightly rolled t-shirts and pairs of undies, a bra, socks, several pens, a crossword puzzle book, my field guide, and two little notebooks for keeping track of what we saw. The two interior pockets held extra cash and keys to my house and car.

The roll-on held sports sandals, my wide-brimmed birding hat, a water bottle filled with two more pairs of undies, more socks, a big t-shirt for sleeping, a long-sleeved cotton shirt, and two pairs of lightweight pants that were easy to wash out and dried quickly. At the last minute, I made room for a rolled-up polypro top, in case I was still with Charlie when he headed to the mountains.

Staring down at my luggage, I was struck by the enormity of what I was doing. I was committing myself to being alone with someone I barely knew, day and night, for at least a full week. Maybe much more. I liked Charlie, and I thought he liked me, and we had birding in common—but we wouldn't be birding all the time. There would be meals, and driving between camping spots. And evenings. I wouldn't be able to duck upstairs to my room in the evenings the way I did when he stayed at my house.

I took a deep breath. I wouldn't have to stay for his entire northward trip. Maybe there would be a lodge or an inn near one of Charlie's birding places, and I could stay there a few days to give us a break. He could pick me up for the next part of the trip. Or I could just stay put for a week or more, reading and eating humongous meals and walking every single day. Or if things weren't working out, if we were both uncomfortable and it was obvious that I was ruining Charlie's first-ever vacation, I could ask him to drop me off at the outskirts of any one of the big cities of the east coast and I could take a cab or a city bus to an airport and I could just head home. Or to Arizona and the umpteen species of hummingbirds.

Whatever happened, I needed this vacation, and I was going to enjoy it.

Chapter Twelve

There were palm trees below as the plane circled over Jacksonville Airport.

Heatwaves rising from the tarmac.

Airport personnel wearing t-shirts and shorts.

And when I walked up the ramp into the waiting area, in front of me were two forty-foot-tall American Oystercatchers, their brilliant red bills almost neon in the artificial light. I might have set myself up for days and days of uncomfortable silence. But it didn't matter. I was in Florida and not in Vermont.

Charlie was walking toward me, his new tan making his blue eyes even bluer and his gold-and-silver mustaches even more extravagant than usual. For one silly moment, I imagined that there might be a producer, Hollywood or Broadway, right there in the Jacksonville Airport and that producer might walk right up to Charlie and offer him a role as senior pirate in an upcoming movie or play. The producer wouldn't even notice me. A handsome man Charlie's age was still marketable; a woman in her forties was just blah.

The handsome man didn't exactly gush when I said hello, but his mustaches quirked in a smile and he leaned forward and patted my arm. And then I was quick-stepping, following Charlie and my roll-on to the exit. He stashed my bag in the back seat of his truck and I added my backpack, windbreaker, hat and gloves, flannel shirt, and raw silk sweater. There was no way to get rid of my long underwear out there in the parking garage, but it would be a delightful change to be too warm for the first time in months.

We were heading north on I95 before I realized that there was no big dog in the car.

"Is Devon in your camper?"

"Huh?"

"Your dog. Is he behind us in the camper? Splatted out on your huge bed?"

"Nope. He's home in Vermont. Too big for traveling." Charlie glanced over at me. "Allison and Sean are stayin' at my place. Plenty of room. And closer to his school."

"Oh. Perfect then."

"Suggested moving in, a bunch of times now. Make more sense, save her a heap of money. But she says she doesn't want to—" He made his voice almost ladylike "—Infringe on my privacy." He slanted me another look. "Likely she doesn't want her daddy peerin' over her shoulder every time she moves."

"Of course she doesn't, Charlie. You're a private person, and she's your daughter."

"Huh."

Charlie was probably capable of saying nothing else for the whole drive. I didn't care. There was green as far as I could see. Sun glinted on roadside ditches that were full of water, not ice, and not one single branch on one single tree was bowed down with snow.

"Oh!" I craned my neck around. "That was a very large bird!"

"Didn't see it. What'd it look like?"

"It was as big as a Great Blue Heron, maybe taller,

161

and I think a bit heftier, although that could have been the angle. It had a gray head and a huge gray bill."

Charlie's mustache twitched. "Wood Stork. Good introduction to southern birding for you, Beck."

"A life list bird."

Grunt.

There were other birds in the ditches next to the highway. I recognized Great Egrets and a little group of what I thought were coots, but we went by too fast to get good looks at them. I would have plenty of time for every bird, once we were on Jekyll Island. I suddenly felt bubbly with delight and anticipation and relief.

"Did you have good birding in Florida, Charlie? Has the weather been treating you well? And how has the camper been working out?"

"Good birding. Good weather. Camper's great."

"Did you see your friends? Both of them?"

"Pittsburgh. Yes."

"And the other one?"

He turned his head toward me for just a second. "The other one died."

"Oh, no. I'm so sorry."

"Got there, big smile, come to see my old buddy. And his wife burst into tears."

"That is truly awful, Charlie."

"Yeah. It sucked. To use Sean's favorite expression." He sighed. "Shoulda kept up. Been a better friend. The address his wife had for me was twenty years out of date. Couldn't contact me when he died." He gave a little snort. "But you know? It was good to talk about him with his wife, and with their neighbors. Sounds odd. But it was good."

I couldn't think of anything to say.

"Great time with my Pittsburgh friend. Went to the Carnegie Museum of Natural History. Saw a Penguins game."

Penguins must be a sports team, probably hockey because of the ice connection. I didn't feel like asking.

"What did you see? At the museum?"

"Dinosaurs. Monster fish." He flashed me one of his rare smiles. "Then we went to a Chinese restaurant and shared a crispy fish as long as my arm."

"Seems fitting." I hadn't been with Charlie a half hour and I was already talking in partial sentences.

"We thought so."

Silence again.

"Good four days with Claire's sister. Nice husband. Nice kids." He slanted a glance in my direction. "All six of 'em."

"Yikes."

"Good kids. But I was ready to be alone by the time I left."

"I can imagine."

We were quiet again until Charlie got off the highway.

"Only one grocery store on the island. We'll do some shopping here." His mustaches twitched. "Your first Winn Dixie?"

"What? Oh. Yes."

"Welcome to the south."

"We'll split grocery costs."

"Sounds good."

"I ate breakfast way before dawn, Charlie, and I'm ravenous. I looked up Jekyll Island restaurants. I'd like to take you to one before we check in at the camping place."

"Seafood?"

"But of course."

"Sounds good."

****

I asked Charlie to stop at the entrance to Jekyll Island so I could get a photo of the massive gate. Right beside the gate were over a dozen tall wading birds, some of them pure white and others a color like dusty sand.

"White Ibises."

"What are the brown ones?"

"White ibises."

I turned and looked him in the face. "You get a kick out of that, don't you?"

His mustache twitched but he looked innocent. "Out of what?"

"The man of few words persona."

He studied my face for a long minute. "Yup. I do."

"So what are the brown birds?"

"White Ibises. Immature."

"Thank you."

****

I would not have guessed that the sun could possibly look any brighter, or the foliage any greener, but every single thing in my world was better when I walked out of that restaurant with a full belly. And maybe our first meal together would be a predictor of how well we got along for the rest of the trip. We shared two appetizers: crab cakes because we both said we loved them, and fried green tomatoes because Charlie said they were a Southern delicacy. Then we split an entrée served on a platter at least two feet long. The clams went to Charlie because I detest them; the scallops were mine because he hates scallops. We both devoured the fried catfish, grilled shrimp, hush puppies, cheesy grits, and slaw. Neither of us should have been able to walk without groaning when we left the restaurant, but Charlie was carrying a pink box that held a Georgia peach pie. He carefully laid the box on the truck's back seat, and then he got a thermos out of the camper and went back into the restaurant to get it filled.

****

The RV camp was quiet and shaded, with old trees hung with Spanish moss. Charlie backed into a spot at the far end from the entrance, with only one RV nearby and a few empty tent sites.

I got out of the truck and stretched. "I am so happy to be here I could almost burst."

"That's lunch."

"Well, maybe. But I am also truly happy. Hand me out the tent and I'll set it up."

A half hour later, I had the tent set up and the newly-repaired air mattress inflated. Charlie tied a clothesline from one tree to another and hung up the sleeping bags and liners to air. He put the stove and wash pan on the picnic table and settled the big cooler on the ground in the shade, covered with a heavy white fabric that he said reflected light and made ice last longer.

"Walk around the campground?"

"Is this all right?"

"Eh?"

"Is it all right to walk off and leave things out?"

"It's our site."

All the camping I did with Alain was at digs, usually in the middle of nowhere. We knew every single person there. Now I felt uneasy about leaving the stove, the cooler full of food, the sleeping bags on the line. But

Charlie just jerked his head toward the dirt road in front of our site and started walking.

Our stroll ended back near the camper, in a little fenced-in area with a sign "Bird Sanctuary—Quiet Please." We sat side by side on one of the benches, looking at a small pool and bird feeders and nesting boxes. We had avian company within minutes, some at the feeders and some on the ground eating dropped seed. The first were familiar to me: a Northern Cardinal, two Chipping Sparrows, a handsome male Eastern Towhee.

"Is that a grackle? It looks unusually big."

"Grackle yes. But not what we see in Vermont. Boat-tailed Grackle."

"I think there were several of those at the airport."

"Probably."

I almost fell asleep, sitting there in that quiet little garden. Chickadees came and went and I heard Charlie mutter something about Carolina versus Black-capped. Then he nudged me with his elbow.

"Shrub just right of the red feeder."

I blinked and tried to focus. "That small bird? What is it?"

"Orange-crowned Warbler. Looked for one in Florida but missed out."

"I am glad there's one here then." I got to my feet. "I'm heading back, Charlie."

"Me too."

We should not have wanted anything more to eat, not after our shared gluttony only a few hours before. But Charlie got out two folding chairs, I started a fire in the little fire pit, he poured two mugs of coffee from his thermos, and we sat down with the Georgia peach pie and two forks.

"These are nice sounds. The camping area in the evening."

"Where'd you and Alain go? For camping?"

"We never stayed at actual campgrounds. All of our camping was at digs."

"Huh."

Around us we could hear snippets of quiet conversations from nearby RVs. Laughter, a short protest from a small child who didn't want the day to be over. Bullfrogs.

"Hear that?" Charlie was whispering.

"What an odd noise. What is it?"

"Chuck-will's-widow. Says its name."

"I've never heard one before." We both were quiet, listening as the bird went from a single song to a long stream of noises. "He really wants everyone to know his name."

"Yup."

"What a wonderful end to the day, Charlie. And now I'm ready for sleep. I headed for the airport at four-something this morning."

"You can have the big bed tonight."

"No way. That's your bed, tonight and every night." I picked up our coffee mugs and put them in the dish pan. "With that extra special mattress all the way from Canada."

"Thought we were takin' turns."

"You thought wrong. I am going to sleep in the tent. Unless, of course, you decide you'd like to be outside sometime, in which case I'll use Sean's bunk."

"Huh."

It was so wonderfully familiar to crawl into the tent, our tent, where Alain and I had cuddled together and slept together, where we woke up in each other's arms, looking at each other's faces, knowing we would be together all day.

And if I had to pee in the middle of the night, I wouldn't have to worry about disturbing Charlie's sleep.

****

"Low seventies by afternoon. You sure you need these?"

I turned away from making sandwiches to see Charlie standing by the open back door of the truck, holding a fuzzy fleece hat and warm gloves in two fingers and grimacing as if he was repelled by the slightest reminder of winter in Vermont.

"I forgot all about those." I turned back to the sandwiches. "I meant to leave them in the car but Speedy Sal's son-in-law was raring to go."

"Huh. Words with no meaning."

I grinned, reaching for the foil wrap. "Sally is a co-worker of mine. People call her Speedy Sal, maybe because she talks a mile a minute or maybe because she drives even faster. When Speedy Sal heard about my trip, she said I could leave my car at her daughter's house, which is only three blocks from the airport. I planned to drop off the car and walk, so I had on my warm hat and gloves. However, as soon as I pulled into their driveway, her son-in-law burst out of the house, pulling a coat over his pj's, and said he was going to drive me. So I stuffed those things in my backpack and then took them out when we got here so I wouldn't be carrying anything unnecessary."

"Lots more words, and admirably clear."

I could tell he was smiling without even turning around. "Thank you."

"Seafood pasta for supper?"

"That sounds wonderful, Charlie."

"Frozen fish in the cooler. Gotta use it tonight or give it the gulls tomorrow."

****

The next week was everything I hoped for, everything I needed. It was the perfect antidote to the dark and worry-filled months before. Jekyll Island had miles of sandy beach, sun, wind, gentle ocean waves, birds and birds and more birds. I was often apart from Charlie, each of us meandering at our own pace. He had a new camera and he spent the mornings hunkered down in front of shorebirds, or staring at driftwood and trying different settings, completely engrossed. Whenever our paths crossed, when we ran into each other on the long beaches, we shared what we had seen, what we'd been thinking about, and then we watched the shorebirds feeding only a few yards away. Some were similar to the sandpipers Ivy had pointed out on that awful drawdown day, when nine dead chickens were waiting for me at home. But there were also new species. My favorites were the Sanderlings, little flocks that ran together after each receding wave and then raced back up the beach when the next wave came in.

"Clockwork toys. That's what everybody always says."

"Very apt."

Taller, more dignified shorebirds paced slowly, occasionally dipping their heads to catch and eat tiny crabs or other delicacies. I got out my field guide but I wasn't in any hurry to identify them. I was, for the first time in months, maybe the first time since Alain's death, completely, utterly at peace. I loved waking up in the tent. I loved the almost wordless breakfasts. I loved climbing up into the high front seat of the truck without even knowing where we were going. I loved being by myself in nature for an hour, two hours, all morning. I loved walking the beaches, sometimes staring down at my bare feet, at the thousands of tiny prints made by birds and crabs, sometimes looking at the waves, watching them roll in, mesmerized and unthinking.

I loved picnic lunches in shaded parks. I loved the afternoons when we explored the interior of the island, strolling by nineteenth century "cottages" with more than a dozen rooms plus extensive attics for the servants. And the late afternoons back at our campsite, when I sat and read or did crossword puzzles and Charlie set up his laptop and looked at his photos and sent a few to Sean and to the other Vermont birders.

A couple of hours at the Georgia Sea Turtle Center were, for me, a rollercoaster of emotions. I was fascinated and charmed by the turtles that ranged from the size of a Vermont painted turtle up to a magnificent yard-wide creature slowly swimming a few inches from my nose. I was touched and impressed with the veterinarian who kept up a constant stream of quiet comments while she patched a deep slash in a massive carapace, explaining to those of us watching on the other side of glass that the turtle had been hit by a boat propellor. I was appalled during a recorded lecture about the dangers that threaten not only individual sea turtles but could result in the extinction of entire species.

"Gotta come back here. Bring Sean."

"I wish we could bring whole busloads of kids. From all over the country. They're the ones who might do a better job protecting all of nature than we have."

Charlie steered me into the nearby gift shop and I browsed while he bought two books and a deck of cards with sea turtles on the fronts and facts on the reverse sides.

The next afternoon we slowly walked The Wanderer Trail, reading every sign, sobered by the history of the last slave ship to the island and by the stories of those who survived its sinking.

And I enjoyed the busier, more talkative evenings, when Charlie and I fixed supper together and then sat at the picnic table with full plates and glasses of ale or beer or wine or lemonade. I loved sitting around the little fire pit after supper, staring at the flames and the glowing embers, listening to the campground settling down around us, sometimes hearing the Chuck-will's-widow insistently telling us its name.

****

"What made you decide to be an accountant?"

"Safety."

"What?"

Charlie refilled his coffee mug. "I was a cop. Montpelier. Right outa high school."

Oh. That's why he and Officer McCauley were so chummy.

"I think you would be a very good policeman."

Grunt.

"But you're not one now."

He slanted a look at me.

"Why not?"

"Made the decision all at once. One night."

I wondered if he had been shot at, but I didn't want to say anything yet.

"My wife, Claire, lost our first baby. She was

171

alone." He turned toward me, his blue eyes full of pain. "I was working crazy hours. Overtime. Lots of nights. Tryin' to make a name for myself. Get respect from the older cops." He shook his head. "But after that night, after Claire lost that baby when she was all alone, I promised myself, and I promised Claire, that I would quit the very next day."

"And you did."

"I did." He frowned. "Never had a single fear for myself. Invincible. Strong young buck. Courageous defender of law and order." His mustache twitched. "In Montpelier. Not exactly crime capital of the northeast."

"No. But law enforcement is potentially dangerous anywhere."

"True." He took a long drink of coffee. "Never once thought of danger to Claire, to my wife. Never once thought about what she'd do if I got hurt. Or killed." He shook his head again. "She sure worried though. She told me, after I quit, she told me she was scared every single time I walked out the door to go to work." He shrugged. "I was already doing the books for the volunteer fire department. Added the police, then the bakery, then the bookstore. Eventually got my C.P.A. Turned out good for Claire and me both."

We were still for a while, listening to the neighborhood bullfrog.

"Did you and Claire have any other children, after the miscarriage?"

One of those slanting looks, under heavy eyebrows.

"Oh. Of course you did. Sean's your grandson."

"Sean's mother. Allison. Then we had another miscarriage, and then we decided it was too risky for Claire to try for more."

"I'm glad for you that Sean and his mother live close by."

"Me too. Me too." His face tightened and he suddenly looked fierce. "Seventeen when her mother died. Allison. Always wondered if that was why she hooked up with that man. I thought she was handling Claire's illness, her death, pretty well. But I was wrong." He leaned forward and stabbed at the fire. "Got pregnant, moved to South Carolina with a guy who wasn't worth one of her little toenails. Two years later, she's back and he's in jail, someplace down here, in the south. Never said what happened."

"She has done a great job rearing Sean. He's an exceptional youngster."

"That he is. That he is." Charlie slapped his hands on his knees, his signal that he was ready to call it a night. "Hankering for fried."

"What?"

"Fried clams. Fried oysters. A mountain of fried stuff. Hard to deep-fry stuff when you're camping."

"So let's eat out tomorrow."

"My thought exactly."

****

The crab cake appetizer that next evening was even better than the one we shared the first night. I wanted to let each bite melt on my tongue before I finally had to give in and swallow. After the crab cakes, Charlie ordered the monster plate of fried oysters that had been calling his name. I gave thought to the fried shrimp po-boy, but then the man at the table next to ours asked about the fish of the day and by the time the waitress finished her rhapsodic description of grilled mahi-mahi I knew that was what I had to have.

My phone started vibrating just as we left the restaurant. I stepped to the end of the long porch, and rejoined Charlie a few minutes later.

"That was odd."

"Eh?"

"That was Ivy. From Vermont. She wanted to know if I will be birding with you tomorrow, and if so where we will be."

"What'd you say?"

"I told her we both wanted to go back the beach and scrubby area on the south end."

"St. Andrew's."

"I couldn't remember the name so I just said the south end. And she said thanks, and she hung up."

"Vicarious."

"What?"

"Forecast for Montpelier. Another storm. Quarter inch of ice and then a foot of snow. Ivy was going stir-crazy weeks ago. Must be achin' for someplace warm by now."

"Poor woman. Poor birders. Poor everyone."

****

Months after Alain died, I spent an afternoon talking to him, walking around our property and letting his ashes fall, one handful at a time. Now, as I walked on Georgia beaches, I wondered about all the elements that once were part of him, the bits that might have been caught by a Vermont wind and blown away. Was part of Alain in that proudly strutting Great Black-backed Gull? Was part of him nourishing that shrub?

He told me once that I should develop friendships so I would have someone when he was gone. I didn't want to think about his ever being gone, and I didn't need friendships, not then. But that night, sitting looking into the dying fire while Charlie was at the restroom, I talked aloud to Alain.

"I think you would be pleased, my love. I am starting to have friends!"

Chapter Thirteen

Even at a distance, even with their backs to us, three of the four people were unmistakable. Two women, a tall one wearing a tan birding vest and a tiny one with bouncy egret-white curls, and a lanky man with broad shoulders and hair that glinted red where the sun touched it. Charlie saw them first, and his shout was warm with humor and pleasure.

"I knew it! I knew FATSO was headin' south!"

That whole day was one of my favorites ever, from Charlie's delighted yell, through the hugging and manly handshakes, and all the hours when Charlie and I showed off "our" shorebirds, and the leisurely lunch on the deck at their rented condo. Then Molly's Ed stayed behind while the others visited our campsite, sat for a quiet half hour in the Bird Sanctuary, and took a leisurely walk beyond the old amphitheater so Charlie could get close-up photos of Black Vultures, Wood Storks, Anhingas, Roseate Spoonbills, and Yellow-crowned Night Herons.

And then warblers, scores of warblers, and we became a FATSO group with Ivy in the lead. "Palm!" she called out, and we watched a chestnut-capped bird strolling around on a small patch of mowed lawn.

"It's on the ground."

"You'll often see Palm Warblers on the ground, Beck. And… Oh! Parula in that scraggly-looking tree."

In the next five minutes, we saw redstarts and Black-

and-white Warblers and Common Yellowthroats, birds that we might see in Vermont if winter ever ended, and an exotic Yellow-throated Warbler diving into a thick patch of gray-green moss.

"They build their nests in Spanish moss. To hide from predators."

Way before we got back to the cars, Ivy was hugging herself and anyone near her, full of delight at the day and the birds and the company. "Let's do this again tomorrow! And the day after, and every single day we're here!"

"Tomorrow definitely." I met Charlie's eyes. "But then we'll be leaving."

"No! Not fair! Not fair in the extreme! We've got five more nights."

Charlie reached his arm out and pulled her into a shoulder hug. "And you'll relish every minute."

"I am so glad we overlapped. This has been thoroughly wonderful!" I looked at their faces, realizing with a jolt that I loved seeing these people, loved talking with them and being with them. "It's too bad Jack couldn't join you."

"Are you kidding? He's completely besotted with that new baby. He even found someone to substitute for him on those driving-all-over FATSO days!" Ivy looked from me to Charlie and then back to me. "You're both going to leave? There might be a room for you, Beck, where we're staying."

"Jekyll Island is wonderful but I think I'm up for more traveling. I'm going to burden Charlie for a bit longer, this time in the Blue Ridge Mountains. Oh! My pocket is buzzing."

At home, months and months go by without a single

personal call. But as we all walked back toward the cars, my phone vibrated for the second time in two days.

"Beck? I don't quite know how to begin…"

"Letitia? Oh, no. I'm so sorry."

Out of the corner of my eye, I saw Molly stop and clutch Ivy's sleeve.

"No! It's good! It's very good! He just called me by my name!"

"Molly and Ivy are right here. May I put you on speaker?"

"Yes! Of course! I just tried to call Ivy but it went to voicemail."

"Your brother is awake? And he knows who you are?"

"Yes! He called me Letty, like he used to when we were kids. I don't think he knows where he is, or why, but he said my hair is longer than it used to be." There was a thump. "Sorry. I had to sit down."

"I can understand why. I am so pleased for you, Letitia. For both you and your brother." I looked at the others. "We're all happy! What's next, do you think, for Joseph?"

"Well, this kind of, of coming to… coming out of a coma… It was a possibility all along but it had been looking less and less probable. But Joseph had another brain scan yesterday and it looks like there's nothing that should get in the way of more progress. There's damage, of course, but nothing new." She made a noise like a groan. "It will be a long haul, though. You probably know about that, Molly."

Molly nodded and then realized Letitia couldn't see her. "Yes," she said aloud. "Physical Therapy. Speech Therapy. Occupational Therapy."

"The whole nine yards."

"Still, if he knows who you are and called you by name, that's a very important step."

"I know!"

"It must feel as if you have your brother back." Molly's voice was still strong but she had teared up.

"For the first time in years and years. Yes."

I put the phone up close to my face again. "Thank you for calling me. For calling us. Oh!" I realized she thought we were all in Vermont. "We're in Georgia right now, all of us! Charlie's in the middle of a really long trip, escaping winter. I joined him for some birding, and Ivy and Molly and their menfolk are here too for a few days. Your call makes everything even brighter, for all of us."

"Is it warm there?"

"Hot! And gorgeous!"

"Will you send me a postcard?"

"Better. I'll e-mail you some photos."

"Thank you. That would be great."

"And you will keep us posted about your brother?"

"Yes. Definitely. Bye."

But as I ended the call, I looked over at Molly and Ivy, and I knew I didn't want her to keep us posted.

"I like her. Letitia." I said slowly. "But I want to forget Josef. Joseph. Completely and forever."

"Me too." Molly's white curls flew around her face with her vigorous nodding. "Oh, me too."

****

"Again—How didja all end up down here?" Charlie handed the dessert menus to the waitress. We were all stuffed to the gills but we still ordered Key Lime pie and chocolate peanut butter pie and pecan pie and two pieces of peach pie. Molly's Ed was the only wise one among us.

Molly gave the happy whinnying laugh that we had all missed for so many months. "You sent pictures, Charlie. And Beck sent pictures. And there we were, up there in the land of unending cold and ice." Her eyes sparkled as she looked over at Ivy. "So we two women talked to our two men, and we all started making phone calls, and we lucked into the condo. Six nights on Jekyll Island." She heaved a dramatic sigh. "And then back to winter's icy grip."

"But we're here now!" Ivy's smile was infectious. "And actually, the cruddy weather in Vermont helped."

"I cannot possibly guess how."

"It's not good to close the store during April or May because spring migration is when lots of people start noticing birds and they all head for the store to ask questions and buy field guides and get better binoculars and stuff."

Molly hooted again. "But there's not even a tiny hint of spring yet! We figured we could miss the middle of April and nobody would even notice!"

"And besides…" Ivy looked uncharacteristically shy. She glanced at Hugh, and I was intrigued to see that he too looked a bit embarrassed. "And besides, Hugh and I wanted a… a second sort-of honeymoon."

"Ivy! Hugh!"

"You remember we went to Newfoundland last fall, to watch seabirds?"

I didn't remember, but we all nodded anyway.

"We decided, we decided…"

Hugh's deep voice took over. "We decided to get married up there."

"Not married up there! Hugh and I decided, in Newfoundland, to get married in Montpelier. But then that awful thing happened and we couldn't... It didn't seem right to have a festive marriage ceremony..."

"And we wanted to wait for good weather..."

"That too. So we talked about a spring wedding." She gave a long happy chortle. "Maybe with a bird theme. Like—"

"No," Hugh interrupted firmly. "We JOKED about having a bird theme."

"Spoilsport." She leaned over and kissed his cheek. "So, anyway, we're not married yet but we feel like we are. Newfoundland was our first sort-of honeymoon, and this is our second."

My cheeks hurt from smiling so widely. "Congratulations to you both!"

Charlie was also grinning ear to ear. "Happy for you. Happy, happy, happy."

Molly laughed with delight. "Jekyll Island. Sun. Heat. Birds. Friends. And a sort-of, not really, second pre-honeymoon! This could not be a better vacation!"

****

Charlie added two more sticks to our nightly campfire. "You have any idea Hugh and Ivy were gonna get married?"

"No. But it seems like they have been living together for ages now. And there's no question they are good for each other. Good with each other."

"They are. They are. Molly and her husband seem good too."

"I agree."

"Tell me more about your husband. Alain."

I took a deep breath. "Where to begin?"

"How'd you meet?"

"All right. How we met... Alain taught the beginning archaeology class I took when I was an undergraduate. I was a science major." I raised my eyebrows. "Hard science, Charlie. Not any of those wimpy *social* sciences all of us real scientists sneered at. But I loved that archaeology class. So the summer before my senior year I signed up as—well, they called it an intern but I was really just a grunt laborer on a dig. I loved the whole experience. The heat, the sweat, the dirt, the mud, the excitement of being where people had lived hundreds and even thousands of years ago. Touching things they had touched, things they had made and used and maybe cherished. I felt... connected, I guess is the word. Connected to people I never met."

Charlie did his chin-dip nod.

"So I took two more archaeology classes in graduate school, one with Alain and one with another professor whose name I've forgotten. I knew I could never make a living as an archaeology assistant, and I knew I didn't want to go back and take enough additional classes to get a degree in that subject. And I enjoyed my work in hydrology. But I was sure that once I got a real job, once I got on my proper career path, as my graduate advisor always called it, I probably would never do archaeology again in my life. So after I finished my Masters work, I decided I would take a year, just one year, to play around in ancient history. That year turned into three, all of them working with Alain. In the field whenever he was, transcribing his notes and editing his articles. I even worked as a TA and got to teach a few small-group seminars."

"Sounds like you loved him."

"I didn't. I don't think so. But I almost worshipped him. Professor Charbonneau. He knew his stuff, of course, but he also knew how to teach, and he cared passionately about teaching. Even teaching undergrads, which isn't a given with many college professors. All his classes were full and there were usually wait lists. I never thought of him as a, a lover. Good lord no. He was ten years older, for one thing, and he was married. And he was Dr. Charbonneau. Professor Charbonneau."

"Off-limits."

"Yes. And when someone is off-limits, when they're taboo, I think something self-protective clicks in. I never realized how I was beginning to feel about him."

"Want the last drops of coffee?" Charlie held out his thermos.

"No. Thanks."

"So there's you. And Professor Charbonneau. Off limits. What next?"

"Then one day... We were both in his office, two separate desks, two separate pieces of the same project. Someone brought in the mail and he started sorting through it. A few seconds later, he made an odd sound, like a little grunt, and pushed most of the mail off his desk onto the floor. I looked up and he was, he was frozen, Charlie. He was completely still. Then he slit open the one envelope that was still in his hands, in slow motion, and he took out some papers. He was quiet for so long that I asked him if anything was wrong. He looked up at me. These are my divorce papers, he said.

"He and his wife had been married as long as I'd known him, and way before that. It was just part of the reality about Professor Charbonneau, that he was married." I shook my head, back in that breathless, confusing, life-changing moment. "I didn't know what to say. I suppose I said I was sorry. But he shook his head. Then he repeated that he was divorced. We sat staring at each other for the longest time. I didn't have a lot of experience but I wasn't a complete innocent. I knew that Professor Charbonneau was looking at me like a man looks at a woman. For the first time." I took a deep breath. "This sounds melodramatic, I know. But for those seconds, or maybe minutes, I would have sworn that nothing on earth was moving. Or breathing. Or making any sounds at all. I was pinned to my chair. I thought I should look away and get back to work but I didn't. I had never thought of him by his first name but I think I whispered 'Alain'. And he continued to look at me. And then he said it again. 'My divorce is final. I would very much like to make love to you, now that I can.'"

"Not wasting any time, huh?"

"Neither one of us did. He asked if I would go with him to his house and I said yes. I think that was all either one of us said. He stood up, I stood up, we went downstairs and out to his car, he drove a few miles, we went into his house…" I smiled a little. "The same house where I still live. And we started taking off our clothes. Sex with Alain, kissing Alain, touching him, was like coming home. It was like everything that was good and true in the world. All I ever wanted was right there, in my arms."

I inhaled again, my eyes and nose prickling.

"I cried. He cried. We made love again. We had some supper…" I laughed, suddenly remembering. "Popcorn and cheddar cheese. And some olives. It was the very best supper I've had in my entire life. We made love again and then we slept like the dead. I don't think either of us moved all night. We were exhausted from sex but even more from the enormity of what was happening. Our bodies were tight together all night long and I think we both were smiling, even in our sleep. I moved my things into his house the next day."

There was a long silence. I could feel Charlie watching my face, but I wanted to be in control again before I looked up.

"What happened?"

"We had fifteen years. And four months. Sometimes I think I must be idealizing those years. But I don't think so, Charlie. I think we truly did have fifteen years of perfection. We worked together. We lived together. I helped him with his third book. I worked with him in the field during the summers. We shared worries and wonderings and, and triumphs about his work and my work. We talked, Charlie, so many millions of words that came without effort and that the other one of us always understood."

"When did you become a state hydrologist?"

"After we'd been married about three years. My old honors advisor contacted me about a part-time job with the state. It was perfect because I still had lots of time to be with Alain, and I was also doing what had intrigued me in grad school. And I was making money, earning my own way."

"He was happy with that? With you working and being alone out in the field?"

"Of course. He… He really loved me, Charlie. The whole me. He was pleased that I had a job that gave me such satisfaction."

I leaned forward, poking at the fire. "I wasn't with

him when being with him might have given us more years together." I felt the anger again, the impotent rage. "He was doing a survey in the Champlain Islands, getting ready for a possible dig that summer. We'd been out there all morning together, with a few grad students. Then I got a call that the next day's dentist appointment had to be cancelled but they could take me in two hours." I gulped back the tears, the sense of failure, the grief that I always felt about Alain's last afternoon. "So I went to my dentist appointment."

Charlie reached his hand out and touched mine, just for a second.

"Most of the grad students called it a day a few hours after I left. Alain wanted one more look at the soil. He stepped down into the end of a trench and it collapsed. The walls collapsed. One grad student was at the other end of the site, getting into his car, and he heard a noise and when he couldn't see Alain, he ran back. But it was too late." I picked up a paper napkin and blew my nose. "If I had been there, I would have been right with him. We could have dug him out in time."

"Maybe."

"I know. Maybe."

"Sorry that happened to you. To Alain and you."

"Me, too. Still."

The Chuck-will's-widow called three times, this night sounding more mournful than insistent.

"I didn't have exactly the same feeling you did, Beck. The first time I kissed Claire. My wife. It wasn't like coming home. It was *finally*! Yayuh!"

I knew that Charlie was trying to lighten things up, and I was grateful.

"Claire and I grew up next door to each other. We

probably made mud pies together, but I don't remember that. We were in the same grade at school. Both of us were on the newspaper staff in junior high. In the high school marching band." He got up to get another good-sized log. "Claire was always part of my life. Not like a sister, exactly. I sure noticed when she started developing. But she had dates in high school, and I had dates, and one time we sat on the river bank and compared."

My laugh was a bit shaky, but it was a laugh. "Compared your dates and hers?"

"Yup. What was your worst date ever? What was the stupidest thing you ever said on a date? I wondered how far she went but I didn't dare ask. She was my friend Claire. My best friend. Except for my beagle."

"Your beagle. Of course. So what finally got you two together?"

"Well… I went off to the Police Academy, she went to St. Mike's, we saw each other at Christmas time. Party at someone's house. We danced together once. Then summer came and Claire was working at Sandy's Sundae Shoppe. And I was strutting around in my spankin' new uniform and feeling damn studly."

"I can imagine."

"Thought about asking her out for a hamburger or something, but I got nervous and found myself asking if she'd like to go fishing with me."

"Romantic."

"I brought a picnic lunch. And a big blanket."

"Getting better."

"She caught four fish to my one. We ate the picnic lunch. Then I reached across the blanket and hauled her close and kissed her. And that was that. I knew. She knew. We got married two months later."

"Did you go on fishing together?"

He laughed. "Every chance we got! And she always caught more than I did."

"What did she die of, Charlie?"

"Cancer. Pancreas. Went fast. Diagnosed in August, dead before Thanksgiving."

"I'm so sorry."

"Me too. Still."

Chapter Fourteen

Charlie's photos, my snapshots, my little purple birding notebook, even the name Jekyll Island, will always and forever mean peace to me. Quiet, happiness. An idyl. There were enjoyable moments in the week that followed also, but the overriding recollection is of fog, rain, and foolish fear.

****

Charlie had reservations at a small private campground on the edge of the Blue Ridge Mountains. The sweet-faced, roly-poly woman who checked us in apologized in advance for the noise.

"Your site is right close to the picnic area. Not much happening there November through March, but this weekend all the way through October it's busy, busy, busy."

"We'll be out acting like tourists most days."

"You won't have a bit of a problem then! The day-use area closes at 8 p.m. and the nights are quiet, quiet, quiet. Rain, though, toward the end of your stay."

"We won't melt."

She patted Charlie's arm. "That's the spirit!"

Our site was right up against a fenced-in day-use area that held picnic tables, the parking lot, and restrooms. The barrier didn't block the shrieks of children and the loud laughter of adults, or the smoke and smells of cooking meat that wafted over to our site like ground mist. But, as the woman promised, the day-use lot emptied out and was locked soon after we finished supper, and the campground settled into quiet.

****

When I climbed out of the tent early the next morning, I was greeted by my first-ever Hooded Warbler, at the top of a mountain laurel. The bird's golden face glowed in the first slanting rays of sun. I whispered good morning, and the warbler responded with just a few whispery notes of song before it stretched its wings and flew. That bird was a feathered promise, a harbinger of the migratory wave that Charlie predicted. The next three days were filled with whirlwinds of birds. Our lunchtime peanut butter sandwiches drew in Brown-headed Nuthatches, a year-round species there but one that was never seen in Vermont. Both kinds of kinglets made odd noises from the tops of trees whenever we walked a few yards into the woods along the Blue Ridge Parkway. Eastern Phoebes darted from tree branches to catch flying insects. A Scarlet Tanager sang for us during one picnic stop.

On our third morning, we were walking on a forested trail covered with fallen leaves and needles when I caught a flash of orange up ahead. I scanned the treetops with my binoculars, and then I heard Charlie gasp. The shrubs around us were full of birds, alive with birds, hung about with birds like Christmas trees with brightly-colored ornaments. My orange flash was one of several Blackburnian Warblers, the males with throats of flame. There were Black-throated Green and Black-throated Blue Warblers, Yellow Warblers, Chestnut-sided Warblers, as well as larger Indigo Buntings and Rose-breasted Grosbeaks. We stood, transfixed, as the birds gobbled down tiny caterpillars, sometimes from the undersides of new leaves, sometimes from the bud ends of twigs. I didn't even get out my field notebook until, with a whoosh, the whole flock moved on, and I took my first deep breath in many minutes.

"That was extraordinary, Charlie. I've heard of warbler waves and migration fall-outs, but I never imagined anything like that."

His bright blue eyes sparkled and he was chuckling. "That wasn't a fall-out. Just your everyday wave. And not over yet." He pointed toward the forest floor where three or four Ovenbirds were scratching around. Another sang "cherTEEE cherTEEE" from a branch eight or ten feet off the ground. A Wood Thrush scuffled in dead leaves, so intent on its search for insects that I don't think it even noticed two humans standing and watching and wondering if that very bird would excite winter-weary Vermonters in just a few weeks.

A hundred yards farther, we stopped to watch two Blue-headed Vireos foraging in the understory, close enough so Charlie got at least a dozen photos.

"Solitary Vireos. That's what they used to be called. Better name, I think."

"What's that, Charlie? Left of the vireos, at about your height."

He frowned, scanning. "Can't find your bird. Still there?"

"Yes. It's… In a sapling with a big spider web. The bird has a hint of spectacles, but not as definite as the Blue-headed Vireo. And look at its colors!"

"Got it. Yellow-throated."

"Yellow-throated what?"

"Vireo. We get 'em in northern Vermont, but not

very often. Typical habitat. Gap in dense woods."

"Another first for me. And another truly beautiful little bird."

We were almost back to the parking lot when Charlie made a "pssst" noise behind me. I turned to see him crouched, every line in his body taut, staring through his binoculars into a wild rhododendron just off the trail. I lifted my binoculars and took three cautious steps in his direction, afraid of scaring away whatever he was looking at. I saw the striped head first. Another Ovenbird? No. Charlie liked Ovenbirds, of course, but they were common in Vermont in spring and summer. This had to be something different.

The bird moved. It was smaller, less rounded, than an Ovenbird, and there were no black spots on its breast. The whole head was buffy-orange, with dark stripes from the base of the bill back through the eye and over its crown. We watched as it took a spider from a web, then another and a third. Charlie cautiously lifted his camera and got few photos before the bird took flight.

"Documentation."

"Of what?"

Charlie turned to me with a wide grin. "Worm-eating Warbler! Thought we'd see one on the island but we didn't."

"That one was chowing down on spiders, not worms."

"Bad name. Eats mostly caterpillars, like just about every other small bird. And beetles and grubs." He grinned again. "And spiders."

If I had been alone, I might have yielded to my urge and tilted my head to the sky and hugged myself and maybe even twirled my whole body around a few times.

But I settled for a quiet comment.

"I am so happy, Charlie, to be right here. Where it's already spring. To beat spring back to Vermont."

"Me too, Beck. Me too."

****

Heavy fog was forecast for the fourth morning. We decided to do some grocery shopping a few miles away, and maybe spend the afternoon walking the loop trail next to the campground. We were unloading groceries when a van pulled into the day-use area and two men began unloading boxes.

A minute later the park's owner bustled into our site. "Sorry, sorry, sorry. I meant to let you know yesterday but things got just crazy. There's a bachelor party booked into the day-use area all afternoon. It'll be just them." She twinkled at us. "Nice, nice boys. Well not boys, more like thirty now I'll just bet, but I think of them as boys. I know two-thirds of them. The groom used to work right here at the campground every summer till he graduated college."

She kept talking as the men unpacked cases of beer, an impressive array of liquor bottles, and an equally impressive assortment of tumblers and glasses.

"The bar's just for the party, of course, liquor laws and all, and the guys know to stay inside the fence but I wanted to let you know ahead of time and then I just forgot. Totally forgot! Slipped my mind entirely! Busy, busy, busy."

Charlie managed to get in a word. "We're planning to leave in a few minutes and walk that loop trail through the woods."

"Oh, good, good, good! The party'll be over by five so we can open the day-use area for picnic suppers and all, and it'll be quiet by eight as usual. Nothing but peace and blessed, blessed quiet."

"You have a very popular place here."

"I know. I know. Thanks to my late husband and his good planning. He was always planning. I just wish he was here to see what his ideas come to. Well, gotta be going." She twinkled at us again. "Stop moving and the rust'll set in." And she bustled off.

I got sandwich things out of the cooler while the two men next door finished setting up a well-stocked bar on a picnic table.

"Huh. That's not usually seen in a campground."

"I'm sure there have been bars in campgrounds before."

"Not that." Charlie was looking over my shoulder. I turned around as three long black limousines pulled to a stop.

"Oh my goodness! They are doing things up royally!"

A dozen large, loud, and jovial young men piled out, most of them carrying brightly wrapped packages and tote bags. They piled the presents on the cement pavilion at one end of the picnic area, dropped the tote bags on the ground, and headed for the makeshift bar.

"Wanna guess who's the groom?"

I scanned the group. "The crewcut with the glittery tiara?"

"That'd be my guess."

He held out two long-necked bottles of ale. "Wanna join the party, from a distance?"

"That is a lovely idea."

By the time we sat down to eat, most of the group next door had taken their seats, drinks in front of them, and were looking expectant. We watched, amused, as the bartenders opened the tote bags, stepped back a few yards, and started lobbing foil-wrapped cylinders into waiting hands.

"High school football team alum. Betcha."

A young man wearing a t-shirt decorated with neon pink flamingos burst through the gate and jogged toward us.

"Hate to bother," he called out. "We forgot knives."

Charlie got up and walked over to the camper.

"Some of us, names not going further than our group alone, must be feeling their advanced age." He shook his head dolefully. "They won't eat a two-foot grinder without cutting it first."

He was flushed, excited, happy and healthy, and I found myself grinning. "You look pretty crowded over there. It might be awkward eating food that long, with elbows out and hitting other elbows and such," I said.

"That is a point I had not considered. You have convinced me and I thank you." He nodded to Charlie as he took a handful of steak knives. "I will cut my grinder, just this once."

****

The fog rolled back in just as we rounded the far end of the loop trail and headed back toward camp. When Charlie stopped abruptly ahead of me, I thought he might be going to get his poncho out of his backpack. But he was staring fixedly up into a white oak, and he made a gesture with his hand telling me to come closer.

"Cerulean," he whispered.

I was utterly blank. Cerulean. Cerulean Blue was my favorite crayon in that big box of sixty-four I had when I was nine or ten years old. Then I remembered the warbler pages in my guidebook. Cerulean Warbler. Another bird I had never seen and, if I remembered correctly, another species in sharp decline. I peered up into the oak and caught sight of a small yellow-green bird with two pale wing bars.

"It's not blue."

"Female."

"Oh. Of course."

"I'm gonna want a picture. If I can." He was muttering more to himself than to me. "Need a setting for fog and mist. Tricky."

I was suddenly, uncomfortably, reminded of Josef and his money shots.

"I'm heading back, Charlie. I'll see you at our site."

He grunted.

I shook off Josef thoughts. I forced myself to think of something different. Didn't a forest in fog take on a magical aspect? Wouldn't some people see that bent sapling as a satyr? Couldn't that white birch, almost invisible in the white mist, be a unicorn? Maybe Hansel and Gretel would come traipsing along the path on their way to the woodcutter's hut.

There were two shapes ahead of me, blocking the trail, and they looked much more like real humans than fantastical imaginings. One of the shapes moved toward me. I thought it said something. I couldn't see clearly. I couldn't hear through the loud rushing sound filling my head.

After a frozen eternity, I breathed.

"Didn't mean to startle you, ma'am. But didja hear what I said? About the dire calamity that has befallen all us bachelors and our almost-not-a-bachelor?"

Ah. Two of the young men from the party.

196

"Roger screwed up in a HUUUmungous fashion," the closer one said earnestly. "He didn't get us a stripper. Can you imagine that? A bachelor party without a stripper?" He reached out and grabbed my arm. "But then we go walking and lo and behold! A beauteous lady! How about it? Will you be our stripper? Pleeeeeeezzz?"

The other one laughed. "You can't ask a complete stranger, moron!"

"But we neeeeeeed a stripper."

"We'd get kicked out of here so fast, if we had a stripper. Come on."

They were both drunk, but they weren't dangerous. Of course not. I was being idiotic. I took a step backward and freed my arm.

"When is the wedding?" I was pleased, proud, to hear my voice, my normal voice.

"Tomorrow morning. Ten o'clock. Ten o'clock SHARP! Thass what the groom says."

The other one snorted. "Over and over and over, that's what the groom says."

"Don't you worry about ush, ma'am. Limos'll be back to pick ush up. Five. Three limos, five o'clock. Take ush right to our doorsh. No drunk driving." He shook his head at the wonder of it all. "Hit the shack and shleep it off and fine and dandy in the morning."

"That sounds like an excellent plan." I wanted to be back at our site, to go inside the camper and latch the door, but I didn't want to walk past them. "Aren't you worried you might be missing something back at the party?"

He gasped, opened his eyes wide, and clutched his chest with both hands. "Thash right! We might be missing shumthing." He turned to his friend. "What are we doing out here in the woods?"

"C'mon, moron. It was your idea to go looking for a stripper."

"Oh. Right. Rightshu-are."

They turned around and headed back toward the campground. Moron stumbled a few times, but they both quickly disappeared into the fog.

I counted five whole minutes before heading after them.

****

"You okay, Beck? You look pale."

"I'm a little tired. I guess."

"Pardon me. Once again." The same polite young man as before was holding out Charlie's steak knives in one fist and two of the foil-wrapped sandwiches in the other. "We're hoping you can use these. They're extras. They haven't been touched, and they're really good."

"That is so nice of you. Thank you. Did you have a good party?"

"It was the best. The very best. I hate like heck to lose another one of us to that dreaded M word, matrimony, but I have to say we gave him a fine send-off."

"I'm glad." I put the grinders on the picnic table. "Have a nice wedding!"

****

The harmless encounter on the trail frightened me beyond all logic. I was shaky and I was upset and I was furious with myself for overreacting. It wasn't even nine o'clock when I crawled into the tent, took off my shoes, and wiggled into my sleeping bag with all my clothes on.

I listened as Charlie added sticks to the fire, lowered himself into one of the folding chairs, turned the pages of a magazine. I listened as he walked away, heading for the restrooms, and came back a little while later. I heard him douse the fire, open the camper, climb the stairs, and close the door again.

It was so quiet in the campground that I could hear toilets flushing, seven sites away from ours. Once I heard a child cry out and then a soothing adult voice. I thought I could hear trucks out on the highway. I listened as some late arrivals drove in, found their sites, talked quietly, made coffee or tea or cocoa, got ready for bed. I heard a distant Great Horned Owl, and then something small that ran through the campsite and, a while later, a larger animal snuffling and rooting around under the picnic table. Skunk, I thought. It's just a skunk.

I couldn't sleep. I was afraid to close my eyes.

And then I heard footsteps. Or maybe I imagined footsteps. The measured sound was first out on the circular drive, and then it was right outside our site. I couldn't believe that my imagination could conjure up the sound. I had been spooked earlier, but I wasn't crazy. There were footsteps, I was sure, and they were slow and heavy and they were getting closer.

Whoever it was would hear me if I unzipped the sleeping bag, but I could not just lie there and wait. I grabbed my heavy flashlight, struggled out of the bag, unzipped the tent and shone the light all around in front of me and to the sides and out past the camper. Nothing. No heavyset plodding walker, no dark shadowy shape.

The fog wasn't as heavy as before. It wasn't thick enough to hide a person. But I could not get back in that tent. I couldn't zipper it closed with me inside, zippered into a sleeping bag, helpless. I ran the few steps to the camper, grabbed for the door handle, hauled myself up the steps, and almost slammed the door shut behind me, gasping.

"Beck?"

"I'm sorry I woke you up."

I switched off my flashlight and reached up to put it on Sean's bunk.

"Are you okay?"

"No. I am not okay. At all. I would… This sounds idiotic. I know it does. But I would feel much safer if I could get into your bed. Just for a while."

"Sure." I could see him sitting up, pushing back the opened sleeping bag that he used like a quilt. "I'll go out in the tent. Guard against nighttime bogeymen."

"No. I mean I would like to get in with you." I moved closer, until my knees touched the bed. "You don't have to hold me or anything. I just need to know that you're there." My voice broke and I felt like a fool. "We can lie back to back. I'll feel your, your warmness. I will know you're here, while I'm sleeping."

"Something did happen today, in the woods."

"It was nothing, Charlie. I got scared by something that would not have frightened a, a seven-year-old, let alone a professional woman in her forties."

He lifted the covers, and I cautiously eased down on the very edge of the bed.

"Good god, Beck." He pulled me back against him and rubbed his big hands up and down my arms. "You're stiff as a board. You're freezing cold and you're shaking. Talk."

"No. It's…" I forced out a little laugh. "As I said, it's idiotic."

Oh god. The warmth felt so good. The knowledge that Charlie would keep me safe felt so good. I knew I could fall asleep and sleep for hours. I didn't want to talk.

"It was nothing. Really. It was foggy and two of the young men from the bachelor party were on the trail. In front of me. I couldn't see them clearly and I had… Never mind. Go back to sleep. I am fine now."

"Keep talking."

"I had a, a flashback or something. I couldn't see clearly and for a few seconds I couldn't hear either. My head was all… There was a roaring sound. Just for a few seconds. And then…" This laugh was a little more believable. "It was quite funny, Charlie. One of them asked if I would be their stripper. For the party."

"Were they drunk?"

"One was. The other not so much. The whole episode… It doesn't even deserve that word. Episode. The whole thing was over in two minutes. The less-drunk guy pulled the other one away and I walked back to camp and that was all. It was over."

Charlie's hand moved to my legs, massaging rough denim against cold skin.

"It isn't over. It's still affecting you."

I shook my head, exasperated with myself. "But it doesn't make sense, Charlie. I should be over that. The whole thing was back in November. I am not some asinine cowering wimp." My voice broke a little on "cowering" and that made me angrier.

"That's true. You're not whatever you said. An asinine wimp."

"You left out cowering."

"You're not that either." He pulled the sleeping bag up, and his heat surrounded me. "You had a traumatic experience. You're gonna have leftovers for a while. Maybe even years. It's just a fact."

I inhaled on a sob. "I don't like that fact, Charlie."

"Understood."

****

"Might want to move on earlier than planned."

"I thought you were loving the mountains."

"I am. I do." Charlie was staring down at his phone. "But not in frigid temps and pouring rain."

"I'm fine with anything, Charlie."

"Looks like we got twenty-four more hours." He fiddled with something on the screen. "I'm gonna see if we can check in early at the next site. Outer Banks."

We didn't get twenty-four more hours. That night the temperature plummeted from almost eighty to just above freezing. I woke up cold, with a howling wind finding every bit of mesh, every grommet in the tent. I wasn't going to barge into Charlie's bed again. I thought about Sean's bunk, but I didn't think I could get into it without the ladder and I had no idea where the ladder was stashed.

I crawled out of the tent, battled the wind over to the camper and opened the door just wide enough to reach in and grab the truck keys. Then I pulled my sleeping bag out of the tent and tossed it into the back seat of the truck.

Even with the air mattress inside it, the tent was lifting a few inches off the ground with every gust. I had visions of tent and mattress both ending up in the next county by morning. There was no way I could get the pegs out of the ground without Charlie's hammer, and I didn't want to wake him up. I stood there shivering, conscious of the absurdity of the situation and feeling giggly. Finally, I collapsed the poles and laid them and the two picnic benches on top of the flattened tent.

"You stay!" I said aloud. Then I got into the back

seat of the truck, crawled into my bag and fell deeply asleep.

It started to rain before first light, rain that slashed horizontally across the campground, driven by wind that was even stronger than in the night. When I sat up and peered outside, Charlie was standing in the door of the camper and staring at the collapsed tent.

"Oh good. You're not still in it."

There was no point in getting out rain gear. We were drenched in seconds. He grabbed the stove and put it in the truck. I crouched down, reached into the collapsed tent and opened the air mattress valves. Both of us wrestled the mattress outside, knelt on it until it deflated, and got it into the back seat. Both of us got the sopping tent folded and stuffed into the truck. The wet folding chairs went into the camper along with the cooler, water containers, and dishpan with all the dishes and cutlery and pots.

"I'm going to the restroom," I yelled, splashing and sliding toward the dirt road.

When I got back, Charlie had changed into dry clothes and was already in the driver's seat. I changed and then made a mad dash for the truck cab.

"THAT," I gasped as I threw myself into the seat. "THAT was an adventure."

"You think?"

We looked at each other and burst out laughing.

Chapter Fifteen

"Charlie." I reached across the table at the diner and almost touched his hand. "I have been thinking that I never properly thanked you."

"It's been good having you along. Nothing to thank."

"For saving me from my own fears the night before last. Or from the bogeyman. Or the night terrors. Or whatever."

"A question."

"What?"

"Would you have done the same for me?"

"I… Of course I would."

"Well then." He caught the eye of the tired-looking waitress. "Let's order."

Pancakes, sausages, bacon, scrambled eggs, home fries, juice, white toast and rye toast, biscuits, one cherry muffin, and two side orders of cheesy grits advertised as *real* deep South. The waitress asked if we were waiting for anyone else and raised her eyebrows when we said no.

"So tell me what's next. What will we find in the Outer Banks?"

"We'll be in one of the smallest campgrounds. Got some trees so we won't be in the sun all day." He slapped the hand down on the table, startling me and the couple in the next booth. "Duh! Duh! Duh!"

"Another Sean-ism?"

He tilted up on one hip so he could get his phone. "Shoulda thought of this earlier. You ever try fishing?"

"I have, a few times."

"Might be able to get you on the charter boat with me. All day trip." He waggled his eyebrows. "Possible marlin, definite pelagic birds. "

That was a treat I hadn't expected. I sipped the truly wonderful coffee and waited, but it was soon evident from Charlie's side of the conversation that the marlin and pelagic birds were not going to happen for me.

"Full up. With a waiting list."

"So I'll drop you off and then go birding on the islands."

"Day before that, though, you could join me for a few hours of pier fishing. Don't need a state fishing license for that. Rent equipment right at the pier."

"I might do that."

****

We were both silent as Charlie drove down Route 12 on the narrow strip of barrier islands called the Outer Banks. After we'd been through Rodanthe and Salvo and Avon, he said what I was thinking.

"Well, we got to see sane waterfront development on Jekyll Island. Now we're seein' insane."

ATVs and dune buggies roared back and forth on narrow beaches lined with multistory buildings. Tattoo parlors, sex shops, tacky motels, and decrepit-looking amusement parks broke up the view on both sides of the road. The "campgrounds" we passed didn't offer anything I would ever call camping, just rows of RVs with a few yards between them and pop-up tents set right down on fragile dunes.

There were, though, lots of people fishing, and every other vehicle had fishing poles sticking up from the bumpers. And we passed a National Wildlife Refuge. And there was the ocean. It would be only six nights, five days.

****

"Can't stay here." Charlie was frustrated and irritated when he climbed back into the truck. "Flooded. Guy found us another site but it's in one of them that didn't look good."

"So what do you want to do?"

"Gonna take it, I guess. A few days anyway."

"Your fishing trip is day after tomorrow?"

"Charter trip. Yeah."

"Then we have to stay at least that long."

He looked right at me for the first time. "You're a good person to travel with, Beck."

"Thank you, Charlie. You are too."

****

The so-called campground looked like the sales lot of an RV dealer. Our site was so small we could have reached into the next RV and borrowed the salt right off their table.

It took us over an hour to take care of our sopping belongings. We spread the tent over the hood of the truck and then inflated the air mattress and set it on end. There were no trees and no room for a clothesline, so we draped sleeping bags, liners, and wet clothes from the rearview mirrors and the top of the camper. There was no place to set up the tent, so I would be sleeping in Sean's bunk for the next few days.

"What time tomorrow, Charlie? For the pier fishing?"

"After breakfast. No hurry. You gonna come?"

We had passed several piers, every one crowded with people, folding chairs, coolers, and extremely loud boom boxes filling the air with angry-sounding rap music.

"I'd rather walk around that refuge we passed."

"Pea Island."

"And the next day, while you're out to sea catching monster marlins, I think I'll take the ferry to that other island, the one you said was less crowded."

"Ocracoke."

"Pea Island and Ocracoke. I'm set."

Charlie looked away from me, making unnecessary adjustments to the sleeping bags and scowling.

"You gonna be okay? Alone?"

"What?"

Now he looked stubborn. "You are gonna be alone, Beck, at Pea Island and on Ocracoke. Are you sure you'll be okay?"

"Charlie. I am forty-three years old. I have a job that requires me to be alone outdoors, a hundred days or more every single year. I live alone. I got scared back there, in the mountains. I know I worried you, and I am sorry for that. If I get scared again, I will just lock myself in the camper and shake for a while and then I will go back outdoors into the sun. I'll be fine."

"Well. Good, then."

****

"Can't even shave down there. Too crowded."

I looked up from making coffee as Charlie stomped into our site and slammed his shaving bag down on the picnic table.

"Dozens of RVs, only two restrooms. You mind if I

shave here?"

"Of course not."

For some reason, I hadn't thought of Charlie shaving even though his cheeks and chin were always smooth. I suppose the immensity of his mustaches led me to think of him as a generally hairy person.

I used to like watching Alain shave, watching all the facial contortions, the mouth twisted to one side and then the other, the chin jutting forward, the eyes now squinty and now wide. I kept glancing at Charlie as I finished making the coffee and started on breakfast, and he was doing those same contortions. Then he lengthened his upper lip until it almost disappeared into his mouth and trimmed the part of his mustache between mouth and nose. When he noticed me watching, he muttered, "How I'm gonna look when I'm old and toothless."

I didn't answer. I had just noticed, for the first time, how lovely his mouth was, how firm and well-shaped.

Charlie picked up a metal can about the size of Alain's shoeshine wax. I watched, fascinated, as he opened it, took out a little dab of something and massaged it into his fingertips, and rubbed his fingers down first one and then the other of the long dangling mustaches.

I picked up the can. Beard Balm. Itch-free Grooming. Lasts all day.

"Gettin' a bit of a mountain man look. You mind trimming the back of my hair?"

He was indeed getting shaggy. I took the clippers and stood behind him.

"Tell me how to use these."

"Just sorta drift 'em up about a inch from my scalp."

I drifted. It worked! Little ends of hair lifted up and

then fell softly to the ground. I drifted the clippers up again, and one more time. His hair felt downy against my fingers.

"I'm afraid to do more."

Charlie lifted a hand and felt the back of his head. "Just once more sorta toward the sides.... Yup. That's good. Thanks."

****

My memories of the Outer Banks are like a kaleidoscope. Turn it one way, and there's ugliness and crowding and noise. Turn it again and there's the softness of Charlie's hair against the back of my hand. And my growing awareness of him as a physical being, with hair and skin and muscles.

Turn the kaleidoscope again and there's Ocracoke Island and sixteen miles of undeveloped coastline with not a single building on the beach, just sand and wind and waves and space. And then Charlie walking off the pier carrying a plastic bag of cleaned fish that we pan-fried the minute we got back to camp. Another twist and there's Pea Island National Wildlife Refuge, and me using the field guide I bought in Ivy's store so many months earlier. Identifying my first-ever Whimbrel, my first-ever American Avocet. Almost stepping on a copperhead that was longer than my arm and bigger around than my wrist. Sitting on a piece of driftwood and watching more than a dozen windsurfers, every single kite a different brilliant color.

Another twist of the kaleidoscope and we are eating out for two breakfasts and a supper because the busy restaurants were quieter than our site. Chatting with a local waitress who lived her whole life on the Outer Banks and kept shaking her head over all the new buildings, all the crowding. Lingering over coffee and dessert while we watched the sun set on the darkening ocean, sailboat masts gradually turning from white to gray and finally disappearing in the dark. And the next morning watching the shadowy shapes of the dozen men gathered at the dock in the still-dark when I dropped Charlie off for his charter boat trip. Nine clients, the captain, and two men whose job it was to make sure the paying customers got their money's worth. And the realization that Charlie might have been older than half the men there but he had a better build than any of them.

****

It felt more intimate sharing the camper, with me in Sean's bunk, than it had the night I slept so securely in Charlie's bed, in his warm arms. That night, when I was so frightened and so upset with myself for being frightened, I had not even wondered what he was wearing. Nothing mattered except knowing I was safe. But lying in Sean's bunk, I was very aware of Charlie only a few yards away. Aware of him as he took off his shirt and undid his belt. Aware when he sat down to remove his shoes and socks. Aware as he dropped his chinos and laid them across the end of his bed. We both washed out some of our clothes during our time in Georgia, and hung things on a line, so I knew Charlie's white briefs. But I didn't know then how he looked wearing them, and now I did. After he got into his bed and under the covers, I lay awake for a long time, cocooned in that camper with Charlie's breathing, the still-busy and still-noisy campground a world away.

****

"Think I got a plan."

I looked up from drizzling fake maple syrup over a

stack of blueberry pancakes.

"I am never, ever traveling again without bringing some of the real stuff. *Maple* syrup, not cane sugar or corn syrup or—Sorry, Charlie. What were you saying?"

"Got a plan about where to go next."

I took the first bite. Not bad. There were lots of blueberries, and the butter melting all over the top of the stack was real.

"I thought you had everything worked out before you left Vermont."

"Not the last stops. Waiting to see how far north the migrants were."

"That makes sense." I held out a forkful. "This is surprisingly tasty. Try it."

"I'll stick to bacon and eggs. But thanks."

"I never make pancakes at home. By the time the pan is the perfect temperature, I've already made eight or ten that aren't all that good." The unexpected, and unwelcome, thought occurred to me that Gilbertie Grouse or others of his kind might have been happy to eat the rejects.

"You sound just like Claire. When we were first married, she made pancakes for company but never for the two of us." His smile was soft, reminiscent. "But from the time Allison was, oh, maybe four or five, Claire made pancakes every single Sunday. Blueberry. Strawberry and pecan. Elderberry. Apple and ham. Those were my favorite. Banana sometimes, but Allison was the only one who liked 'em. Claire would make two whole batches of batter and the three of us would finish every single one." He chuckled. "Maybe you and I should just eat now. Too hungry to talk plans."

"Very good idea."

When we were finally sated, he took a little notebook out of his shirt pocket.

"No point staying here the full six nights."

"I agree wholeheartedly."

"And no point driving through the mess around Baltimore or DC."

"Complete agreement there also."

"So we head northwest, do some birding in Virginia." He flipped the notebook open. "Two nights at some place called Dutch Gap. Birding hotspot. Then coupla nights in southern Ohio, and then straight up to the south shore of Erie. Miles of natural migrant traps. Birders from all over the world." I must have grimaced because he assured me, "No, not like this place. Different kind of crowding. Boardwalks with a birder every coupla yards."

"That sounds good to me." I hesitated. "Charlie, you do know that you're not saddled with me for the whole trip, don't you? If you would rather be alone for the next stops, you can drop me off somewhere."

"Just drop you off, huh? Drop you by the side of the road and go on my merry way." He took a long swig of coffee, gazing at me over the rim of the mug. "Gonna hitchhike up to Montpelier? That your plan?"

"Of course not. You drop me not far from an airport, I call a taxi, and I get a flight."

"You want to do that?"

I felt myself getting irritated and flustered. "No, I don't want to do that! But this is your big trip, Charlie. I invited myself along and you've been more than accommodating. I want to make sure you know you're not stuck with me if you'd rather not be. That's all."

He set his mug down. "I am not stuck with you,

Beck. I am enjoying you. I like getting to know you better. And you are, as I said before, a good traveling companion." He scowled. "So no more talk about heading home early."

My smile started as a little pull at the corners of my mouth and just kept growing.

"I promise, birder's honor, that I will never ever mention it again."

"Good."

****

"That call from Josef's sister."

We had been silent ever since we left the Outer Banks, lost in our own thoughts while I drove and Charlie looked out the window. Now he said five words and stopped.

"Yes?"

He turned to look at me. "You said you were happy for Josef. That true?"

I hesitated.

"That's a good question. I am glad he didn't die, but that's because of Molly and Ivy. And I'm pleased for his sister. I like her." A very inappropriate grin pulled at my mouth. "And I'm pleased for the U.S. healthcare system. Josef won't be a vegetable, hanging on for decades while other people tend to all his physical needs."

"If he's in a home, an institution, it'll still be pricey."

"True."

"Gotta ask, Beck. Why Josef? Why not some other man?"

My laugh was just a little puff of air. "Josef was the only man who ever asked."

"Hard to believe."

I shot him an incredulous look. "I had two 'affairs'

213

in college, Charlie. A one-night stand and a two-night stand. Then Alain. And absolutely no come-ons or temptations while we were married. And then Josef. I am not exactly a siren."

We were quiet again as a few more miles of rural Virginia rolled by outside the car.

"You know that mermaid statue? Little mermaid? Copenhagen?"

I gave a spurt of laughter. "That is a non sequitur if ever I heard one."

"It's not. Put you on that rock. No clothes. Legs curled around you. Lookin' out to sea." He looked over at me. "A very good siren."

I had no idea how to respond.

"Gotta have your hair down though."

More silent miles.

"But why'd you let him stay?"

The little goldfinch feather hanging from the rearview mirror fluttered when I sighed.

"You know, Charlie, I cannot make sense of that. I never actually invited him to stay. He came the day we met and we… We had sex. He came the next day and we had sex again. He came by and we went to bed almost every day for the next few weeks. Then he said he was going to move in until his book came out."

"And you just went along? You don't seem like a person anyone can just ride roughshod over."

"I would like to think that I'm not. But I did. I did just go along. I didn't realize…" I could feel my face getting pink. "I missed Alain fiercely, every single day. As my love, my husband, my partner, my best friend, my mate. I didn't… I suppose I didn't allow myself to miss him physically as well."

"Makes sense."

"It does?"

"When the other one is dead, you can hate being alive. Healthy. Breathing. So you go—" He made a short waving motion with his left hand "—outside your body. You don't pay attention to your living body. Don't notice you're hungry. Get dehydrated 'cause you don't know you're thirsty. Don't know when you're tired. Even if you get injured, sometimes. How can you possibly be alive when she's not?"

"Oh. That's true. I lost almost thirty pounds the year after Alain died. It… I couldn't bear to have food taste good when he wouldn't ever…" Surely I had cried all the tears I would ever cry about my husband, but now they were clogging my throat and prickling behind my eyes and nose. "When he would never taste anything again."

"And the other part is sex. You want sex 'cause you're human. But you're disgusted with yourself. Horrified that you want it when the person you loved to have sex with is dead." He looked away, out of his side window. "Makes that first time you have sex again pretty darn powerful."

"That's another true thing, Charlie. For days and days, weeks even, after I met Josef, I could not think of anything but sex. I wasn't easy in my mind about it. I didn't like the man. Not really. I couldn't understand myself, my own body. But, still, I felt like a full sexual woman again."

I concentrated on passing a huge slow-moving RV that was having trouble making it up the first hill we'd seen since leaving the seacoast.

"And sex was the only time I saw him, for the first four, almost five months. I was working Monday through

Friday and often on Saturdays. He worked four evenings plus all day Saturday and sometimes Sunday as well. He was asleep in his room when I got up and gone when I got home. We didn't eat meals together, or watch TV together, or sit reading together. Or anything."

"And then what?"

"Then he cut down on his hours at the Photo Emporium. He said he needed more time to devote to the book. I hated—" I startled both of us by slamming my fist against the steering wheel. "*Hated* having him around all the time. Before that, it was still my house, Alain's and mine. Now Josef was, I don't know, contaminating it."

"So why didn't you ask him to leave?"

"Because." I took a deep breath. "Because I was stupid, Charlie. I can't even blame sex. That stopped being good after the first, oh, six weeks or so, and it pretty much stopped entirely by the fifth month. But Josef didn't have an apartment anymore. And what I saw of the book did look impressive. And I heard him on the phone with his publisher. I believed what he said about leaving soon. All of that combined, and I just crossed my fingers and waited until he left of his own accord." I grimaced. "I think I had an asinine image of myself as some sort of patron of the arts. But I could hardly wait until that 'artist' was gone."

A few miles passed in silence.

"Well. If that was stupidity, mine was lunacy."

"Your what?"

"My one affair. Since Claire's death. Sheer lunacy." He winced. "Bad choice of words. The woman was nuts. Clinically."

"Oh dear."

"Supposed to be taking medication but wasn't going to get her prescription refilled." He shot me a wry look from under his brows. "Said she didn't want to support Big Pharma."

"Oh dear again."

"Self-medicated with brandy. Said her granddaddy was just like her and he did it with brandy and he was still farming in his nineties."

"How long did you and she…"

"Date. Slept together only three times. Dated almost a year. Snowshoeing once, a few movies, supper." He snorted. "Sean's fifth grade play. I liked it. She didn't." He twisted his head to get a look at something we just passed. "Mockingbird."

"There was one just outside Montpelier last summer."

"I remember." He gave a gusty sigh. "It was Sean who brought me to my senses."

I waited.

"She was upfront, I'll say that for her. Told me right at the start she had mental health problems. Said she had 'em under control. Next left."

"What? Oh. Thanks."

"Wondered how much of that medicinal brandy she was takin'. But she was lively and fun. And I was lonely." He snorted again. "And I got a kick outa dressin' up, getting' my hair trimmed. Spendin' time with a woman again."

I made the left from pavement to dirt, from traffic to quiet. "So how did Sean…"

His hand tightened on his thigh until the knuckles were white.

"One day she saw him walkin' home from school.

Stopped and gave him a ride. She was drunk. Scared the hell outa him. The only time he's ever yelled at me, ever. Told me she coulda killed him. Told me he kept asking to get out of the car, but she wouldn't stop. Told me she kept laughing at him and swerving all over the road."

I glanced over at Charlie. His blue eyes were narrowed, fierce, pained.

"Skinny little runt, face all screwed up, tears fallin' down. Making fists at me. Told me I shouldn't ever see her again. And I didn't."

A fuel oil truck was stopped on our side of the road, right near the crest of a hill.

"I can't pass, so we might as well sit here and wait."

"Good thinkin'."

I turned and looked at Charlie. "I'm sorry, Charlie. For you and for Sean. That must have been a very frightening experience."

"She died a coupla months ago. Drunk driving. Didn't kill anyone else. Just her."

He twisted his mouth and I watched, fascinated, as one of his mustaches got shorter than the other. "Of course Sean couldn't resist."

"Told you so?"

"Oh yeah. Reminded me I was lucky to have broken off with her. Reminded me I wouldn't have done it without his advice." His low rumble could have been either a chuckle or a groan. "Advice. Hah. Near-hysteria I'd call it."

"He loves you, Charlie."

"He does, he does. And I'm crazy about him."

For a few long seconds, I just looked at his face. His strong face, his kind face. His tanned skin and blue eyes. The gold and silver mustaches that struck me as so ridiculous when I first met him.

"Driver's back in the oil truck."

"Oh."

****

According to the brochure we picked up when we checked in, twenty-three years ago Mrs. Patricia Owens-Smith had a big night at bingo and spent her entire winnings to buy two-point-three acres of land a half mile down the road from a popular campground and then make it into a nature sanctuary. We explored the place together the first afternoon, walking along narrow winding dirt paths with dense undergrowth on both sides, by an astonishing variety of trees and shrubs and perennial gardens, by two water features and at least a dozen bird feeders and more than a dozen nesting boxes.

"I wonder if Mrs. Smith-whatsie ran out of money."

"Eh?"

"She put up that impressive hurricane fence along the front of her sanctuary, eight feet tall, strong enough to stop a charging moose. With a fancy coin-operated lock. But I don't think there's any fence at all on the other three sides of the place."

"Hmmm." He turned slowly in a full circle. "Mebbe she figured it'd be easy to walk in from the road but any other side you'd have to bushwhack. Lotsa foliage, hobblebush, brambles."

"Maybe."

We went back to the sanctuary for much of the next two days, but mostly apart. Charlie spent hours at the feeders and the water features, photographing returning migrants. I walked the trails and sometimes strolled a few miles along the dirt road, lost in nature almost as wonderfully as I had been on the sandy beaches of Jekyll

Island. The first leaves of spring were opening. I walked with my head tilted back, staring up into the arching canopy of foliage, until I got a crick in my neck. It seemed implausible that greens, just greens, could be so diverse, so different one from the other. Everywhere I looked there was green, and every single green was different from all the others.

The second afternoon my attention was caught by rustling to my right. It was too much noise for a thrush or a sparrow. Maybe it was more than one bird. Maybe it was a flock of White-throated Sparrows filling up on insects before flying north to the mountain ridges of Vermont. But the crackly, rustling, scuffling noise sounded too big even for those possibilities. I wondered if a bear might be rooting around on the forest floor, trying to find the acorns and butternuts and beech nuts buried last fall by squirrels. I could see shadows, movement, screened by the dense undergrowth. And then one shadow moved closer.

"Well, hello," I breathed. "Aren't you splendid?"

A cock pheasant moved into the dappled sunlight, followed by five hens. I stood without moving as the parade left the woods and slowly crossed the road. The cock paused before re-entering the woods and turned its head toward me, iridescent blue and green and almost black, with scarlet red around its eyes. The black and brown hens ignored me. I watched until the birds disappeared entirely into the undergrowth.

"I've never been close to a pheasant before," I whispered. "Thank you."

****

Other people, I suppose, might have predicted that I would start noticing Charlie's body. He was a dramatic-looking man, with a good build, and I was just emerging from six months of misery and anxiety and fear. I was hundreds of miles from the patch of Vermont woods where three women fought against a man with a gun. I was far from the stairs where a grouse raced toward me twice a day, lurching from side to side like a cartoon sailor with a peg leg, where the grouse leaned against me and listened to me talking and made whispery clucking noises while he preened his feathers. I was sleeping eight or nine hours every night. I was spending all day outdoors. I was walking miles and miles. I was healthy for the first time since November. I was, maybe for the first time in several years, happy.

And it was spring. Sap rises in the spring.

I had not predicted it, however, and I didn't like it. I wanted Charlie to go on being my friend, just my friend. Trustworthy, safe. I wanted the days to continue unchanged, relaxed and relaxing, easy and effortless. I wanted many more nights of the kind of sleep that was so gloriously different from those fitful and haunted nights that left me grouchy and sore for months.

Sleeping out in the tent again helped. I couldn't hear him getting undressed, hear every rustle and every zipper. I couldn't watch through almost-closed eyes as he got out of bed and stretched, his ribcage beautiful in the early morning light. I could enjoy the awareness without finding it overwhelming.

I wouldn't tell him. I wouldn't do anything about it. But I would enjoy looking at him. And maybe when we were back in Vermont, I would invite him for dinner. Or ask him if he would like to see a movie with me. Maybe we would add a new dimension to our friendship.

Maybe.

Chapter Sixteen

The next day, as Charlie drove, I was aware of him every time he straightened his back, every time he cleared his throat, every time he sighed. As we checked into a campground that was buffeted by cold wind-driven rain off Lake Erie, I longed for an impossibility. I wanted the temperature to hit ninety-eight, with humidity at ninety-eight percent, just so my birding buddy Charlie would unbutton his shirt and toss it on the picnic table.

****

"What have you been thinkin'?"

I was crouched in front of the fire, rearranging little bits of wood that didn't need rearranging, lost in my thoughts. The rain had stopped a few hours earlier but it was still chilly and our evening campfire was bigger than usual.

"What? Oh. Thoughts. Yes." I stood and went to sit in what had become my chair, the green one to the left of Charlie's orange one.

"I am uncomfortable about what I've been thinking, Charlie. I think you might be uncomfortable too." I looked over at him and took a deep breath. "I was thinking that I have never touched you. And I would like to."

An interminable moment passed. He sat unmoving, staring into the fire, leaning forward with his elbows on his knees. I couldn't read his expression. Then he put his hand on the arm of my chair.

"So touch me."

In all my imaginings about Charlie, I never once imagined touching his hand first. I felt suspended between the familiar world, in which the two of us had never experienced the texture of each other's skin, and a breathtaking new world in which touching each other might be a normal part of every single day.

After an eternity, I traced the broad back of his hand with my fingertips. I caressed his clean flat fingernails. I touched the soft and vulnerable insides of his long fingers, one at a time, and he spread his hand so I could reach. The little hairs on the back of his hand and on his knuckles lifted as I touched them, becoming glittery gold in the flickering light from the fire. I had been so hungry to touch all of him, but now I wanted this to go on forever. He turned his hand over, so our palms met. Slowly, we interlaced our fingers. Then we sat, looking into the fire, holding hands, feeling nothing in the world but the warmth from our joined hands.

"I been thinkin' too."

I waited.

"A lot of thinkin', truth be told."

I did some more waiting. The comfort, the relaxation of the minute before was ebbing away. I had to say something.

"One doesn't hear that phrase very often. 'Truth be told'."

"Ayup."

"Not 'ayup' either."

"Nope."

I gave a nervous spurt of laughter. "I am wondering, Charlie. How much of that old-time Vermonter act is just that? An act."

His deep chuckle sounded wonderfully familiar, normal.

"You're onto me."

"Why, though?"

"Well. Had to shave off my mustache when I signed on with the P.D. Nice mustache. Small and neat. But I still had to cut it off." He sounded aggrieved. "I started growin' a new one the day after I quit. And this one was gonna be big."

More quiet. The butterflies in my stomach were settling down a bit.

"So the mustache goes with the Vermontisms?"

"Well, yeah! Tried talkin' like Yosemite Sam but all that growling made my throat hurt." He gave me a sly look out of the corners of his eyes. "So started droppin' mah final 'g's. Sayin' things like truth be told."

"And cay-unt hardly git thay-uh from hee-uh."

"'Zactly."

"And Jeezum crow."

"Nope. Never said jeezum crow. Claire said it was blasphemous."

"Oh."

Laughter, amused laughter, bubbled up and spilled out of me. I tightened my grasp and Charlie did too, and we both sat, watching the fire and the shadows, breathing in the night air. My voice, when I started talking, felt like part of the night.

"Alain almost never said anything that hurt me. Nothing that bothered me even. But one time he said, almost in passing, that the two of us never belly-laughed." I met Charlie's now-somber eyes. "I thought about that comment for days. It was true. We worked and read and talked together, and cooked and gardened and made love and… and made a home. But we didn't ever get silly. Not once, I don't think. We were… We were professorial, even with each other." I gave myself a quick shake and tried to lighten up. "Or maybe we just didn't have any shared sense of humor."

"You were happy, though."

"Very."

"That's all that matters."

"Yes." I felt my mouth widening until I thought my face might burst as I smiled into the darkness around us. "Still, Charlie, it was fun to laugh just now."

"Ayup."

"So. Charlie. You been thinkin'. A lot, truth be told. About what?"

His fingers tightened again.

"About touching. Same as you. And about sharing that air mattress with you."

"Oh."

"Or my bed. Either one."

"Oh."

"That's all? Oh?"

I turned toward him. "I like what you've been thinking. Truth be told, I love it."

"Gonna be cold tonight. Come in the camper with me?"

"I would like that."

"Wait'll the fire dies a bit?" His grin was very white in the dark. "Anticipate?"

"I'd like that too, Charlie."

****

The fire was too big, and it was taking too long to die back. Charlie stood up after twenty minutes.

"Going to the restroom."

"Me too."

We walked back hand in hand. Sometimes our thumbs rubbed each other's skin. Charlie was right. The anticipation, the building tension, was wonderfully exciting. But when we were back in the camper, together, I was anxious and uneasy all over again.

"It is possible, Charlie, that one of us, or maybe both of us, won't find this, um, all that interesting. All that exciting. If so, I think we should stop. All right? It won't hurt our friendship to admit that it didn't work."

He was looking at me solemnly, under his brows.

"I mean, not every friend, friendship, makes for good, um, for good sex partners. We know each other well enough by now. We could just agree that making love might not fit us. Might not be as good an idea as it seemed out there by the fire. And that would be all right."

"Just look at each other and shrug and say, huh, well, that didn't work?"

"Something like that. Yes."

"That's quite a suggestion, Beck." His hands were warm on my shoulders. "Let's see if there's any interest. Any excitement."

I put both hands flat on his chest, as if I might push him away. But there was no possibility of that.

His mouth was gentle at first, firm and mobile against mine. My body softened and I slid my hands around his rib cage to his back. Someone walked by outside the camper. Our kiss deepened, opened.

"Interest and excitement over here. How about you?"

"Me too," I whispered. "Both of those things."

Undressing was easy, comfortable. We just took off

our clothes, like an old married couple getting ready for bed. And then he sat on the edge of the bed and I stood between his knees and we kissed, many more minutes of kissing. And touching. And rubbing against him. And feeling him.

"Oh no! Charlie..." I took a step back, breathing hard. "I'm not, I stopped taking the pill after Josef left." My short laugh was a bit desperate. "And I don't have a whole lot of enthusiasm for being the sixty-something mother of a high school student."

"Well, sexy woman. Tomorrow we'll go by a drug store and get some condoms. But tonight..." He reached for me again. "Tonight we're still gonna make love."

His hair felt silky in my hands, and his face looked incredibly dear in the dim light.

"I have one more, um, concern, I guess. Worry. And then I promise I'll stop talking."

"Shoot."

It was difficult to think with his big hands cupping my bottom and the hairs on his chest tickling my breasts.

"I told you that sex with Josef stopped being good a long time before he left. I have wondered... I wondered then, and I still wonder, if maybe I passed some... that maybe I had that one brief flurry and then I got past my, my prime age. For sex."

"You didn't like him."

"True. And that probably was part of it."

"Big part."

"But I still worry that things might not work anymore, the way they should."

Charlie grunted. "Man a year past fifty, Beck. I'm the one who should worry about things not working."

I felt his fingers gentle between my legs.

"You're wet."

"Oh."

"And soft. And warm. Hot."

I gasped.

"But with Josef—" His fingers moved and I gasped again. "Sometimes I would be ready and then, a few minutes later, I wasn't."

"Dry?"

I turned my head away and looked blindly out the little window on the side of the camper. "You don't dodge anything embarrassing, do you?"

"Well?"

"Yes. Dry."

"Try lubrication?"

"Of course. I wanted things to work. But it pissed Josef off. He..." I pulled his head down, against my breasts. "That's all I'm going to say about it, Charlie. I don't want Josef in here with us."

"Agreed."

"I've got... I have Vitamin E oil. If I need it ever."

His mouth was making it very hard to think, to talk.

"If *we* need it. We."

"Oh. Yes."

"One thing, Beck."

"What?"

"If we ever need it, you put it on me. On my cock."

"Oh. Yes." I moved just enough so I could touch his chest, his abdomen, his penis. "Oh yes indeed."

****

Charlie laid the box of condoms on the picnic table.

"There when we want 'em, Beck."

I looked at the box and then back at him. "I believe now is an excellent time."

"Tent?"

"I'd like that."

He looked around, at the picnickers in the little green opposite our site, at the two lanky kids playing toss and catch. "Nope. Too many people around. Might be a little more private in the camper." His eyes sparkled as he grinned at me. "Still have to be careful about noise though."

"Those signs don't address noise. Just motion."

"Signs?"

"The ones we keep seeing. If this rig's rockin', don't come knockin'."

He kept his face deadpan as he nodded. "We should get one."

"Maybe—wait—How about this? If you hear screamin', no intervenin'. No! This is better. If you hear a moan, go right back home."

"If you hear screamin', somebody's creamin'."

"Charlie!" Humor bubbled up in me again. "If you hear yelling, something's been swelling."

He raised both eyebrows. "Somethin' is. Time to get inside."

****

This time we undressed each other, slowly, taking time to look and pet and taste. And this time Charlie reached up and unfastened my hair and let it fall around my shoulders and I could feel it cool and tickling against my back. As soon as we were both naked, as soon as I could see him in the light, I pushed him down on the bed and straddled him.

"Beck." Charlie arched up under me. "We're skippin' something important."

"Foreplay. I know." I reached for him. "Can we do

it later? I need to know…"

He grabbed my hands. "What do you need to know?"

"I said. It didn't work last time. The last several times. And I'm older than last time."

"Works that way."

"What does?"

"Time. Being older than last time." His words were quick, breathless, guttural, but he was laughing up at me.

"So I need to know, right now, if it still works."

"Fine. But I meant something else. Something else we're forgetting."

"What? What?" I reached for him again, wanting him so much it hurt.

"Reach over and grab that box."

"Oh god, Charlie. I forgot. I forgot entirely." Now I was laughing too. "I can see it now. Huge big belly, waddling around those muddy fields, doing my job."

"Quite a picture."

I got the box and watched him tear it open.

"You, Charlie, are far too attractive. You have interrupted my usually logical thought processes."

He handed me a condom. "And you, logical and sexy woman, are going to put this on me. Right now."

His whole body stiffened when I started rolling it down. "Christ almighty."

As hungry as I was, as desperate to feel him inside me, still I rocked back on my heels and just looked. At his thick cock in the glistening condom. At his belly, his rib cage, his tiny nipples raised and hard. His mustaches that almost reached his shoulders. His mouth, his eyes. His eyes.

I took a deep breath, got us positioned right, and

slowly lowered myself onto him.

We didn't make a sound, either one of us. In complete silence we fucked, intent on every gliding sensation. I had to close my eyes. I simply could not process the way he felt in me, the emotions, the heat, and see at the same time.

After many long, slow, silent minutes, I whispered, "Charlie?"

He made a low noise in his chest.

"Things are working."

I felt his deep chuckle against my body and inside my body.

"Gotta agree."

****

"Two problems."

We were lying together, still in Charlie's bed, our bodies now bathed in slanting afternoon light.

"What problems?"

"One. I'm gonna want to do that again. Soon."

"That is not a problem, Charlie."

"Good." His fingers stroked my belly. "Two. You didn't come this time. You came yesterday but not today."

"I am aware of that."

"You pushed my hand away…"

"I'm aware of that too."

"Why?"

"I don't want to…" I raised up on one elbow. "I wasn't wet anymore. Sometimes… Fingers can hurt if I'm not wet."

"So we get your, what was it? Vitamin oil."

"But I feel great, Charlie. I don't need—"

"Don't you feel uncomfortable? A man would."

231

"Blue balls?"

"Exactly."

I looked out the window at two identically dressed people walking two identical little dogs that were wearing identical little blue jackets.

"Well, I won't. My body will know that we had sex and I didn't have an orgasm. And I will be horny, yes. But I like being horny. It's a very alive feeling." I traced the line of his lips with my finger. "I have been feeling horny for many days now, ever since the Outer Banks. I didn't feel that way for months and months and months. It is quite wonderful, Charlie."

"Alive, huh?"

"Sort of simmering. And female. I am very aware, every minute, that I'm a woman. As I said, Charlie, that is not bad at all."

"Huh."

"Sometimes with Josef I would… I faked orgasms. Sometimes. It worked just as well as the real thing for him. Sex was pretty much just about him anyway. But I hated it."

Charlie reached up and caressed my cheek and I had a sudden urge to cry.

"Lying to someone about… about this, it's disrespectful, I think." My loose hair flew all over as I shook my head. "The first few times I felt sorry for him, that he was so dumb he couldn't tell if a woman was pretending. That he was so damnably self-centered. But then it turned into contempt."

"Not a good thing when it's mixed in with love-making."

"Tell me about it." I smiled down at his dear face. "I don't want to fake an orgasm with you. Not ever."

"Glad to hear it."

"And that means that sometimes, maybe, I won't come. And that's all right."

"Raspberries. Big beautiful raspberries."

"Did you hear me?"

"Yup." His fingers were tweaking my swollen nipples. "Heard you."

He sat up, pushing me onto my back.

"And you don't have to come. But I have to do this."

His tongue made a long wet line down the middle of my body.

"Spread your legs for me, sexy woman."

I felt his mustache first, then his tongue, his lips, even his teeth. I was able to watch for only a few seconds before arching back, my head pushing into the pillow, my eyes shut tight, gasping, reaching, wanting, striving. My hands were full of his hair and then digging into his shoulders and then pounding on him.

And then I made noise, and I didn't give a single thought to the dog-walking couple outside.

Chapter Seventeen

Charlie's description of birding on the Erie shore was accurate. The parking lot at Magee Marsh was full of cars, trucks, vans, and motorcycles, with license plates from at least twenty different states. There were birders every few yards along the boardwalk, alone or in clumps, with occasional congestions of many more. Ages ranged from a white-haired man using a walker to a precocious little blond boy who was helping his parents find and identify warblers. We saw two trios of eager teenagers who gave each other high fives for every new species. We saw family groups wearing the nineteenth-century clothing of local Amish farmers. We heard at least four languages other than English.

But Magee Marsh was delightfully, excitingly, wonderfully different from the crowded piers and beaches of the Outer Banks. People walked along slowly. They talked quietly or not at all. There were no skateboards, no yapping dogs, no loud laughter, no boom boxes. And there were birds everywhere. In our first ten minutes on the boardwalk, I listed more than twenty species in my little birding notebook. By our third day, I had so many pages of notes that it was going to take several hours to sort through them all, and Charlie had over five hundred photos that he hadn't even looked at yet.

"Charlie, I am so happy to be here. It's like a feast.

An overwhelming, exciting, and totally satisfying feast."

"Weather helped."

Only a birder would say that. Our first three days in Ohio were overcast, with wind and occasional spitting rain, and that was the forecast for at least one more day. Birders who had been at the marina reported that waves on the big lake were over six feet high, racing west to east—and every single person near us cheered. What might seem like dreadful weather to nonbirders was a gift for us. Birds newly arrived from the south and intent on flying farther north would stay put and wait for better weather before attempting to cross the lake. They would be around at least today and tomorrow, filling the trees with color and movement and occasional song.

"Something exciting up there," Charlie murmured.

There was a traffic jam of sorts ahead, a few dozen people with binoculars up and all pointed in the same direction. A man at the near end of the group noticed us coming and beckoned to us urgently.

"Proto... Protho... Prato... Warbler! You know!"

Apparently Charlie did know. He muttered "Lifer" and raised his binoculars, and I raised mine too although I didn't know why.

"Prothonotary Warbler," Charlie muttered. "Don't find it yet. Ah! Yeah! 'Bout six feet left of that guy's bald head. Same level as his chin. Dropped now. Even with knees. Yellow."

"Oh my goodness."

"'Zactly."

The warbler glowed with the color of a monk's saffron robes. It had silver-gray wings, a shiny black bill, and big black eyes. It was a relatively large warbler, easy to find and impossible to forget. All around us there were quiet gasps, whispers, and the clicks of cameras and cell phones. The bird ignored it all, foraging along small twigs, dropping to the ground a few times, climbing up the trunk of a small tree, picking up minuscule insects. I was about to mention what I thought was a second Prothonotary deeper into the brush when the whole boardwalk began shaking and heaving. On the far side of the crowd, a heavyset man pounded closer and closer, his face flushed and sweaty. He was carrying a camera with a lens as long as his arm.

"Still here?" he gasped. His muttered "'scuze me" sounded polite but the way he shoved himself to the front of the group wasn't. It was illogical of me to pay attention to him. I should have spent more minutes with the beautiful golden warbler. But I watched the newcomer as he elbowed two men aside and inserted his considerable bulk between a lanky teenager and a gray-haired woman. When he used his hip to move her out of the way, she lost her balance and teetered with one foot off the boardwalk before grabbing the railing and pulling herself upright.

Oblivious, the man continued making his way toward Charlie and me, jostling other birders with his shoulders, hips, and elbows. He glanced at Charlie, must have decided he looked unmovable, and veered in my direction, using his beefy shoulder to shove me away from where he wanted to be standing. I stumbled, skidded on a little pool of water, lurched against him, grabbed his arm to keep from falling, and ended up bringing my foot down hard on his toes.

The photographer's sports sandals were no match for my hiking shoes. He sucked in an agonized breath, forgot all about the warbler, and turned on me.

"I am SO sorry, sir. You pushed me off-balance. Sorry. Sorry."

He peered over his camera at his injured foot. "You broke my toe. Toes! All of 'em! You broke them all!"

"Oh my goodness. Perhaps you should find some ice to put on them. Fast."

"Ice! Hah! Probably have to find a hospital!"

The whole group turned and watched him limp away, toward the parking lot.

"Awesome move, dude!"

I turned to see the teenager raising his palm in the air in a long-distance high-five. The gray-haired woman with him chortled, hooted, and said she hoped I had broken every one of that man's toes.

"Warbler's gone," said a disgruntled voice—and the crowd started disbanding, spreading out along the boardwalk in ones, twos, and small clusters.

Charlie pulled me into a one-armed hug. "Gotta ask. Accident?"

"Not entirely."

"You, Beck, are an amazing woman."

"I, Charlie, was an irritated woman." I grimaced. "And now I'm feeling a bit foolish."

"No reason. Guy was a jerk."

I reached across and kissed his cheek. "Thank you."

****

"You take your regular white sauce. You know?" The waitress cocked her head toward me and I nodded. "And you add a blob of mayo, a squirt of yellow mustard, and a couple spoonfuls dill pickle juice."

"That doesn't sound all that delicious."

"Believe me, hon. It's the most popular thing we got on the menu. Tell you what. You get the perch, I'll put the mustard sauce on the side. But I betcha like it."

I looked at Charlie. "All right. We're going to try the two specials then, on your recommendation. Pecan-crusted walleye with corn cakes and slaw, and fried perch in cornflake crumbs with mustard sauce, with a side of scalloped potatoes."

As she walked away, I shook my head. "I am highly dubious about the perch."

"No worry. If you hate it, I'll eat it."

"No. We both will. When in Rome."

****

"What a truly lovely day, Charlie. From first light…"

He looked sideways at me and raised one eyebrow, and I felt my face get warm.

"… to all the birds and all the birding. And then more fish than I thought we could possibly eat, even after our displays of gluttony on Jekyll Island. And now the most beautiful sunset I've ever seen."

"Glad we went local."

"What?"

"Fish."

"Oh. Me too. And the waitress was right. That perch was delicious. Cornflakes, mustard, dill pickle juice, and all."

We rode in silence for a few minutes, wind-burned, full of fish, and happy.

"You know, Charlie?"

"Eh?"

"This morning, when you reached up to take the sleeping bag off the top of the camper, your shirt pulled out."

"Yeah?"

"And I got light-headed, staring at that little strip of skin."

Charlie raised both eyebrows this time.

"I am not exaggerating, Charlie. I have always assumed that swooning was caused by poor nutrition. And tight corsets. I might have to revise that assumption. It is possible that a woman might swoon from desire and…"

"Frustration. Sexual frustration."

"I am not frustrated."

"Humph. Mebbe not. But I keep feelin' guilty. All I gotta do is look at you now and I'm ready to come. Gotta be hard on a person's system to have sex and not finish up."

"I told you before, Charlie. I am very much enjoying sex with you, whether or not I have an orgasm." I turned to him, now serious. "I cannot tell you how much I appreciate the fact that you didn't push me this morning. That you didn't keep trying when I wanted to stop. I don't want…" I hesitated, looking for the right words. "I don't want to be thinking that there's something I'm *supposed* to be doing. Supposed to be feeling. I don't want to lie there, with you trying and me trying, and knowing that it might not happen." I reached up and touched his cheek. "I want to just relax and feel. And enjoy."

He was staring straight ahead at the road, scowling. "Before. When you were married. You ever come just from intercourse, with nothing else?"

"Sometimes. But not regularly. I think that's true for many women."

"That's what Claire said too." His mouth twisted and I watched, fascinated, as his mustaches took on two entirely different lengths and shapes. "Men. We always think our favorite thing is your favorite thing."

"It's way up there, Charlie, on my personal list of favorite things. Believe me."

"Well. Good then."

****

The weather changed during the night. On our fourth morning in Ohio, I woke up to a warm breeze coming through the open camper window, and I could see a hint of blue sky in the east. I slid out from under Charlie's arm, eased off the bed, pulled on some clothes, picked up my sandals, and went out into the beautiful day. The only sounds were those of birds. Mourning Doves. Chickadees, Carolina or Black-capped, I wasn't sure. A White-breasted Nuthatch. An Eastern Towhee. A cardinal. I measured coffee into the battered camp percolator that Alain said had gone through too much with him to ever be replaced, and then got out eggs and our remaining half-pound of bacon.

A loud raspy "churrrrrr" interrupted my breakfast-making. In the closest tree to our picnic table was a stunning Red-bellied Woodpecker. The species was relatively new to Vermont, and I'd seen only two of them before, and now I was eye to bright beady eye.

"You, bird," I murmured, "are sadly misnamed. Red-crowned maybe. Or Red-nape. No. I think there's a red-naped sapsucker so that might be confusing. But where's your red belly, pretty bird? It is truly not evident."

The woodpecker darted its head forward and I saw the long tongue come out and snatch up what looked like a centipede.

"Happy breakfast."

It turned its head just far enough to fix me with what I was sure was a warning look out of one eye.

"Don't worry, bird. I will be sticking with bacon and eggs."

"Me too." Charlie was coming down the stairs from the camper. "And coffee. And the rest of those pastries."

"Good morning. Good beautiful morning!"

The woodpecker stayed where he was until the bacon and eggs were ready and we sat down to breakfast. Then it made another "churrrrr" and flew away.

"I think it was guarding its insects until it was convinced we would be breakfasting on something else."

Charlie nodded gravely. "Prob'ly." He plopped four brochures onto the table and looked through them while we ate. "Try some of the other places? Little Portage?"

"Is that another marsh, like Magee?"

"Partly." He looked up. "Some meadows. Lots of wetlands and dikes with bridges over 'em. Walking trails. Fewer people." He folded the brochure and stood to slip it into his back pocket. "Probably fewer birds too, but maybe waterfowl. Maybe plovers."

"That sounds good, Charlie. But I'd love to head back to Magee and Black Swamp tomorrow, for our last day."

"Good with me."

I put my plate and fork in the plastic wash bin. "Do you think the birds we saw yesterday left early this morning, riding this wind up into Canada?"

"Mebbe." He grinned his rare but wonderful Charlie grin, so wide that his long mustaches made an open V instead of hanging parallel to each other. "And lots more of 'em will ride the wind up from the south."

"Excellent."

****

Ivy and Jack frequently had lively debates about which bird deserved the honor of being dubbed BOD—bird of the day. Jack invariably chose something showy: a male Scarlet Tanager, a Great Egret, a Baltimore Oriole in the sun. But Ivy always argued for a bird that showed us some characteristic behavior, a bird that taught us something about the species and how it lived its life. For Charlie and me, there was no contest about the BOD on our second-to-last day in Ohio.

When I first glimpsed the trio of big white birds, I thought they were Snow Geese, although it didn't make sense that they hadn't left yet for the far north. Or maybe swans. We had seen two Trumpeter Swans overhead as we drove to Magee Marsh the first day. But then I focused on the huge bright-colored bills.

"Charlie! Hurry. Aren't those pelicans?"

"Looks like it."

"But what are they doing here? I thought they were coastal birds."

"Brown Pelicans are. Like the ones we saw in Georgia." He was staring through his binoculars. "Still, it's sort of surprising to see White Pelicans here. Thought they stayed further west. Great Plains. Prairie Provinces. Didn't expect 'em here."

"White Pelicans. Amazing."

"Cooperative. Watch."

The three big birds were swimming in a line now, moving toward the dike, flapping their long wings.

"What are they… Oh my goodness! Are they trying to drive fish in to shore?"

"'Zactly."

When the pelicans were almost at the dike, they

dipped their bills and then raised their heads in unison, water pouring from the sides of their oversized beaks as they threw back their heads and swallowed.

"This is amazing, Charlie. This whole trip has been one wonder after another. What next, some Asiatic falcon? Or… Wait! I've got it. I predict that the next life list bird for either or both of us will be a, a Willow Ptarmigan. Dressed in winter white, making it doubly extraordinary at this time of year."

We never saw a ptarmigan, in winter white or summer camouflage, but I added to my life list one brick-red Orchard Oriole singing in a tree. And we stood for many minutes watching a large mixed flock of waterfowl: Blue-winged Teal, Gadwalls, American Wigeons, Mallards, American Coots, and handsome Northern Shovelers with their implausibly large bills. And then came the insect-eaters, flycatchers and swallows gorging themselves on a massive hatch of midges swarming above one of the man-made impoundments. It was almost dizzying to watch them all, phoebes and kingbirds darting out from perches all around the water, and at least five species of swallows dipping and swooping from the sky. A Willow Flycatcher, apparently sated for the moment, sat on a branch not far from Charlie's head and "sneezed" repeatedly. "Fitz-BEW! Fitz-BEW!" I felt a rush of pleasure that I knew the song belonged to Willow Flycatchers and not to any one of several look-alikes; that I remembered that fact from one of Ivy's walks.

But for the first time, watching those swarming, hungry, active birds, I realized that the idyllic existence of the past month was going to end, very soon.

"Charlie."

"Eh?"

"I am not ready to go home." I turned to him, letting him see my confusion and unhappiness. "I have always loved my home. It's always been *home*. Truly my home. My center. The place I always wanted to be, at the end of every day. I am so sad, Charlie, that I'm not feeling that way now."

We both stopped walking.

"The months before this trip were hard on you."

"That is putting it exceedingly mildly."

"And that's clouding your feelings right now." He reached out and pushed back a bit of hair that the wind had worked loose from my bun. "But I am willing to bet, Beck, that once you see that house, once you walk inside, you will feel at home. In your home again."

"I hope so." I gave an impatient headshake. "No doubt you're right. And it is far too beautiful today to be moping." I tried a grin. "And maybe another lonely bird will adopt me when I get home. That would help."

"Ivy said you got that grouse to eat out of your hands."

"Not quite. I put the grain in an old dog dish and then sat on the bottom of the porch stairs with the dish between my feet. You saw the dish, remember? The grouse would…" I raised my shoulders in a quick shrug. "I still think of the bird as male. He would come wobbling up to me, as fast as he could, and eat right there, between my feet. He seemed completely comfortable with me talking to him all the while. The last couple of weeks he even preened after eating, right at my feet." This time my smile was real. "One time he stepped up onto my shoe to preen and he leaned against my ankle."

"That was a unique and special thing to happen, Beck."

"I know it, Charlie. And I should be happy that it did happen, instead of mourning that it didn't keep on happening forever."

He pulled me close with one arm and gave me a hard hug.

"I like your attitude, woman."

****

Toilets and showers were in a good-sized building in the center of the campground, men on one side and women on the other. The first time we saw the neat little paintings on the doors, we stopped in our tracks and we both laughed. Now I didn't even notice as I pushed open the door with a drawing of a little cloud with a neat rain shower falling straight down onto a small potted plant. The men's door had a cloud also, but the rain from that one was shooting horizontally out of the side, widening into a fine spray and falling on a sizeable patch of flowers, grass, and weeds.

Charlie's shower cost him twenty-five cents. Five minutes for a quarter. I had a whole handful of quarters in my bag with the soap, shampoo, conditioner, and a change of clothes.

"I'll meet you back at camp, Charlie."

In honor of our warmest Ohio evening so far, I walked back through the campground after my shower in nothing but sandals, loose hiking shorts and a sweatshirt.

There was no fire going, and no Charlie. When I climbed the stairs to the camper, he was stretched out on the bed, naked, his hands under his head.

I stopped with one foot still on the stairs. "Well,

245

hello."

"Yesterday. You said you swooned from desire and… I cut you off. Desire and what?"

"I did not say I swooned. I said I felt light-headed." I closed the door behind me. "What I was feeling, and enjoying very much, was desire and delight. Delight in your body. Delight that I am getting familiar with your body."

"Then come closer and get more familiar."

I pushed off my sandals, took two steps, unfastened my shorts and let them drop.

"Shirt too."

"Later." I smiled into his eyes and then slowly looked down his long body. "I am feeling a strong need to spend some time, maybe a great deal of time, kissing you first."

"No argument here."

I bent and he reached up to meet my mouth, but I moved almost at once to the hollow below his Adam's apple. And the sides of his neck. And out along his shoulders, one at a time, relishing the taste and touch of skin stretched taut over bone.

I sat on the edge of the bed and kissed down his sternum. I took some of his yellow-white chest hairs between my teeth and tugged. When I ran my tongue around his nipple, he bucked and groaned and he brought one hand off the bed to grab my hip.

"I have developed quite a crush on your rib cage, Charlie."

He grunted, and I traced each rib with my tongue and then with kisses.

"Your abdomen is quite appealing also. I might need to spend many minutes here."

He sucked in his belly and muttered something. His fingers tightened and clutched and dug into me as I kissed and nipped and sucked and licked. I skipped the part of him I wanted the most and moved my mouth to his leg, kissing and nibbling the top of his thigh, licking his hairy knee and calf, kissing my way back up the inside of one leg and then the other.

"Oops." I sat up. "Forgot your feet. Oh! And your arms. This might take a while."

I used to rub Alain's feet but I don't think I ever kissed them. Now I put my mouth against Charlie's high arch. I ran my tongue between his toes and his whole body arched off the bed. I lifted one foot and kissed underneath and then I took one big toe into my mouth and nibbled.

I sat up again and kissed from his right wrist to the soft thatch of long hairs under his arm. I kissed his hand, his wonderful broad strong hand, the back of his hand and then the palm and then the fingertips. A pale beam of light from another camper's distant lamp made a diagonal stripe across his belly. His chest and head were in shadow but I could see the gleam of his eyes.

"You know, Charlie?"

He made a low growling sound.

"I think I will save your left arm for some other time." I bent my head to him. "I think that right now…"

I was fascinated by the coarse curly hair. It was a darker gold than on his head or in his mustache, and the silver there was more a slate gray. When his swollen cock brushed against my cheek, I rubbed back and forth against it, and his fist closed around a handful of my wet hair.

"God almighty, Beck. Don't stop there."

In slow motion, holding my breath, I slid my hand up his inner thigh and then bent my head to do what I wanted to do from the beginning. Charlie was the second man I'd ever taken in my mouth. I didn't with Josef. Only with Alain and Charlie. Only with two thoroughly wonderful people.

"God, Beck." I barely heard his agonized whisper over the still concentration in my head. His fingers tightened in my hair and he tried to pull me up and off from him.

"Condom."

****

I have always enjoyed touching more than being touched. Alain said it was because I was in control, so nothing could surprise me and disturb my concentration. My whole body, thoughts, emotions, the tingling of nerve endings, sight and smell and touch and taste and even hearing, everything is focused when I am doing the touching. And those long minutes touching Charlie, exploring the textures of his skin and hair with my palms, my fingertips, my wrists and lips and tongue started a heavy knot growing in my belly.

The knot expanded as he came into me and widened with every thrust. It pushed out to my hip bones. It filled my belly, heavy and aching. I moved my legs up his back but it wasn't enough. When Charlie maneuvered both of us around so he could put his feet on the floor, I raised my legs straight up onto his shoulders and he moved faster and I was panting, and the heaviness grew unbearable until it covered the whole world and I was pounding on his back with my heels and I was gasping, sobbing.

And then it shattered. Lightning streaked to every

part of me, to my toes and fingers and throat and ears and elbows and the top of my head. I couldn't breathe for the throbbing, the pulsing. Charlie grabbed my bottom and I heard him shout.

****

I lay motionless, boneless, tingling. The sudden absence of sound and movement was startling. When I opened my eyes, Charlie was still standing, still grasping me, looking as stunned as I felt.

"I haven't... It hasn't... I haven't felt like that since Alain. And not every time with him." I made a noise that was a laugh, sob, gasp. "Just sometimes."

"It's not gonna happen every time with us either, Beck." He reached up and rubbed his thumb over my wet cheek. "Glad we had it this time."

"Me too."

Chapter Eighteen

Won't happen every time with us.

I replayed those six words in my head for two hundred miles.

I had not wondered, not even once, what might happen when we were back home in Vermont. But now Charlie had said it wouldn't happen every time with us, and I realized he expected us to continue making love, to go to his bed or my bed together, to meet as lovers even after we were home.

Yes. I wanted that too.

I didn't want to move to his house or to have him move into mine. But I wanted this to continue, our comfort with each other, our conversations, our laughter. Meals together. Making love. Waking up feeling his arm around me.

"You wanna drive?"

"What? Oh. Yes."

We had an unspoken rule that we would pull over every couple of hundred miles, get out of the car, walk around a bit, and change drivers.

"What happened to our beautiful day?"

Charlie grunted. "Left it in Ohio."

"We're already in Pennsylvania?"

His mustache twitched. "You were lost in thought, weren't you?"

"I was indeed."

The bright sun was gone. The sky above us was a dozen colors of gray, and wind sent bits of trash scuttling across the highway ahead of us.

"Ready for a sandwich?"

"I am. Yes."

He pulled into a truck stop parking lot and went inside to fill his thermos with coffee. Then we sat in the camper and ate the onion rolls we bought on our way out of Port Clinton, filled with meat and cheese and vegetables and pickles.

"When do you think we'll get back to Vermont?"

"Eleven hours Port Clinton to Burlington, plus one for stops like this. So I should drop you off at your car by nine-thirty. Maybe ten."

I turned in my seat and looked at his now familiar face. "I have to work Monday through Friday."

He raised one eyebrow.

"And I will probably take work home with me, too. That will be my focus for the next five days. But Saturday, would you come for supper? And would you stay overnight?"

His smile started in his eyes, moved to his cheeks and the corners of his mouth, and then spread wide.

"I would love to, Beck."

****

The sky darkened while we were eating lunch. Black thunderclouds piled up and there were distant rumbles of thunder. A half hour later, back on the highway, we were buffeted by wind that rocked the camper and whitened my knuckles on the steering wheel. Then the rain began, driving across the road in steel gray sheets and reducing visibility to a quarter mile. I sagged with relief when I made out a sign for an upcoming Rest Area.

"Let's wait this one out, just for a while."

"Good idea."

The sound from wind and rain and thunder was deafening. Charlie and I sat staring out the window at a dark that was almost as black as night.

"Scary."

"It is, Charlie. But it's… I always feel excited. Awed. Almost like laughing out loud."

He nodded. "Me too."

At last, the rain slackened.

"Give it a few more minutes, Beck."

"Yes."

"Uh oh."

The darkness was lit by red and blue lights flashing by on the highway. Then more lights. Then an alarming stream of emergency vehicles all heading east.

"Let's definitely stay put."

"Right."

The rain let up a bit more and we could see a long line of unmoving red, the brake lights of cars that weren't moving at all.

"Accident."

Some minutes later, a vehicle with flashing blue on top stopped across the exit ramp from the rest area.

Charlie grunted. "Nobody's leaving any time soon."

More emergency vehicles passed the line of stopped cars, sometimes in the passing lane, sometimes rocketing along the shoulder, sirens wailing.

"Since we're going to be here for a while, I am going to avail myself of the facilities."

The wind didn't want me to open the door, and it battled me again when I tried to close it. The noise outside the truck was staggering, a rising keen like wolves in a horror movie, with a deeper roar underneath. I struggled toward the little building, my head bent, my arms wrapped around me keeping Charlie's poncho from flying away, and I wondered if Pennsylvania ever had tornados.

Like so many highway rest areas, this one had coffee and a few vending machines and, glorious to see, a tray with cookies that looked homemade. Before heading back out into the tempest, I filled a super-sized paper cup with coffee, put a plastic lid on it, took six huge cookies, and put into the jar three times the suggested donation.

"Here," I gasped, holding the coffee cup toward Charlie. "Take it, quick."

Closing the door again was as challenging as the first time. I slid onto the seat, struggled out of the poncho and tossed it into the back.

"I know…" I gave Charlie a very stern look and quoted him. "We should never get coffee in throw-away cups when there is a perfectly good thermos right here in the truck. But I think this counts as an emergency."

"I do too, Beck."

"It really is, Charlie. The woman at the desk said there was a multi-vehicle accident a mile from here. The highway is closed and might stay closed for a while."

"Lucky you pulled off when you did."

"We are." I dug the cookies out of my pocket. "Sustenance. A bit smushed but they look delicious."

"Put 'em away. Might need 'em for breakfast."

"Goodness. I hope not."

We sat passing the coffee back and forth and listening to the rain and the howling wind. Emergency vehicles continued flashing by, in both directions now.

"I know accidents happen every day, and most of the

time I don't even think of the people involved. But when it's this close, it's... It's almost as if we can't miss the fear, and the pain, that people must be feeling up ahead. As if it's hanging in the air around us."

Charlie grunted again and put his warm hand over mine.

A state police car pulled off the highway into the rest area and slowed to a crawl. Charlie opened his window so we could hear the trooper's loudspeaker. The booming voice repeated, over and over, that the highway would be closed for several hours, that we should sit tight and be patient, and that any stranded motorist who might be having a medical emergency should turn on four-way flashers. When no flashers came on, the trooper drove down the exit ramp and stopped next to the cruiser already there. The two drivers shouted a few sentences to each other and the earlier one left.

"I remember that kind of duty. Traffic duty." Charlie looked over at me. "Part of me wanted to be where the action was. Other part was relieved. Didn't have to cope with the blood and the crying. And then guilty about bein' relieved."

"Did you ever have to go to a big accident, like this one?"

"Two. One on the interstate and one on Route 15. Interstate's easier to get to, usually. Fifteen's narrow. Lotsa places there's nowhere for cars to pull over." He scowled. "And there's always idiots who don't pull over at all."

"They can get fined, right?"

"Sure. And they do, sometimes. But traffic arrests aren't the main job right then."

"Oh. Of course not."

Charlie crumpled the empty coffee container and tossed it in back of him. "Last exit was three or four miles back, right?"

"I'm not sure, but that sounds accurate."

"Troopers might organize a caravan. Lead everybody the wrong way back to that exit, wrong way down the on-ramp, and onto some secondary road. Clear that jam ahead." He frowned. "But they might be needing every available responder at the scene."

At the end of the first hour, the rain was no longer pounding down and the sky was lighter. Another hour, and the rain stopped entirely. A weak sun struggled to make itself seen through the clouds. People started leaving their cars, walking to the restrooms, coming back with soda cans and cups of coffee and wrapped snacks. Two people walked their dogs. A trio of college-age kids got out a frisbee and started tossing it back and forth.

Next to our camper, a harried-looking young woman knelt down, talking earnestly to two little children who looked as if they'd been crying.

"Whatta you think, Beck? Offer them something to eat?"

"That's a very kind thought, Charlie."

He opened his window. "Ma'am. We're wonderin' if you and your kids might be ready for a snack."

The taller of the two, either a boy or a short-haired girl, looked up eagerly.

"We got peanut butter and jelly, some bread, some stale crackers, coupla apples…" He looked at me. "Anything left in that box of newtons? Yup, and a few cookies."

The woman's expressive face showed the battle going on inside. She didn't want her children accepting food from strangers, ever. On the other hand, they were stuck here for an unknown amount of time.

"We were expecting to be at my parents' house over an hour ago so I didn't bring anything to eat." She leaned closer as if needing to see who else was in the truck with Charlie. "My kids aren't supposed to…"

"I know." He looked at both little ones with a fierce look on his face. "Taking food from strangers is dangerous. Even talking to strangers can be dangerous. But your mom's right here with you."

I got out of the truck. "We've been camping for the past month. It might take me a minute to find everything."

"Thank you, both of you."

After handing over a paper bag of odds and ends, Charlie and I made three walking loops around the rest area, on the pavement, over the wet lawn, around and around, stretching our legs.

"That was very yummy, sir. And missus."

It was the younger of the two children, a tiny person with tousled blond curls and a face smeared with strawberry jam.

"Glad you liked it." Charlie met the mother's eyes. "You keep anything that's left over. We all might end up havin' breakfast here."

"I dearly hope not." She heaved a huge sigh. "But at least we aren't in that mess up ahead. It makes me shudder to think of it."

"Agreed."

By the end of the third hour, the frisbee players were back in their car. Most of the stranded people had talked to at least a few others, sharing stories about friends waiting for them and missed appointments and places they no longer thought they would reach by nightfall. Two groups of four sat at picnic tables, one group playing cards and the other with some sort of game board anchored down with rocks. Several people, some in and some out of their cars, were almost constantly on their cell phones, their expressions ranging from worry to excitement to irritation to humor.

Charlie struck up a conversation with a nearby trucker and came back with details about the accident. Just a few minutes after the start of the heavy rain, a semi braked to avoid plowing into a slow-moving car, and jack-knifed. The truck clipped the car, then other cars hit the truck. By the time the chain reaction was over, it involved at least one other big rig, a couple of panel vans, a tour bus, and more than thirty cars.

"No fatalities. At least none reported yet. Most of the vehicles were going slow because of the rain. Plenty of injuries, though. Lots of people thrown around on the tour bus. The trucker says more than two dozen ambulances got called." He looked over at me. "You think your work can wait one more day?"

"You don't expect to get home tonight?"

"Mebbe. But if we do, it'll be after midnight."

"All right. One more day."

So our trip, our idyl, wouldn't end in a few hours after all. I felt giddy with relief and pleasure, and then immediately chagrined to be rejoicing about something that resulted from the misery of many other human beings.

"What happens, Charlie, when all those people get stranded on a highway without functional cars?"

"Cops'll call for buses. There'll be a school gymnasium or the basement of a church. Red Cross or

Rotary or somebody'll have hot drinks and food, maybe cots and blankets. Phones available for anyone who doesn't have a cell." He was looking out the window, his eyes unfocused, and I wondered if he was back in his days as a police officer. "Some folks'll find rental cars. Some'll go to a motel for the night. Most, though, are probably local. Just on their way to Walmart or Home Depot. Didn't know they'd be stuck here on the highway for most of the day. They'll have family or friends come pick 'em up."

"I never thought about what this kind of accident involves in terms of logistics."

"A lot."

My first call, to my supervisor, went to voicemail. If he was finally taking the fishing vacation he kept talking about, he might not check his phone for days. I tried the office manager next and left another message. Then I tried Speedy Sally and got her on the first ring. She listened, gasped, oohed, gasped again, and then rattled off that she'd let everyone in the office know.

"And if it's a slow news night, maybe we'll see something about the accident on CAX. Big accident like that, human interest story, you know. And we'll all thank our lucky stars you weren't part of it!"

"Thank you, Sally."

Charlie had his phone out too. "Campsite less than an hour away. Sound sensible?"

"Yes. Very."

"Next door to a pizza place."

"Even better."

"I'll reserve us a spot."

****

Charlie was right. An hour later, the state police led

everyone in the rest area back to the last exit, down the ramp, and onto a paved side road. We found the pizza place, shared a large pie with sausage, mushrooms, spinach, olives, and extra cheese, drove to the small campground, and sat in front of our own campfire for one more evening. One more evening lying together in Charlie's camper, in his bed, listening to the quiet sounds of other people getting ready for bed, dousing their fires, walking the dog one last time, saying good night to their neighbors. One more night to make love in intense silence. One more morning waking up with Charlie's warmth at my back.

We were on the road early, after coffee and left-over pizza and the last of the rest area cookies. We stopped in the Adirondacks for lunch and a walk, and we were driving over the Champlain Bridge by early afternoon.

"Your car's in South Burlington?"

"Yes."

"Saturday. What time?"

I was focused on my mental to-do list: get the car, drive to Montpelier, stop and get a few groceries, unlock my cold and empty house, get some heat going, check for messages on the landline. And then four frantic days at work. Now I felt a delighted smile spread across my face.

"Saturday. Any time at all, Charlie. No, anytime past 10 a.m. because I will probably sleep late."

"Mighty early for supper."

"What about lunch and supper both? Sunday breakfast too."

"Sounds good to me."

****

There were still isolated pockets of dirty snow,

under the big pine tree, against the north side of the house, around the garage, piled up at the end of the driveway. Snow, the end of the first week in May. I was glad, again and powerfully, that I hadn't spent the last four weeks in Vermont.

But even with the snow, my house and land looked good to my eyes. Solid, sturdy, safe. Welcoming. I got out of the car and stretched, taking a deep breath and slowly turning almost a full circle.

The door to the chicken coop was open. I had a distinct, and unpleasant, recollection of wading through mountains of snow, losing the padlock, shoving the door closed until it was tight against the warped sill, sobbing in the cold and wind and drifts. Now the door was open, moving back and forth in the gentle breeze.

I walked down the slope, skidding once on wet mud, and pulled the door wider. The two bags of grouse food were ripped open and almost empty. Seed lay scattered across the floor, mixed with an inch or so of muddy snow that was covered with a hodgepodge of tracks. I recognized the delicate prints of mice, larger tracks that might have been weasels and squirrels and maybe a skunk, and a few canine tracks from a fox or a small coyote that would have entered the coop not for the seed but for the smaller mammals.

There were bird tracks of several different sizes. Blue Jays would be daring enough to go into the building, especially a few weeks ago when snow still covered much of their natural food. And crows, definitely: some of the tracks were large enough for crows. And there were some mid-sized tracks from birds smaller than crows but bigger than all the others. I spent several fruitless seconds searching for a clear set of those specific tracks, irritated that prints from my hiking shoes now covered some of the chaos on the floor.

I backed out, and froze. To the left of the door there were two pairs of tracks from a mid-sized bird that walked with its right foot turned out.

"Not possible."

I leaned back into the chicken coop, peering into the dark corners as if there might be a gimpy Ruffed Grouse hiding in there.

"It makes absolutely no sense. I know that, logically. You cannot possibly still be alive. Although I suppose I might have jumped to the wrong conclusion that day, when I saw your feathers and the fox tracks."

I straightened my shoulders and inhaled sharply, exasperated with myself.

"This is idiotic. I have had a marvelous month. I have recovered from..." I sighed. "Charlie's right. I will call it trauma. I have recovered from the trauma of that day in the woods. And I have recovered from losing that grouse. It is idiotic for me to be standing out here, talking aloud, behaving as if I am communicating with a dead bird."

Logic didn't matter. After I took my roll-on and backpack into the house, and after I turned up the thermostats, I got the dog dish from the far corner of the porch where I had hidden it from my view. I walked back down to the chicken coop and used my hands to scoop up what was left of the corn, oats, and field peas. Then I went back to the house, sat on the bottom step, and waited.

"I am talking aloud, again. To myself. But if you are still around, grouse, maybe you will hear my voice. So... So I am going to tell you where I've been. What I've been doing. I, grouse, have had an adventure. Not a hair-raising one, like you and that fox. A wonderful and restorative adventure. I have seen places I never saw before. I have walked miles on nearly empty beaches. You wouldn't have liked the beaches, though. They were too hot and too open, with no cover anywhere. Not Ruffed Grouse habitat. But I truly loved them."

I scanned the dead weeds around the garage, the snow by the chicken coop, the viburnums next to the driveway.

"I have seen birds, Gilbertie, that could hide your whole body in their beaks. Yes. That's true, although I agree with you that it sounds highly unlikely."

Did the hydrangea bush move? I wanted to get up and investigate but I stayed put and I kept talking, reaching into my pants pocket to get my cell phone so I could take a picture, on the slim chance the bird might appear.

"And you might not believe this either, Gilbertie Grouse. I have laughed. Me. Somber Beck. I have been silly. I have giggled, on more than one occasion."

Yes. The hydrangea was moving. I leaned forward and stared, and then sagged back when two gray squirrels chased each other out from behind the shrub.

"It is probably cruel of me to mention this part, grouse, but I ate amazing, diverse, delicious food. All those weeks when you've been up here munching moldy grain."

It was getting chilly on the wooden stairs.

"I got scared one time, grouse. Terrified, to be accurate. And I will admit, to you anyway, that I might get sc… terrified again, sometime in the future, probably when I don't expect it and don't see it coming. But now

I know I can get over it."

I shivered. The breeze wasn't strong but it was from the north.

"You are lucky, Gilbertie Grouse. You never have to wish you'd worn something warmer. You just fluff up your feathers and make your own insulation."

I considered going inside for a heavier jacket.

"Just a few more minutes, grouse, if you're there. What else can I tell you? Oh. Of course. I just spent one whole month, and one extra day, with a truly wonderful person. A good, decent, honest, caring, gentle man. He can look fierce. And I am sure he can be fierce, in defense of friends and loved ones. But he is usually mild. And he is extremely sexy."

Fifteen minutes had passed. I sat, now shivering almost constantly but still scanning the shrubs and weeds and driveway, and still talking.

Twenty-five minutes.

And then, from way down the driveway, a lurching shape started running toward me.

I wanted to cheer, to laugh aloud, to sob, but I gulped it all down for fear of scaring him off. I kept talking, telling the bird what a wonder he was, and how delighted I was to see him, and how happy I was that he had been able to get at the food in the chicken coop.

The grouse stopped twenty feet from me. For long minutes, he looked toward me and then toward the coop and then toward the distant woods and then back at me. I lifted my phone in slow motion and snapped three pictures.

"I understand. You are pretty sure you know me. But I abandoned you. For a whole month. Maybe I am not a safe part of your world anymore. That's all right, grouse.

In just a few minutes, I will go back up the stairs and maybe you'll feel safer. I'll keep watch, though, to make sure nothing beats you to the food."

The grouse made a little running dash, ending six feet away.

"Although, of course, you don't need this food. You could just go back to the chicken coop and share with the rodents."

Another foot closer. My cheeks were wet with tears and I was smiling ear to ear.

"Tomorrow morning I'll add nuts. And on the way home from work, I will make another stop at the grocery store and get all sorts of good things specifically for you. Nuts and raisins and, and sesame seed crackers. And I'll get a bag of birdseed. It will be so much better than the wet and muddy glop down there in the chicken coop."

Gilbertie Grouse took the remaining steps and lowered his head to the dog dish. From that angle, I could see that his tail looked lopsided.

"Something wrong with your tail, too? As well as your foot?"

Yes. There were more feathers on the left side of the bird's tail than on the right.

"So those were your feathers in the snow. You had a close call, Gilbertie."

The bird kept eating, and I kept talking, until the dog dish was empty.

"Of course, you might just be molting. I have no idea what time of year grouse molt. I'll look it up. Or I'll ask Ivy."

The grouse, my grouse, took two steps back and raised its head to look at me. Then he took to the air, flying low over the ground past the chicken coop and into the little patch of woods beyond.

"Thank you, thank you, grouse. Thank you for not being dead. Thank you for remembering me. Thank you for bringing me so much delight. And, right now, thank you for so much, SO much relief."

****

Charlie might not be home yet. He might have stopped to get groceries. Or he might be unloading the camper, getting his duffel bag full of clothes and toiletries, hanging up the sleeping bags and liners to air.

I would see him in just a few days. It would be foolish to call him and interrupt whatever he was doing.

I went into my warm house, my home, and sat down at the kitchen table and e-mailed photos of my grouse to my best friend, my lover.

A word about the author…

Maeve Kim is a teacher, nature guide, gardener, musician and writer. In her fourth novel, a traumatized woman escapes from the endless Vermont winter and from her recent fears and finds friendship and then erotic love with a self-contained widower who shares her love of nature.

Thank you for purchasing
this publication of The Wild Rose Press, Inc.

For questions or more information
contact us at
info@thewildrosepress.com.

The Wild Rose Press, Inc.
www.thewildrosepress.com